The Author

THE NEW CANADIAN LIBRARY

General Editor: David Staines

Leonard Cohen

BEAUTIFUL LOSERS

With an Afterword by Stan Dragland

M&S

Copyright © 1966 by Leonard Cohen
Afterword copyright © 1991 by Stan Dragland

This book was first published in Canada
by McClelland & Stewart in 1966.

New Canadian Library edition 1991

National Library of Canada Cataloguing in Publication
Cohen, Leonard, 1934-
Beautiful losers

(New Canadian library)
Includes bibliographical references.
ISBN 0-7710-9875-8

I. Title   II. Series.

PS8505.O44B42 1991   C813'.54   C90-095215-6
PR9199.3.C628B42 1991

Lyrics quoted on pages 78-81 are from "It Hurt Me Too" by M. Gaye and
W. Stevenson. © 1962 Jobete Music Co., Inc. All rights reserved.

We acknowledge the financial support of the Government of Canada
through the Book Publishing Industry Development Program and that of
the Government of Ontario through the Ontario Media Development
Corporation's Ontario Book Initiative. We further acknowledge the
support of the Canada Council for the Arts and the Ontario Arts
Council for our publishing program.

Printed and bound in Canada

McClelland & Stewart Ltd.
The Canadian Publishers
481 University Avenue
Toronto, Ontario
M5G 2E9
www.mcclelland.com/NCL

6 7 8 9 10   07 06 05 04 03

Contents

Somebody said lift that bale.

– RAY CHARLES singing "Ol' Man River"

Book One

The History of
Them All

CATHERINE TEKAKWITHA, who are you? Are you (1656-1680)? Is that enough? Are you the Iroquois Virgin? Are you the Lily of the Shores of the Mohawk River? Can I love you in my own way? I am an old scholar, better-looking now than when I was young. That's what sitting on your ass does to your face. I've come after you, Catherine Tekakwitha. I want to know what goes on under that rosy blanket. Do I have any right? I fell in love with a religious picture of you. You were standing among birch trees, my favorite trees. God knows how far up your moccasins were laced. There was a river behind you, no doubt the Mohawk River. Two birds in the left foreground would be delighted if you tickled their white throats or even if you used them as an example of something or other in a parable. Do I have any right to come after you with my

3

dusty mind full of the junk of maybe five thousand
books? I hardly even get out to the country very often.
Could you teach me about leaves? Do you know anything about narcotic mushrooms? Lady Marilyn just
died a few years ago. May I say that some old scholar
four hundred years from now, maybe of my own blood,
will come after her in the way I come after you? But
right now you must know more about heaven. Does it
look like one of these little plastic altars that glow in
the dark? I swear I won't mind if it does. Are the stars
tiny, after all? Can an old scholar find love at last and
stop having to pull himself off every night so he can get
to sleep? I don't even hate books any more. I've forgotten most of what I've read and, frankly, it never seemed
very important to me or to the world. My friend F. used
to say in his hopped-up fashion: We've got to learn to
stop bravely at the surface. We've got to learn to love
appearances. F. died in a padded cell, his brain rotted
from too much dirty sex. His face turned black, this I
saw with my own eyes, and they say there wasn't much
left of his prick. A nurse told me it looked like the inside
of a worm. Salut F., old and loud friend! I wonder if your
memory will persist. And you, Catherine Tekakwitha, if
you must know, I am so human as to suffer from constipation, the rewards of a sedentary life. Is it any wonder I have sent my heart out into the birch trees? Is it
any wonder that an old scholar who never made much
money wants to climb into your Technicolor postcard?

2.

I am a well-known folklorist, an authority on the A———s,
a tribe I have no intention of disgracing by my interest.
There are, perhaps, ten full-blooded A———s left, four of
them teen-age girls. I will add that F. took full advan-

tage of my anthropological status to fuck all four of them. Old friend, you paid your dues. The A——s seem to have made their appearance in the fifteenth century, or rather, a sizable remnant of the tribe. Their brief history is characterized by incessant defeat. The very name of the tribe, A——, is the word for corpse in the language of all the neighboring tribes. There is no record that this unfortunate people ever won a single battle, while the songs and legends of its enemies are virtually nothing but a sustained howl of triumph. My interest in this pack of failures betrays my character. Borrowing money from me, F. often said: Thanks, you old A——! Catherine Tekakwitha, do you listen?

3.

Catherine Tekakwitha, I have come to rescue you from the Jesuits. Yes, an old scholar dares to think big. I don't know what they are saying about you these days because my Latin is almost defunct. "Que le succès couronne nos espérances, et nous verrons sur les autels, auprès des Martyrs canadiens, une Vierge iroquoise—près des roses du martyre le lis de la virginité." A note by one Ed. L., S.J., written in August 1926. But what does it matter? I don't want to carry my old belligerent life on my journey up the Mohawk River. Pace, Company of Jesus! F. said: A strong man cannot but love the Church. Catherine Tekakwitha, what care we if they cast you in plaster? I am at present studying the plans of a birch-bark canoe. Your brethren have forgotten how to build them. And what if there is a plastic reproduction of your little body on the dashboard of every Montréal taxi? It can't be a bad thing. Love cannot be hoarded. Is there a part of Jesus in every stamped-out crucifix? I think there is. Desire changes the world! What makes

the mountainside of maple turn red? Peace, you manu-
facturers of religious trinkets! You handle sacred material! Catherine Tekakwitha, do you see how I get carried away? How I want the world to be mystical and
good? Are the stars tiny, after all? Who will put us to
sleep? Should I save my fingernails? Is matter holy? I
want the barber to bury my hair. Catherine Tekakwitha,
are you at work on me already?

4.

Marie de l'Incarnation, Marguerite Bourgeoys, Marie-
Marguerite d'Youville, maybe you could arouse me if I
could move out of myself. I want to get as much as I
can. F. said that he'd never once heard of a female
saint he wouldn't like to have screwed. What did he
mean? F., don't tell me that at last you are becoming
profound. F. once said: At sixteen I stopped fucking
faces. I had occasioned the remark by expressing dis-
gust at his latest conquest, a young hunchback he had
met while touring an orphanage. F. spoke to me that
day as if I were truly one of the underprivileged; or
perhaps he was not speaking to me at all when he mut-
tered: Who am I to refuse the universe?

5.

The French gave the Iroquois their name. Naming
food is one thing, naming a people is another, not that
the people in question seem to care today. If they never
cared, so much the worse for me: I'm far too willing to
shoulder the alleged humiliations of harmless peoples,
as evidenced by my life work with the A——s. Why do I
feel so lousy when I wake up every morning? Wondering if I'm going to be able to shit or not. Is my body
going to work? Will my bowels churn? Has the old ma-

chine turned the food brown? Is it surprising that I've tunneled through libraries after news about victims? Fictional victims! All the victims we ourselves do not murder or imprison are fictional victims. I live in a small apartment building. The bottom of the elevator shaft is accessible through the sub-basement. While I sat downtown preparing a paper on lemmings she crawled into the elevator shaft and sat there with her arms around her drawn-up knees (or so the police determined from the mess). I came home every night at twenty to eleven, regular as Kant. She was going to teach me a lesson, my old wife. You and your fictional victims, she used to say. Her life had become gray by imperceptible degrees, for I swear, that very night, probably at the exact moment when she was squeezing into the shaft, I looked up from the lemming research and closed my eyes, remembering her as young and bright, the sun dancing in her hair as she sucked me off in a canoe on Lake Orford. We were the only ones who lived in the sub-basement, we were the only ones who commanded the little elevator into those depths. But she taught no one a lesson, not the kind of lesson she meant. A delivery boy from the Bar-B-Q did the dirty work by misreading the numbers on a warm brown paper bag. Edith! F. spent the night with me. He confessed at 4 a.m. that he'd slept with Edith five or six times in the twenty years he'd known her. Irony! We ordered chicken from the same place and we talked about my poor squashed wife, our fingers greasy, barbecue-sauce drops on the linoleum. Five or six times, a mere friendship. Could I stand on some holy mountain of experience, a long way off, and sweetly nod my Chinese head over their little love? What harm had been done to the stars? You lousy fucker, I said, how many times, five *or* six?

Ah, F. smiled, grief makes us precise! So let it be known that the Iroquois, the brethren of Catherine Tekakwitha, were given the name Iroquois by the French. They called themselves Hodenosaunee, which means People of the Long House. They had developed a new dimension to conversation. They ended every speech with the word *hiro*, which means: like I said. Thus each man took full responsibility for intruding into the inarticulate murmur of the spheres. To *hiro* they added the word *koué*, a cry of joy or distress, according to whether it was sung or howled. Thus they essayed to pierce the mysterious curtain which hangs between all talking men: at the end of every utterance a man stepped back, so to speak, and attempted to interpret his words to the listener, attempted to subvert the beguiling intellect with the noise of true emotion. Catherine Tekakwitha, speak to me in *Hiro-Koué*. I have no right to mind what the Jesuits say to the slaves, but on that cool Laurentian night which I work toward, when we are wrapped in our birch-bark rocket, joined in the ancient enduring way, flesh to spirit, and I ask you my old question: are the stars tiny, after all, O Catherine Tekakwitha, answer me in *Hiro-Koué*. That other night F. and I quarreled for hours. We didn't know when morning arrived because the only window of that miserable apartment faced into the ventilation shaft.

—You lousy fucker, how many times, five *or* six?

—Ah, grief makes us precise!

—Five or six, five or six, five or six?

—Listen, my friend, the elevator is working again.

—Listen, F., don't give me any of your mystical shit.

—Seven.

—Seven times with Edith?

—Correct.

—You were trying to protect me with an optional lie?

—Correct.

—And seven itself might just be another option.

—Correct.

—But you were trying to protect me, weren't you? Oh, F., do you think I can learn to perceive the diamonds of good amongst all the shit?

—It is all diamond.

—Damn you, rotten wife-fucker, that answer is no comfort. You ruin everything with your saintly pretensions. This is a bad morning. My wife's in no shape to be buried. They're going to straighten her out in some stinking doll hospital. How am I going to feel in the elevator on my way to the library? Don't give me this all diamond shit, shove it up your occult hole. Help a fellow out. Don't fuck his wife for him.

Thus the conversation ran into the morning we could not perceive. He kept to his diamond line. Catherine Tekakwitha, I wanted to believe him. We talked until we exhausted ourselves, and we pulled each other off, as we did when we were boys in what is now downtown but what was once the woods.

6.

F. talked a great deal about Indians, and in an irritating facile manner. As far as I know he had no scholarship on the subject beyond a contemptuous and minor acquaintance with my own books, his sexual exploitation of my four teen-age A——s, and about a thousand Hollywood Westerns. He compared the Indians to the ancient Greeks, suggesting a similarity of character, a common belief that every talent must unfold itself in fighting, a love of wrestling, an inherent incapacity to unite for any length of time, an absolute dedication to the idea of the contest and the virtue of ambition. None of the four teen-age A———s achieved orgasm, which, he said, must be characteristic of the sexual pessimism of the entire tribe, and he concluded, therefore, that every other Indian woman could. I couldn't argue. It is true that the A———s seem to present a very accurate negative of the whole Indian picture. I was slightly jealous of him for his deduction. His knowledge of ancient Greece was based entirely on a poem by Edgar Allan Poe, a few homosexual encounters with restaurateurs (he ate free at almost every soda fountain in the city), and a plaster reproduction of the Akropolis which, for some reason, he had coated with red nail polish. He had meant to use colorless nail polish merely as a preservative, but naturally he succumbed to his flamboyant disposition at the drug-store counter when confronted with that fortress of bright samples which ranged the cardboard ramparts like so many Canadian Mounties. He chose a color named Tibetan Desire, which amused him since it was, he claimed, such a contradiction in terms. The entire night he consecrated to the staining of his plaster model. I sat beside him as he worked. He was humming snatches from "The Great Pretender," a song which was to change the popular music of our day. I could not take my eyes from the tiny brush which he wielded so happily. White to viscous red, one column after another, a transfusion of blood into the powdery ruined fingers of the little monument. F. saying: I'm wearing my heart like a crown. So they disappeared, the leprous metopes and triglyphs and other wiggly names signifying purity, pale temple and destroyed altar disappeared under the scarlet glaze. F. said: Here, my friend, you finish the caryatids. So I took the brush, thus Cliton after Themistocles. F. sang: Ohohohoho, I'm the great pretender, my need is such I pretend too much, and so on—an obvious song under the circumstances but not inappropriate. F. often said: Never overlook the obvious. We were happy! Why should I resist the exclamation? I had not been so happy since before puberty. How close I came, earlier in this paragraph, to betraying that happy night! No, I will not! When we had covered every inch of the old plaster bone F. placed it on a card table in front of a window. The sun was just coming up over the sawtooth roof of the factory next door. The window was rosy and our handicraft, not yet dry, gleamed like a huge ruby, a fantastic jewel! It seemed like the intricate cradle of all the few noble perishable sentiments I had managed to preserve, and somewhere safe I could leave them. F. had stretched out on the carpet, stomach down, chin in hands supported by wrists and elbows, gazing up at the red akropolis and the soft morning beyond. He beckoned to me to lie beside him. Look at it from here, he said, squint your eyes a bit. I did as he suggested, narrowed my eyes, and—it burst into a cool lovely fire, sending out rays in all directions (except downward, since that was where the card table was). Don't weep, F. said, and we began to talk.

—That's the way it must have looked to them, some early morning when they looked up at it.

—The ancient Athenians, I whispered.

—No, F. said, the old Indians, the Red Men.

—Did they have such a thing, did they build an akropolis? I asked him, for I seemed to have forgotten everything I knew, lost it in stroke after stroke of the small brush, and I was ready to believe anything. Tell me, F., did the Indians have such a thing?

—I don't know.

—Then what are you talking about? Are you trying to make a damn fool of me?

—Lie down, take it easy. Discipline yourself. Aren't you happy?

—No.

—Why have you allowed yourself to be robbed?

—F., you spoil everything. We were having such a nice morning.

—Why have you allowed yourself to be robbed?

—Why do you always try to humiliate me? I asked him so solemnly that I scared myself. He stood up, covered the model with a plastic Remington typewriter cover. He did this so gently, with a kind of pain, that for the first time I saw that F. suffered, but from what I could not tell.

—We almost began a perfect conversation, F. said as he turned on the six o'clock news. He turned the radio very loud and began to shout wildly against the voice of the commentator, who was reciting a list of disasters. Sail on, sail on, O Ship of State, auto accidents, births, Berlin, cures for cancer! Listen, my friend, listen to the present, the right now, it's all around us, painted like a target, red, white, and blue. Sail into the target like a dart, a fluke bull's eye in a dirty pub. Empty your memory and listen to the fire around you. Don't forget your memory, let it exist somewhere precious in all the colors that it needs but somewhere else, hoist your memory on the Ship of State like a pirate's sail, and aim yourself at the tinkly present. Do you know how to do this? Do you know how to see the akropolis like the Indians did who never even had one? Fuck a saint, that's how, find a little saint and fuck her over and over in some pleasant part of heaven, get right into her plastic altar, dwell in her silver medal, fuck her until she tinkles like a souvenir music box, until the memorial lights go on for free, find a little saintly faker like Teresa or Catherine Tekakwitha or Lesbia, whom prick never knew but who lay around all day in a chocolate poem, find one of these quaint impossible cunts and fuck her for your life, coming all over the sky, fuck her on the moon with a steel hourglass up your hole, get tangled in her airy robes, suck her nothing juices, lap, lap, lap, a dog in the ether, then climb down to this fat earth and slouch around the fat earth in your stone shoes, get clobbered by a runaway target, take the senseless blows again and again, a right to the mind, piledriver on the heart, kick in the scrotum, help! help! it's my time, my second, my splinter of the shit glory tree, police, firemen! look at the traffic of happiness and crime, it's burning in crayon like the akropolis rose!

And so on. I couldn't hope to write down half the things he said. He raved like a lunatic, spit flying with every second word. I guess the disease was already nibbling at his brain, for he died like that, years later, raving. What a night! And from this distance, how sweet our argument now seems, two grown men lying on the floor! What a perfect night! I swear I can still feel the warmth of it, and what he did with Edith matters not at all, indeed, I marry them in their unlawful bed, with an open heart I affirm the true right of any man and woman to their dark slobbering nights which are rare enough, and against which too many laws conspire. If only I could live in this perspective. How quickly they come and go, the memories of F., the nights of comradeship, the ladders we climbed and the happy views of simple human clockwork. How quickly pettiness returns, and that most ignoble form of real estate, the possessive occupation and tyranny over two square inches of human flesh, the wife's cunt.

7.

The Iroquois almost won. Their three major enemies were the Hurons, the Algonquins, and the French. "La Nouvelle-France se va perdre si elle n'est fortement et promptement secourue." So wrote Le P. Vimont, Supérieur de Québec, in 1641. Whoop! Whoop! Remember the movies. The Iroquois was a confederation of five tribes situated between the Hudson River and Lake Erie. Going from east to west we have the Agniers (whom the English called Mohawks), the Onneyouts, the Onnontagués, the Goyoqouins (or Goyogouins), and the Tsonnontouans. The Mohawks (whom the French called Agniers) occupied a territory between the upper reaches of the Hudson River, Lake George, Lake Champlain, and the Richelieu River (first called the Iroquois River). Catherine Tekakwitha was a Mohawk, born 1656. Twenty-one years of her life she spent among the Mohawks, on the banks of the Mohawk River, a veritable Mohawk lady. The Iroquois were composed of twenty-five thousand souls. They could put two thousand five hundred warriors in the field, or ten per cent of the confederation. Of these only five or six hundred were Mohawks, but they were especially ferocious, and not only that, they possessed firearms which they got from the Dutch at Fort Orange (Albany) in exchange for furs. I am proud that Catherine Tekakwitha was or is a Mohawk. Her brethren must be right out of those uncompromising black and white movies before the Western became psychological. Right now I feel about her as many of my readers must feel about pretty Negresses

who sit across from them in the subway, their thin hard
legs shooting down from what pink secrets. Many of my
readers will never find out. Is this fair? And what about
the lily cocks unbeknownst to so many female American
citizens? Undress, undress, I want to cry out, let's look at
each other. Let's have education! F. said: At twenty-
eight (yes, my friend, it took that long) I stopped fucking colors. Catherine Tekakwitha, I hope you are very
dark. I want to detect a little whiff of raw meat and
white blood on your thick black hair. I hope there is a
little grease left in your thick black hair. Or is it all
buried in the Vatican, vaults of hidden combs? One
night in our seventh year of marriage Edith coated herself with deep red greasy stuff she had bought in some
theatrical supply store. She applied it from a tube.
Twenty to eleven, back from the library, and there she
was, stark naked in the middle of the room, sexual
surprise for her old man. She handed me the tube,
saying: Let's be other people. Meaning, I suppose, new
ways to kiss, chew, suck, bounce. It's stupid, she said,
her voice cracking, but let's be other people. Why
should I diminish her intention? Perhaps she meant:
Come on a new journey with me, a journey only
strangers can take, and we can remember it when we
are ourselves again, and therefore never be merely ourselves again. Perhaps she had some landscape in mind
where she always meant to travel, just as I envisage a
northern river, a night as clean and bright as river
pebbles, for my supreme trip with Catherine Tekakwitha. I should have gone with Edith. I should have
stepped out of my clothes and into the greasy disguise.
Why is it that only now, years past, my prick rises
up at the vision of her standing there so absurdly
painted, her breasts dark as eggplants, her face re-

sembling Al Jolson? Why does the blood rush now so
uselessly? I disdained her tube. Take a bath, I said. I
listened to her splashing, looking forward to our midnight snack. My mean little triumph had made me
hungry.

8.

Lots of priests got killed and eaten and so forth. Mic-
macs, Abénaquis, Montagnais, Attikamègues, Hurons:
the Company of Jesus had their way with them. Lots of
semen in the forest, I'll bet. Not the Iroquois, they ate
priests' hearts. Wonder what it was like. F. said he
once ate a raw sheep's heart. Edith liked brains. René
Goupil got it on September 29, 1642, first victim in
black robes of the Mohawks. Yum, yummy. Le P. Jogues
fell under the "hatchet of the barbarian" on October 18,
1646. It's all down there in black and white. The Church
loves such details. I love such details. Here come the
little fat angels with their queer bums. Here come the
Indians. Here comes Catherine Tekakwitha ten years
later, lily out of the soil watered by the Gardener with
the blood of martyrs. F., you ruined my life with your
experiments. You ate a raw sheep's heart, you ate bark,
once you ate shit. How can I live in the world beside
all your damn adventures? F. once said: There is nothing so depressing as the eccentricity of a contemporary.
She was a Tortoise, best clan of the Mohawks. Our
journey will be slow, but we'll win. Her father was an
Iroquois, an asshole, as it turns out. Her mother was an
Algonquin Christian, baptized and educated at Three-
Rivers, which happens to be a lousy town for an Indian
girl (I was told recently by a young Abénaqui who
went to school there). She was taken captive in an
Iroquois raid, which was probably the best lay she ever

had. Help me, someone, help my crude tongue. Where
is my silver tongue? Aren't I meant to speak of God? She
was the slave of an Iroquois brave, and she had a wild
tongue or something because he married her when he
could have just pushed her around. She was accepted
by the tribe and enjoyed all the rights of the Tortoises
from that day on. It is recorded that she prayed inces-
santly. Glog, glog, dear God, hump, fart push, sweet
Almighty, slurp, flark, glamph, hiccup, jerk, zzzzzz, snort,
Jesus, she must have made his life hell.

9.

F. said: Connect nothing. He screamed that remark at
me while overlooking my wet cock about twenty years
ago. I don't know what he saw in my swooning eyes,
maybe some glimmering of a fake universal comprehen-
sion. Sometimes after I have come or just before I fall
asleep, my mind seems to go out on a path the width of
a thread and of endless length, a thread that is the
same color as the night. Out, out along the narrow
highway sails my mind, driven by curiosity, luminous
with acceptance, far and out, like a feathered hook
whipped deep into the light above the stream by a
magnificent cast. Somewhere, out of my reach, my control, the hook unbends into a spear, the spear shears
itself into a needle, and the needle sews the world together. It sews skin onto the skeleton and lipstick on a
lip, it sews Edith to her greasepaint, crouching (for as
long as I, this book, or an eternal eye remembers) in our
lightless sub-basement, it sews scarves to mountain, it
goes through everything like a relentless bloodstream,
and the tunnel is filled with a comforting message, a
beautiful knowledge of unity. All the disparates of the

world, the different wings of the paradox, coin-faces of problem, petal-pulling questions, scissors-shaped conscience, all the polarities, things and their images and things which cast no shadow, and just the everyday explosions on a street, this face and that, a house and a toothache, explosions which merely have different letters in their names, my needle pierces it all, and I myself, my greedy fantasies, everything which has existed and does exist, we are part of a necklace of incomparable beauty and unmeaning. Connect nothing: F. shouted. Place things side by side on your arborite table, if you must, but connect nothing! Come back, F. shouted, pulling my limp cock like a bell rope, shaking it like a dinner bell in the hands of a grand hostess who wants the next course served. Don't be fooled, he cried. Twenty years ago, as I say. I am just speculating now what it was that occasioned his outburst, that is, some kind of smirk of universal acceptance, which is very disagreeable on the face of a young man. It was that same afternoon that F. told me one of his most remarkable lies.

—My friend, F. said, you mustn't feel guilty about any of this.

—Any of what?

—Oh, you know, sucking each other, watching the movies, Vaseline, fooling around with the dog, sneaking off during government hours, under the armpits.

—I don't feel in the least guilty.

—You do. But don't. You see, F. said, this isn't homosexuality at all.

—Oh, F., come off it. Homosexuality is a name.

—That's why I'm telling you this, my friend. You live in a world of names. That's why I have the charity to tell you this.

—Are you trying to ruin another evening?

—Listen to me, you poor A——!

—It's you who feel guilty, F. Guilty as hell. You're the guilty party.

—Ha. Ha. Ha. Ha. Ha.

—I know what you want to do, F. You want to destroy the evening. You're not satisfied with a couple of simple comes and a nice poke in the hole.

—All right, my friend, you've convinced me. I'm perishing with guilt. I'll keep quiet.

—What were you going to say?

—Some fabrication of my guilty guilt.

—Well, tell me, now that you started the whole thing.

—No.

—Tell me, F., for Christ's sake, it's just conversation now.

—No.

—God damn you, F., you are trying to destroy the evening.

—You're pathetic. That's why you must not try to connect anything, your connection would be pathetic. The Jews didn't let young men study the Cabala. Connections should be forbidden citizens under seventy.

—Please tell me.

—You mustn't feel guilty about any of this because it isn't strictly homosexual.

—I know it isn't, I—

—Shut up. It isn't strictly homosexual because I am not strictly male. The truth is, I had a Swedish operation, I used to be a girl.

—Nobody's perfect.

—Shut up, shut up. A man tires in his works of charity. I was born a girl, I went to school as a girl in a blue tunic, with a little embroidered crest on the front of it.

—F., you're not talking to one of your shoeshine boys. I happen to know you very well. We lived on the same street, we went to school together, we were in the same class, I saw you a million times in the shower after gym. You were a boy when you went to school. We played doctor in the woods. What's the point of all this?

—Thus do the starving refuse sustenance.

—I hate the way you try to end everything off.

But I broke off the argument just then because I noticed that it was almost eight, and we were in danger of missing the entire double feature. How I enjoyed the movies that night. Why did I feel so light? Why did I have so deep a sense of comradeship with F.? Walking home through the snow my future seemed to open me: I resolved to give up work on the A——s, whose disastrous history was not yet clear to me. I didn't know what I wanted to do, but it didn't bother me, I knew that the future would be strewn with invitations, like a President's calendar. The cold, which hitherto froze my balls off every winter, braced me that night, and my brain, for which I have always had little respect, seemed constructed of arrangements of crystal, like a storm of snowflakes, filling my life with rainbow pictures. However, it didn't work out that way. The A——s found their mouthpiece and the future dried up like an old dug. What was F.'s part in that lovely night? Had he done something which opened doors, doors which I slammed back in their frames? He tried to tell me something. I still don't understand. Is it fair that I don't understand? Why did I have to be stuck with such an obtuse friend? My life might have been so gloriously different. I might never have married Edith, who, I now confess, was an A——!

10.

I always wanted to be loved by the Communist Party and the Mother Church. I wanted to live in a folk song like Joe Hill. I wanted to weep for the innocent people my bomb would have to maim. I wanted to thank the peasant father who fed us on the run. I wanted to wear my sleeve pinned in half, people smiling while I salute with the wrong hand. I wanted to be against the rich, even though some of them knew Dante: just before his destruction one of them would learn that I knew Dante, too. I wanted my face carried in Peking, a poem written down my shoulder. I wanted to smile at dogma, yet ruin my ego against it. I wanted to confront the machines of Broadway. I wanted Fifth Avenue to remember its Indian trails. I wanted to come out of a mining town with rude manners and convictions given to me by an atheist uncle, barfly disgrace of the family. I wanted to rush across America in a sealed train, the only white man whom the Negroes will accept at the treaty convention. I wanted to attend cocktail parties wearing a machine gun. I wanted to tell an old girl friend who is appalled at my methods that revolutions do not happen on buffet tables, you can't pick and choose, and watch her silver evening gown dampen at the crotch. I wanted to fight against the Secret Police takeover, but from *within* the Party. I wanted an old lady who had lost her sons to mention me in her prayers in a mud church, taking her sons' word for it. I wanted to cross myself at dirty words. I wanted to tolerate pagan remnants in village ritual, arguing against the Curia. I wanted to deal in secret real estate, agent of ageless, anonymous billionaire. I wanted to write well about the Jews. I wanted to be shot among the Basques for carrying the Body into the battlefield against Franco. I wanted to preach about marriage from the unassailable pulpit of virginity, watching the black hairs on the legs of brides. I wanted to write a tract against birth control in very simple English, a pamphlet to be sold in the foyer, illustrated with two-color drawings of shooting stars and eternity. I wanted to suppress dancing for a time. I wanted to be a junkie priest who makes a record for Folkways. I wanted to be transferred for political reasons. I have just discovered that Cardinal ———— has taken a huge bribe from a ladies' magazine, have suffered a fairy attack from my confessor, have seen the peasants betrayed for a necessary reason, but the bells are ringing this evening, it is another evening in God's world, and there are many to be fed, many knees yearning to be bent, I mount the worn steps in my tattered ermine.

11.

The long house of the Iroquois must be clear. Length: varied from one hundred to one hundred fifty feet. Height and width: twenty-five feet. Lateral beams supporting a roof made from large pieces of bark, cedar, ash, elm, or pine. Neither window nor chimney, but a door at each extremity. Light got in and smoke got out through holes in the roof. Several fires in the cabin, four families to each fire. Families arranged so that there was a corridor running down the length of the cabin. "La manière dont les familles se groupent dans les cabanes n'est pas pour entraver le libertinage." Thus Le P.

Edouard Lecompte, S.J., wrote in 1930, whetting our
sexual appetite in his expert Company manner. The
long-house setup did little to "hinder licentiousness."
What went on in the dark tunnel? Catherine Tekakwitha, what did you see with your swollen eyes? What
juices mixing on the bearskin? Was it worse than a
movie theater? F. said: The atmosphere of a movie
theater is a nighttime marriage of a man's prison and a
woman's prison; the prisoners know nothing about it—
only the bricks and gates have combined; in the ventilation system the mystic union is consummated: the smells
absorb each other. F.'s extravagant observation coincides
with something a clergyman told me. He said that on
Sunday morning the odor of semen hangs like a damp
cloud above the men gathered for chapel at Bordeaux
Jail. The modern art-cinema house, made of concrete
and velvet, is a joke, which, as F. said, is nothing but
the death of an emotion. No marriage in these stark
confines, everybody sitting on their genitals because:
silver genitals on the screen. Bring back hidden sex! Let
cocks again rise and twine like ivy round the gold projector beam, and cunts yawn under gloves and white
paper bags of candy, and no naked flashing breasts
lure the dirty laundry of our daily lives into the movie
palace, deadly as a radar signal, no neorealist patent
fucking hang the impenetrable curtains of possibility
between each member of the audience! In the gloomy
long house of my mind let me trade wives, let me
stumble upon you, Catherine Tekakwitha, three hundred
years old, fragrant as a birch sapling, no matter what
the priests or plague have done to you.

12.

The Plague! The Plague! It invades my pages of research. My desk is suddenly contagious. My erection
topples like a futuristic Walt Disney film of the leaning
Tower of Pisa, to the music of timpani and creaking
doors. I speed down my zipper and out falls dust and
rubble. Hard cock alone leads to Thee, this I know because I've lost everything in this dust. Plague among
the Mohawks! In 1660 it broke out, raging along the
Mohawk River, assaulting the Indian villages, Gandaouagué, Gandagoron, Tionnontoguen, like a forest
fire powered by the wind, and it came to Ossernenon,
where lived Catherine Tekakwitha, four years old.
Down goes her warrior father and her Christian mother,
croaking out her final confession, down goes her little
brother, his little prick useless as an appendix forever.
Of this doomed, intermarried family, only Catherine
Tekakwitha survived, the price of admission gouged in
her face. Catherine Tekakwitha is not pretty! Now I
want to run from my books and dreams. I don't want to
fuck a pig. Can I yearn after pimples and pock marks?
I want to go outside and walk in the park and look at
the long legs of American children. What keeps me
here while lilacs grow outside for everybody? Can F.
teach me something? He said that at the age of sixteen
he stopped fucking faces. Edith was lovely when I first
met her in the hotel, where she sold manicures. Her
hair was black, long and smooth, the softness of cotton
rather than silk. Her eyes were black, a solid depthless
black that gave nothing away (except once or twice),
like those sunglasses made of mirrors. In fact, she often
wore that kind of sunglasses. Her lips were not full but
very soft. Her kisses were loose, somehow unspecific, as

if her mouth couldn't choose where to stay. It slipped over my body like a novice on roller skates. I always hoped it would fasten somewhere perfect and find its home in my ecstasy, but off it slipped after too brief a perch, in search of nothing but balance, driven not by passion but by a banana peel. God knows what F. has to say about all this, damn him. I couldn't bear to discover that she lingered for him. Stay, stay, I wanted to shout at her in the thick air of the sub-basement, come back, come back, don't you see where all my skin is pointing? But off she skidded, up the piggy steps of my toes, a leap into my ear while my manhood ached like a frantic radio tower, come back, come back, a plunge into my eye where she sucked too hard (remembering her taste for brains), not there, not there, now grazing the hair of my chest like a seagull over spray, come back to Capistrano sang the knob, up to my kneecap, a desert of sensation, exploring the kneecap so very carefully as if it hid a locket clasp her tongue could spring, infuriating waste of tongue, now descending like laundry down the washboard of my ribs, her mouth wants me to turn over so that it can roller-coast down my spine or some foolish thing, no I won't turn over and bury my hope, down, down, come back, come back, no I won't fold it against my stomach like a hideaway bed, Edith, Edith, let some things happen in heaven, don't make me tell you! . . . I didn't think this would force itself into my preparations. It is very hard to court you, Catherine Tekakwitha, with your pock-marked face and your insatiable curiosity. One lick, now and then, brief warm coronations promising glory, an occasional collar of ermine teeth, then a swift disgrace, as if the archbishop suddenly learned he'd crowned the wrong son, her saliva cold as an icicle as it dried down the length of her exit, and this member of mine rigid as a goal post, hopeless as a pillar of salt in the destruction, ready at last to settle for a lonely night with my own hands, Edith! I broke my problem to F.

—I listen in envy, F. said. Don't you know you're being loved?

—I want her to love me in *my* way.

—You've got to learn—

—No lessons, I'm not going to settle for lessons this time. This is my bed and my wife, I have some rights.

—Then ask her.

—What do you mean "ask her"?

—Please make me come with your mouth, Edith.

—You're disgusting, F. How dare you use that language in connection with Edith? I didn't tell you this so that you could soil our intimacy.

—I'm sorry.

—Of course, I could ask her, that's obvious. But then she'd be under duress, or worse, it would become a matter of duty. I don't want to hold a strap over her.

—Yes you do.

—I warn you, F., I'm not going to take your cowardly guru shit.

—You are being loved, you are being invited into a great love, and I envy you.

—And stay away from Edith. I don't like the way she sits between us at the movies. That is just courtesy on our part.

—I'm grateful to you both. I assure you, she could love no other man as she loves you.

—Do you think that's true, F.?

—I know it's true. Great love is not a partnership, for a partnership can be dissolved by law or parting, and you're stuck with a great love, as a matter of fact, you are stuck with two great loves, Edith's and mine. Great love needs a servant, but you don't know how to use your servants.

—How should I ask her?

—With whips, with imperial commands, with a leap into her mouth and a lesson in choking.

I see F. standing there, the window behind him, his paper-thin ears almost transparent. I remember the expensively appointed slum room, the view of the factory he was trying to buy, his collection of soap arranged like a model town on the green felt of an elaborately carved billiard table. The light came through his ears as if they were made of a bar of Pears Soap. I hear his phony voice, the slight Eskimo accent which he affected after a student summer in the Arctic. You are stuck with two great loves, F. said. What a poor custodian I have been of those two loves, an ignorant custodian who walked his days in a dream museum of self-pity. F. and Edith loved me! But I didn't hear his declaration that morning or didn't believe it. You don't know how to use your servants, F. said, his ears beaming like Jap lanterns. I was loved in 1950! But I didn't speak to Edith, I couldn't. Night after night I lay in the dark listening to the sounds of the elevator, my silent commands buried in my brain, like those urgent proud inscriptions on Egyptian monuments dumb under tons of sand. So her mouth sailed crazily over my body like a flock of Bikini birds, their migratory instincts destroyed by radiation.

—But I warn you, F. continued, a time will come when you'll want nothing in the world but those aimless kisses.

Talking about transparent skin, Edith's throat was like that, the thinnest, softest cover. You thought a heavy shell necklace would draw blood. To kiss her ure was to intrude into something private and skeletal, like a turtle's shoulder. Her shoulders were bony but not meager. She wasn't thin but no matter how full the flesh her bones were always in command. From the age of thirteen she had the kind of skin which was called ripe, and the men who pursued her then (she was finally raped in a stone quarry) said that she was the kind of girl who would age quickly, which is the way that men on corners comfort themselves about an unattainable child. She grew up in a small town on the north shore of the St. Lawrence, where she infuriated a number of men who thought that they should be able to rub her small breasts and round bum simply because she was an Indian, an A—— at that! At sixteen, when I married her, I myself believed that her skin couldn't last. It had that fragile juicy quality we associate with growing things just about to decline. At twenty-four, the year of her death, nothing had altered but her buttocks. At sixteen they had been two half spheres suspended in midair, later they came to rest on two deep curved creases, and this was the extent of her body's decay until she was squashed all at once. Let me think about her. She liked me to rub her skin with olive oil. I complied even though I really didn't like playing around with food. Sometimes she filled her belly-button hole with oil and using her little finger she drew the spokes of Asoka's wheel, then she smeared it, skin darkening. Her breasts were small, somewhat muscular, fruit with fiber. Her freakish nipples make me want to tear up my desk when I remember them, which I do at this very instant, miserable paper memory while my cock soars hopelessly into her mangled coffin, and my arms wave my duties away, even you, Catherine Tekakwitha, whom I court with this confession. Her wondrous nipples were dark as mud and very long when stiffened by desire, over an inch high, wrinkled with wisdom and sucking. I stuffed them into my nostrils (one at a time). I stuffed them in my ears. I believed continually that if anatomy permitted and I could have stuffed a nipple into each of my ears at the same time—shock treatment! What is the use of reviving this fantasy, impossible then as now? But I want those leathery electrodes in my head! I want to hear the mystery explained, I want to hear the conversations between those stiff wrinkled sages. There were such messages going between them that even Edith could not hear, signals, warnings, conceits. Revelations! Mathematics! I told F. about this the night of her death.

—You could have had everything you wanted.

—Why do you torment me, F.?

—You lost yourself in particulars. All parts of the body are erotogenic, or at least have the possibility of so becoming. If she had stuck her index fingers in your ears you would have got the same results.

—Are you sure?

—Yes.

—Have you tried it?

—Yes.

—I have to ask you this. With Edith?

—Yes.

—F.!

—Listen, my friend, the elevators, the buzzers, the fan: the world is waking up in the heads of a few million.

—Stop. Did you do that with her? Did you go that far? Did you do that together? You're going to sit right there and tell me every detail. I hate you, F.

—Well, she stuck her index fingers—

—Was she wearing nail polish?

—No.

—She was, damn you, she was! Stop trying to protect me.

—All right, she was. She stuck her red nails in my ears—

—You enjoy this, don't you?

—She stuck her fingers in my ears and I stuck my fingers in her ears and we kissed.

—You did it to each other? With your bare fingers? You touched ears and fingers?

—You begin to learn.

—Shut up. What did her ears feel like?

—Tight.

—Tight!

—Edith had very tight ears, nearly virgin, I'd say.

—Get out, F.! Get off our bed! Take your hands off me!

—Listen, or I'll break your neck, chicken voyeur. We were fully dressed except for our fingers. Yes! We sucked each other's fingers, and then we stuck them in each other's ears—

—The ring, did she take the ring off?

—I don't think so. I was worried about my eardrums because of her long red nails, she was digging so hard. We shut our eyes and we kissed like friends, without opening our mouths. Suddenly the sounds of the lobby were gone and I was listening to Edith.

—To her body! Where did this happen? When did you do this to me?

—So those are your questions. It happened in a telephone booth in the lobby of a movie theater downtown.

—What theater?

—The System Theatre.

—You're lying! There is no telephone booth in the System. There's only one or two telephones on the wall separated by glass partitions, I think. You did it out in the open! I know that dirty basement lobby! There's always some fairy hanging around there, drawing cocks and telephone numbers on the green wall. Out in the open! Was anyone watching? How could you do this to me?

—You were in the men's room. We were waiting for you beside the telephones, eating chocolate-covered ice-cream bars. I don't know what was keeping you so long. We finished our ice cream. Edith spotted a flake of chocolate sticking to my little finger. In a very charming fashion she leaned over and flicked it into her mouth with her tongue, like an anteater. She had overlooked a flake of chocolate on her own wrist. I swooped in and got that, clumsily, I confess. Then it turned into a game. Games are nature's most beautiful creation. All animals play games, and the truly Messianic vision of the brotherhood of creatures must be based on the idea of the game, indeed—

—So Edith began it! And who touched whose ear first? I have to know everything now. You saw her tongue stretched out, you probably stared. Who started it with the ears?

—I don't remember. Maybe we were under the influence of the telephones. If you remember, one of the fluorescent lights was flickering, and the corner where we were standing jumped in and out of shadows as though great wings were passing over us or the huge blades of an immense electric fan. The telephones kept their steady black, the only stable shape in the shifting

gloom. They hung there like carved masks, black, gleaming, smooth as the toes of kissed stone R.C. saints. We
were sucking each other's fingers, slightly frightened
now, like children pulling at lollipops during the car
chase. And then one of the telephones rang! It rang
just once. I am always startled when a pay phone rings.
It is so imperial and forlorn, like the best poem of a
minor poet, like King Michael saying good-by to Communist Romania, like a message in a floating bottle
which begins: If anyone finds this, know that—

—Damn you, F.! You're torturing me. Please.

—You asked me for the whole picture. I forgot to mention that the lights were buzzing, unevenly, like the
snores of a sinus victim. I was sucking her narrow finger,
careful of the sharp nail, thinking of the wolves who
bleed to death from licking the blood-baited knife.
When the light was healthy our skin was yellow, the
merest pimple exaggerated, and when it failed we fell
into a purple pallor, our skin like old wet mushrooms.
And when it rang we were so startled that we actually
bit each other! Children in a scary cave. Yes, there was
someone watching us, not that we cared. He was watching us in the mirror of the fortune-telling scale which he
was climbing off and on, dropping in nickel after nickel,
dialing various questions, or the same one for all I know.
And where the hell were you? The basement of the
System is a horrible place if you do not stick with the
people you came with. It smells like a desperate clearing in a siege of rats—

—You lie. Edith's skin was perfect. And it smells of
piss, nothing else, just piss. And never mind what I was
doing.

—I know what you were doing, but never mind. When

the telephone rang this fellow wheeled around and stepped off the scale, quite gracefully, I must say, and in that moment the whole eerie place seemed like his personal office. We were standing between him and his telephone, and I feared (it sounds ridiculous) that he would do some violence, pull a knife or expose himself, for his whole weary life among the water pipes and urinals seemed to hang on this telephone message—

—I remember him! He was wearing one of those Western string neckties.

—Right. I remember thinking in that instant of terror that he had conjured up the ring himself with his incessant dialing, that he had been performing a ritual, like rain-making. He was looking right through us as he stepped forward. He stopped, waiting, I suppose, for the second ring, which never came. He snapped his fingers, turned, climbed back on the scale, and returned to his combinations. We felt delivered, Edith and I! The telephone, hitherto so foreboding and powerful, was our friend! It was the agent of some benign electronic deity, and we wanted to praise it. I suppose that certain primitive bird and snake dances began the same way, a need to imitate the fearful and the beautiful, yes, an imitative procedure to acquire some of the qualities of the adored awesome beast.

—What are you trying to tell me, F.?

—We invented the Telephone Dance. Spontaneously. I don't know who made the first move. Suddenly our index fingers were in each other's ears. We became telephones!

—I don't know whether to laugh or cry.

—Why are you crying?

—I think you have ruined my life, F. For years I've

been telling secrets to an enemy.

—You're wrong, my friend. I have loved you, we've both loved you, and you're very close to understanding this.

—No, F., no. Maybe it's true, but it's been too hard, too much crazy education, and God knows for what. Every second day I've had to learn something, some lesson, some lousy parable, and what am I this morning, a Doctor of Shit.

—That's it. That's love!

—Please go away.

—Don't you want to hear what happened when I was a telephone?

—I do, but I don't want to beg. I have to beg you for every scrap of information about the world.

—But that's the only way you value it. When it falls on you from out of the trees you think it's rotten fruit.

—Tell me about Edith when you were telephones.

—No.

—Arrwk! Sób! Ahahah! Sob!

—Contain yourself. Discipline!

—You're killing me, you're killing me, you're killing me!

—Now you're ready. We dug our index fingers in each other's ears. I won't deny the sexual implications. You are ready to face them now. All parts of the body are erotogenic. Assholes can be trained with whips and kisses, that's elementary. Pricks and cunts have become monstrous! Down with genital imperialism! All flesh can come! Don't you see what we have lost? Why have we abdicated so much pleasure to that which lives in our underwear? Orgasms in the shoulder! Knees going off like firecrackers! Hair in motion! And not only caresses leading us into the nourishing anonymity of the climax, not only sucking and wet tubes, but wind and conversation and a beautiful pair of gloves, fingers blushing! Lost! Lost!

—You're insane. I've told my secrets to an insane person.

—There we were, locked in the Telephone Dance. Edith's ears began to wrap around my fingers, at least so it seemed. She was very highly developed, perhaps the most highly developed woman I ever knew. Her ears folded around my throbbing fingers—

—I don't want the details! I see the two of you a lot clearer than you could ever describe. That's a picture I'll never be able to get out of my mind.

—Jealousy is the education you have chosen.

—Fuck you. What did you hear?

—Hear is not the right word. I *became* a telephone. Edith was the electrical conversation that went through me.

—Well, what was it, what was it?

—Machinery.

—Machinery?

—Ordinary eternal machinery.

—And?

—Ordinary eternal machinery.

—Is that all you're going to say?

—Ordinary eternal machinery like the grinding of the stars.

—That's better.

—That was a distortion of the truth, which, I see, suits you very well. I distorted the truth to make it easy for you. The truth is: ordinary eternal machinery.

—Was it nice?

—It was the most beautiful thing I have ever felt.

—Did she like it?

—No.

—Really?

—Yes, she liked it. How anxious you are to be deceived!

—F., I could kill you for what you've done. Courts would forgive me.

—You've done enough killing for one night.

—Get off our bed! Our bed! This was our bed!

I don't want to think too much about what F. said. Why must I? Who was he after all but a madman who lost control of his bowels, a fucker of one's wife, a collector of soap, a politician? Ordinary eternal machinery. Do I have to understand that? This morning is another morning, flowers have opened up again, men turn on their sides to see whom they have married, everything is ready to begin anew. Why must I be lashed to the past by the words of a dead man? Why must I reproduce these conversations so painstakingly, letting not one lost comma alter the beat of our voices? I want to talk to men in taverns and buses and remember nothing. And you, Catherine Tekakwitha, burning in your stall of time, does it please you that I strip myself so cruelly? I fear you smell of the Plague. The long house where you crouch day after day smells of the Plague. Why is my research so hard? Why can't I memorize baseball statistics like the Prime Minister? Why do baseball statistics smell like the Plague? What has happened to the morning? My desk smells! 1660 smells! The Indians are dying! The trails smell! They are pouring roads over the trails, it doesn't help. Save the Indians! Serve them the hearts of Jesuits! I caught the Plague in my butterfly net. I merely wanted to fuck a saint, as F. advised.

I don't know why it seemed like such a good idea. I barely understand it but it seemed like the only thing left to me. Here I am courting with research, the only juggling I can do, waiting for the statues to move—and what happens? I've poisoned the air, I've lost my erection. Is it because I've stumbled on the truth about Canada? I don't want to stumble on the truth about Canada. Have the Jews paid for the destruction of Jericho? Will the French learn how to hunt? Are wigwam souvenirs enough? City Fathers, kill me, for I have talked too much about the Plague. I thought the Indians died of bullet wounds and broken treaties. More roads! The forest stinks! Catherine Tekakwitha, is there something sinister in your escape from the Plague? Do I have to love a mutant? Look at me, Catherine Tekakwitha, a man with a stack of contagious papers, limp in the groin. Look at you, Catherine Tekakwitha, your face half eaten, unable to go outside in the sun because of the damage to your eyes. Shouldn't I be chasing someone earlier than you? Discipline, as F. said. This must not be easy. And if I knew where my research led, where would the danger be? I confess that I don't know the point of anything. Take one step to the side and it's all absurd. What is this fucking of a dead saint? It's impossible. We all know that. I'll publish a paper on Catherine Tekakwitha, that's all. I'll get married again. The National Museum needs me. I've been through a lot, I'll make a marvelous lecturer. I'll pass off F.'s sayings as my own, become a wit, a mystic wit. He owes me that much. I'll give away his soap collection to female students, a bar at a time, lemon cunts, pine cunts, I'll be a master of mixed juices. I'll run for Parliament, just like F. I'll get the Eskimo accent. I'll have the wives of other men. Edith! Her lovely body comes stalking

back, the balanced walk, the selfish eyes (or are they?).
Oh, she does not stink of the Plague. Please don't make
me think about your parts. Her belly button was a tiny
swirl, almost hidden. If all the breeze it took to ruffle
a tea rose suddenly became flesh, it would be like her
belly button. On different occasions she covered it with
oil, semen, thirty-five dollars' worth of perfume, a burr,
rice, urine, the parings of a man's fingernails, another
man's tears, spit, a thimbleful of rain water. I've got to
recall the occasions.

OIL: Countless times. She kept a bottle of olive oil beside the bed. I always thought flies would come.

SEMEN: F.'s too? I couldn't bear that. She made me deposit it there myself. She wanted to see me masturbate for the last time. How could I tell her that it was
the most intense climax of my life?

RICE: Raw rice. She kept one grain in there for a week,
claiming that she could cook it.

URINE: Don't be ashamed, she said.

FINGERNAILS: She said that Orthodox Jews buried their
fingernail parings. I'm uneasy as I remember this. It's
just the kind of observation that F. would make. Did
she get the idea from him?

MAN'S TEARS: A curious incident. We were sunbathing
on the beach at Old Orchard, Maine. A complete
stranger in a blue bathing suit threw himself on her
stomach, weeping. I grabbed his hair to pull him
away. She struck my hand sharply. I looked around;
nobody had noticed so I felt a little better about it.
I timed the man: he cried for five minutes. There
were thousands stretched on the beach. Why did he
have to pick us? I smiled stupidly at people passing,
as if this loony were my bereaved brother-in-law. No-

body seemed to notice. He had on one of those cheap wool bathing suits that do nothing for the balls. He cried quietly, Edith's right hand on the nape of his neck. This isn't happening, I tried to think, Edith's not a sandy whore. Abruptly and clumsily, he rose on one knee, stood up, ran away. Edith looked after him for a while, then turned to comfort me. He was an A———, she whispered. Impossible! I shouted furiously. I've documented every living A———! You're lying, Edith! You loved him slobbering on your navel. Admit it! Perhaps you're right, she said, perhaps he wasn't an A———. That was a chance I couldn't take. I spent the rest of the day patroling miles of beach, but he'd gone somewhere with his snotty nose.

SPIT: I don't know why. In fact, I can't remember when exactly. Have I imagined this one?

RAIN WATER: She got the idea it was raining at two in the morning. We couldn't tell because of the window situation. I took a thimble and went upstairs. She appreciated the favor.

There is no doubt that she believed her belly button to be a sensory organ, better than that, a purse which guaranteed possession in her personal voodoo system. Many times she held me hard and soft against her there, telling stories through the night. Why was I never quite comfortable? Why did I listen to the fan and the elevator?

13.

Days without work. Why did that list depress me? I should never have made the list. I've done something bad to your belly, Edith. I tried to use it. I tried to use your belly against the Plague. I tried to be a man in a padded locker room telling a beautiful smutty story to eternity. I tried to be an emcee in tuxedo arousing a lodge of honeymooners, my bed full of golf widows. I forgot that I was desperate. I forgot that I began this research in desperation. My briefcase fooled me. My tidy notes led me astray. I thought I was doing a job. The old books on Catherine Tekakwitha by P. Cholenec, the manuscripts of M. Remy, Miracles faits en sa paroisse par l'intercession de la B. Cath. Tekakwith, 1696, from the archives of Collège Sainte-Marie—the evidence tricked me into mastery. I started making plans like a graduating class. I forgot who I was. I forgot that I never learned to play the harmonica. I forgot that I gave up the guitar because F chord made my fingers bleed. I forgot about the socks I've stiffened with semen. I tried to sail past the Plague in a gondola, young tenor about to be discovered by talent-scout tourist. I forgot about jars Edith handed me that I couldn't open. I forgot the way Edith died, the way F. died, wiping his ass with a curtain. I forgot that I only have one more chance. I thought Edith would rest in a catalogue. I thought I was a citizen, private, user of public facilities. I forgot about constipation! Constipation didn't let me forget. Constipation ever since I compiled the list. Five days ruined in their first half-hours. Why me?— the great complaint of the constipated. Why doesn't the world work for me? The lonely sitting man in the porcelain machine. What did I do wrong yesterday? What unassailable bank in my psyche needs shit? How can I begin anything new with all of yesterday in me? The hater of history crouched over the immaculate bowl. How can I prove the body is on my side? Is my stomach an enemy? The chronic loser at morning roulette plans his suicide: a leap into the St. Lawrence weighted with

a sealed bowel. What good are movies? I am too heavy
for music. I am invisible if I leave no daily evidence.
Old food is poison, and the sacks leak. Unlock me!
Exhausted Houdini! Lost ordinary magic! The squatting
man bargains with God, submitting list after list of New
Year's Resolutions. I will eat only lettuce. Give me diar-
rhea if I've got to have something. Let me help the
flowers and dung beetles. Let me into the world club. I
am not enjoying sunsets, then for whom do they burn?
I'll miss my train. My portion of the world's work will
not be done, I warn you. If sphincter must be coin let it
be Chinese coin. Why me? I'll use science against you.
I'll drop in pills like depth charges. I'm sorry, I'm sorry,
don't make it tighter. Nothing helps, is that what you
want me to learn? The straining man perched on a circle prepares to abandon all systems. Take hope, take
cathedrals, take the radio, take my research. These are
hard to give up, but a load of shit is harder still. Yes,
yes, I abandon even the system of renunciation. In the
tiled dawn courtroom a folded man tries a thousand
oaths. Let me testify! Let me prove Order! Let me cast a
shadow! Please make me empty, if I'm empty then I can
receive, if I can receive it means it comes from somewhere outside of me, if it comes from outside of me I'm
not alone! I cannot bear this loneliness. Above all it is
loneliness. I don't want to be a star, merely dying. Please
let me be hungry, then I am not the dead center, then
I can single out the trees in their particular lives, then
I can be curious about the names of rivers, the altitude
of mountains, the different spellings of Tekakwitha, Te-
gahouita, Tegahkouita, Tehgakwita, Tekakouita, oh, I
want to be fascinated by phenomena! I don't want to
live inside! Renew my life. How can I exist as the
vessel of yesterday's slaughter? Is the meat punishing

me? Are there wild herds who think poorly of me? Murder in the kitchen! Dachau farmyards! We are grooming beings to eat! Does God love the world? What a monstrous system of nourishment! All of us animal tribes at eternal war! What have we won? Humans, the dietary Nazis! Death at the center of nourishment! Who will apologize to the cows? It's not our fault, we didn't think this whole thing up. These kidneys are kidneys. This is not chicken, this is a chicken. Think of the death camps in the basement of a hotel. Blood on the pillows! Matter impaled on toothbrushes! All animals eating, not for pleasure, not for gold, not for power, but merely to be. For whose eternal Pleasure? Tomorrow I begin my fast. I resign. But I can't resign with a full stomach. And does fasting please or offend Thee? You might construe it as pride or cowardice. I have memorized my bathroom forever. Edith kept it very clean, but I have been less fastidious. Is it fair to ask the intended to scrub the electric chair? I'm using old newspapers, I'll buy rolls when I deserve them. I've promised the toilet much attention if it will be good to me, I'll unblock it. But why should I humiliate myself now? You don't polish windows in a car wreck. When my body starts, the old routines will start, I promise. Help! Give me a hint. For five days, except for that first half-hour of failure, I cannot enter the bathroom. My teeth and hair are dirty. I can't begin to shave, to mock myself with a little deposit of hair. I would stink at an autopsy. Nobody wants to eat me, I'm sure. What's it like outside? Is there an outside? I am the sealed, dead, impervious museum of my appetite. This is the brutal solitude of constipation, this is the way the world is lost. One is ready to stake everything on a river, a nude bath before Catherine Tekakwitha, and no promises.

14.

Into the world of names with us. F. said: Of all the
laws which bind us to the past, the names of things are
the most severe. If what I sit in is my grandfather's
chair, and what I look out of is my grandfather's window
—then I'm deep in his world. F. said: Names preserve
the dignity of Appearance. F. said: Science begins in
coarse naming, a willingness to disregard the particular
shape and destiny of each red life, and call them all
Rose. To a more brutal, more active eye, *all* flowers look
alike, like Negroes and Chinamen. F. never shut up.
His voice has got into my ear like a trapped fly, in-
cessantly buzzing. His style is colonizing me. His will pro-
vides me with his room downtown, the factory he
bought, his tree house, his soap collection, his papers.
And I don't like the discharge from my pecker. Too
much, F.! I've got to hold on to myself. Next thing you
know my ears will be transparent. F., why do I suddenly
miss you so intensely? There are certain restaurants I
can never go to again. But do I have to be your monument? Were we friends, after all? I remember the day
you finally bought the factory, eight hundred thousand
dollars, and I walked with you on those uneven wood
floors, floors which as a boy you had swept so often. I
believe you were actually weeping. It was the middle
of the night and half the lights were gone. We walked
between the rows of sewing machines, cutting tables,
defunct steam pressers. There is nothing more quiet
than a still factory. Every now and then we kicked a
tangle of wire hangers, or brushed a rack where they
hung, thick as vines, and a curious tinkling resounded,
like a hundred bored men playing in their pockets, a
curiously violent sound, as if the men were waiting

among the grotesque shadows cast by the abandoned machines, men waiting for salaries, goons for the word to smash F.'s shut-down. I was vaguely frightened. Factories, like parks, are public places, and it was an offense to the democratic mind to see F. so deeply moved by his ownership. F. picked up an old heavy steam iron which was connected to a metal frame above by a thick spring. He swung it away from the table, dropped it, laughed while it bounced up and down like a dangerous yo-yo, shadows striping the dirty walls like a wild chalk eraser on a blackboard. Suddenly F. threw a switch, the lights flickered, and the central power belt which drove the sewing machines began to roll. F. began to orate. He loved to talk against mechanical noise.

—Larry! he cried, moving down the empty benches. Larry! Ben! Dave! I know you can hear me! Ben! I haven't forgotten your hunched back! Sol! I've done what I promised! Little Margerie! You can eat your tattered slippers now! Jews, Jews, Jews! Thanks!

—F., this is disgusting.

—Every generation must thank its Jews, F. said, leaping away from me. And its Indians. The Indians must be thanked for building our bridges and skyscrapers. The world is made of races, you better learn that, my friend. People are different! Roses are different from each other! Larry! It's me, F., boy goy, whose blond hair you ofttimes ruffled. I've done what I promised you in the dark stock room so many afternoons ago. It's mine! It's ours! I'm dancing on the scraps! I've turned it into a playground! I'm here with a friend!

When he had calmed down F. took my hand and led me to the stock room. Great empty spools and cardboard cylinders threw their precise shadows in the half

light, temple columns. The respectable animal smell of
wool still clung to the air. I sensed a layer of oil forming
on my nose. Back on the factory floor the power belt
still turned and a few spikeless machines pumped. F.
and I stood very close.

—So you think I am disgusting, F. said.

—I would never believe you capable of such cheap
sentimentality. Talking to little Jewish ghosts!

—I was playing as once I promised I would.

—You were slobbering.

—Isn't this a beautiful place? Isn't it peaceful? We're
standing in the future. Soon rich men will build places
like this on their estates and visit them by moonlight.
History has shown us how men love to muse and loaf
and make love in places formerly the scene of much
violent activity.

—What are you going to do with it?

—Come in, now and then. Sweep a little. Screw on
the shiny tables. Play with the machines.

—You could have been a millionaire. The financial
page talked about the brilliance of your manipulations.
I must confess that this coup of yours lends a lot of
weight to all the shit you've been spouting over the
years.

—Vanity! cried F. I had to see if I could pull it off. I
had to see if there was any comfort in it. In spite of
what I knew! Larry didn't expect it of me, it wasn't
binding. My boyhood promise was an alibi! *Please don't
let this evening influence anything I've said to you.*

—Don't cry, F.

—Forgive me. I wanted to taste revenge. I wanted to
be an American. I wanted to tie my life up with a visit.
That isn't what Larry meant.

My arm struck a rack of hangers as I seized F.'s shoul-

ders. The jangling of coins was not so loud, what with
the smaller room and the noise of the machinery beyond, and the thugs retreated as we stood in a forlorn
embrace.

15.

Catherine Tekakwitha in the shadows of the long house.
Edith crouching in the stuffy room, covered with grease.
F. pushing a broom through his new factory. Catherine
Tekakwitha can't go outside at noon. When she did get
out she was swaddled in a blanket, a hobbling mummy.
So she passed her girlhood, far from the sun and the
noise of hunting, a constant witness to the tired Indians
eating and fucking one another, and a picture of pure
Mistress Mary rattling in her head louder than all the
dancer's instruments, shy as the deer she had heard
about. What voices did she hear, louder than groans,
sweeter than snoring? How well she must have learned
the ground rules. She did not know how the hunter rode
down his prey but she knew how he sprawled with a
full belly, burping later at love. She saw all the preparations and all the conclusions, without the perspective set
against a mountain. She saw the coupling but she didn't
hear the songs hummed in the forest and the little gifts
made of grass. Confronted with this assault of human
machinery, she must have developed elaborate and
bright notions of heaven—and a hatred for finite shit.
Still, it is a mystery how one loses the world. Dumque
crescebat aetate, crescebat et prudentia, says P. Cholenec in 1715. Is it pain? Why didn't her vision turn
Rabelaisian? Tekakwitha was the name she was given,
but the exact meaning of the word is not known. She
who puts things in order, is the interpretation of l'abbé
Marcoux, the old missionary at Caughnawaga. L'abbé

Cuoq, the Sulpician Indianologist: Celle qui s'avance,
qui meut quelquechose devant elle. Like someone who
proceeds in shadows, her arms held before her, is the
elaboration of P. Lecompte. Let us say that her name
was some combination of these two notions: She who,
advancing, arranges the shadows neatly. Perhaps, Catherine Tekakwitha, I come to you in the same fashion. A
kind uncle took the orphan in. After the plague the
whole village moved a mile up the Mohawk River, close
to where it is joined by the Auries River. It was called
Gandaouagué, another name which we know in many
forms, Gandawagué, a Huron word used by missionaries to designate falls or rapids, Gahnawagué in the
Mohawk dialect, Kaknawaké which developed into the
current Caughnawaga. I'm paying my dues. Here she
lived with her uncle, his wife, his sisters, in the long
house which he established, one of the principal structures of the village. Iroquois women worked hard. A
hunter never lugged his kill. He made an incision in the
animal's stomach, grabbed a handful of entrails, and, as
he danced home, sprinkled the guts here and there,
this dangled from a branch, that spiked on a bush. I've
killed, he announced to his wife. She followed his slimy
traces into the forest, and her prize for finding the slain
beast was to get it back to her husband, who was sleeping beside the fire, his stomach rumbling. Women did
most of the disagreeable things. War, hunting, and fish-
ing were the only occupations a man's dignity allowed.
The rest of the time he smoked, gossiped, played games,
ate, and slept. Catherine Tekakwitha liked work. All the
other girls rushed through it so they could get out there
and dance, flirt, comb their hair, paint their faces, put
on their earrings, and ornament themselves with colored
porcelain. They wore rich pelts, embroidered leggings

worked with beads and porcupine quills. Beautiful!
Couldn't I love one of these? Can Catherine hear them
dance? Oh, I'd like one of the dancers. I don't want to
disturb Catherine, working in the long house, the
muffled thud of leaping feet tracing perfect burning
circles in her heart. The girls aren't spending too much
time on tomorrow, but Catherine is gathering her days
into a chain, linking the shadows. Her aunts insist.
Here's a necklace, put it on dear, and why don't you
paint your lousy complexion? She was very young, she
allowed herself to be adorned, and never forgave herself. Twenty years later she wept over what she considered one of her gravest sins. What am I getting into?
Is this my kind of woman? After a while her aunts took
the pressure off and she got back to total work, grinding, hauling water, gathering firewood, preparing the
pelts for trade—all done in a remarkable spirit of willingness. "Douce, patiente, chaste, et innocente," says P.
Chauchetière. "Sage comme une fille française bien
élevée," he continues. Like a well-raised French girl! O
Sinister Church! F., is this what you want from me? Is
this my punishment for not sliding with Edith? She was
waiting for me all covered in red grease and I was
thinking of my white shirt. I have since applied the tube
to myself, out of curiosity, a single gleaming column,
useless to me as F.'s akropolis that morning. Now I read
that Catherine Tekakwitha had a great gift for em-
broidery and handicraft, and that she made beautiful
embroidered leggings, tobacco pouches, moccasins, and
wampums. Hour after hour she worked on these, roots
and eelskins, shells, porcelain, quills. To be worn by anyone but her! Whom was her mind adorning? Her wampums were especially cherished. Was this the way she
mocked money? Perhaps her contempt freed her to in-

vent elaborate designs and color arrangements just as
F.'s contempt for commerce enabled him to buy a factory. Or do I misread them both? I'm tired of facts, I'm
tired of speculations, I want to be consumed by unrea-
son. I want to be swept along. Right now I don't
care what goes on under her blanket. I want to be covered with unspecific kisses. I want my pamphlets
praised. Why is my work so lonely? It is past midnight,
the elevator is at rest. The linoleum is new, the faucets
tight, thanks to F.'s bequest. I want all the comes I did
not demand. I want a new career. What have I done to
Edith, that I can't even get her ghost to stiffen me? I
hate this apartment. Why did I have it redecorated? I
thought the table would look nice yellow. O God, please
terrify me. The two who loved me, why are they so
powerless tonight? The belly button useless. Even F.'s
final horror meaningless. I wonder if it's raining. I want
F.'s experiences, his emotional extravagance. I can't
think of a single thing F. said. I can only remember the
way he used his handkerchief, the meticulous folding
to keep his nose away from snot, his high-pitched
sneezes and the pleasure they gave him. High-pitched
and metallic, positively instrumental, a sideways snap
of the bony head, then the look of surprise, as if he'd
just received an unexpected gift, and the raised eyebrows which said, Fancy that. People sneeze, F., that's
all, don't make such a damn miracle out of it, it only
depresses me, it's a depressing habit you have of loving
to sneeze and of eating apples as if they were juicier
for you and being the first one to exclaim how good the
movie is. You depress people. We like apples too. I hate
to think of the things you told Edith, probably sounding
as if hers were the first body you ever touched. Was
she delighted? Her new nipples. You're both dead.

Never stare too long at an empty glass of milk. I don't like what's happening to Montréal architecture. What happened to the tents? I would like to accuse the Church. I accuse the Roman Catholic Church of Québec of ruining my sex life and of shoving my member up a relic box meant for a finger, I accuse the R.C.C. of Q. of making me commit queer horrible acts with F., another victim of the system, I accuse the Church of killing Indians, I accuse the Church of refusing to let Edith go down on me properly, I accuse the Church of covering Edith with red grease and of depriving Catherine Tekakwitha of red grease, I accuse the Church of haunting automobiles and of causing pimples, I accuse the Church of building green masturbation toilets, I accuse the Church of squashing Mohawk dances and of not collecting folk songs, I accuse the Church of stealing my sun tan and of promoting dandruff, I accuse the Church of sending people with dirty toenails into streetcars where they work against Science, I accuse the Church of female circumcision in French Canada.

16.

It was a lovely day in Canada, a poignant summer day; so brief, so brief. It was 1664, sunny, dragonflies investigating the plash of paddles, porcupines sleeping on their soft noses, black-braided girls in the meadow plaiting grass into aromatic baskets, deer and braves sniffing the pine wind, dreaming of luck, two boys wrestling beside the palisade, embrace after embrace. The world was about two billion years old but the mountains of Canada were very young. Strange doves wheeled over Gandaouagué.

—Boo-hoo, wept the eight-year-old heart.

The Heart listened, the Heart which was neither new

nor old, nor, indeed, a prisoner of description, and Thomas sang for all the children, Facienti quod in se est, Deus non denegat gratiam.

—Today you must shine,
  Quills of porcupine;
  Like summer rain
  Beads of porcelain;
  Eternal wreath

This necklace of teeth, sang the Aunts as they dressed the child for the simple wedding, according to their custom, for the Iroquois married children.

—No, no, cried one heart in a village.

Strange doves wheeled over Gandaouagué.

—Go over to him, Catherine, oh, he's a strong little man! clucked the Aunts.

—Ha, ha, laughed the sturdy boy.

Suddenly his laughter ceased, for the boy was frightened, and it was not a fear he knew, not a fear of being whipped or of losing the game, but once, when a Medicine Man had died . . .

—What's the matter with them? asked the family of each child, for the families wished to secure an advantageous union between themselves.

—Roo roo, sang the wheeling doves.

Eternal wreath, this necklace of teeth, her Aunts' song pierced her heart with arrows, No, no, she wept, that is wrong, that is wrong, and her eyes rolled up into her head. How strange she must have appeared to the little savage, her ravished face, her swoon, for he ran away.

—Not to worry, the Aunts agreed among themselves. Soon she will be older, the juices will start to flow, for even the Algonquin women are human! joked the Aunts. We will have no trouble then!

And so the child returned to her life of obedience,

hard work, and cheerful shyness, a source of pleasure
to all who knew her. Nor had the Aunts any reason to
suspect that the orphan would not follow the ancient
course of the Iroquois. Soon she was no longer a child,
and once again the Aunts plotted.

—We will set a trap for the Shy One. We will tell her
nothing!

It was a lovely night for the simple ceremony, which
involved nothing more than a young man entering his
bride's cabin, sitting beside her, and then receiving from
her a gift of food. This was the complete ceremony, the
participants having been chosen without consultation by
an agreement between their respective families.

—Sit still, Catherine, all the chores are done, darling,
we don't need any more water, winked the Aunts.

—How cold it is tonight, Aunts.

The autumn moon sailed over Indian Canada, and
the Three-Whistle Bird discharged his song like aimless vertical arrows from the black branches. Tcheue!
Chireue! Tzeuere! A woman drew a wooden comb
through her thick hair, stroke after stroke, as she mum-
bled phrases of a monotonous mourning chant.

—. . . walk with me, sit beside me on a mountain. . . .

The world moved closer to its little fires and pots of
soup. A fish leaped out of the Mohawk River, and hovered above its splash till the splash sank away, and
still the fish hovered.

—Well, look who's here!

The great shoulders of a young hunter filled the doorway. Catherine looked up from her wampum, blushed,
and returned to her work. A smile played on the sensual
lips of the handsome brave. He licked his lips with a

long red tongue, tasting traces of the meat he had killed and on which he had but lately feasted. Such a tongue! wondered the Aunts, digging their knuckles into their crotches under their sewing. Blood rushed into the young man's groin. He inserted one hand under the leather and seized himself, warm handful, thick as a swan's neck. He was here, the man awaited! He crossed like a cat to where the girl squatted, shivering, working the tiny shells, and he sat beside her, deliberately stretching his body so that thigh and hard buttock were presented to her view.

—Heh-heh, said one Aunt.

A strange fish hovered above the waters of the Mohawk River, luminous. All at once, and for the first time, Catherine Tekakwitha knew that she lived in a body, a female body! She felt the presence of her thighs and knew what they could squeeze, she felt the flower life of her nipples, she felt the sucking hollowness of her belly, the loneliness of her buttocks, the door ache of her little cunt, a cry for stretching, and she felt the existence of each cunt hair, they were not numerous and so short they did not even curl! She lived in a body, a woman's body, and it worked! She sat on juices.

—I'll bet he's hungry, said another Aunt.

So bright! the fish which rose over the river. She felt in her imagination the circle of this hunter's strong brown arms, the circles he would force through the lips of her cunt, the circles of her breasts pressed flat under him, the circle of her bite marks on his shoulder, the circle of her mouth lips in blowing kisses!

—Yeah, I'm starving.

The circles were made of whips and knotted thongs. They bound her, they choked her, they tore her skin, they were shrinking necklaces of fangs. Her tits were bleeding. She was sitting on blood. The circles of love tightened like a noose, squeezing, ripping, slicing. Little hairs were caught in knots. Agony! A burning circle attacked her cunt and severed it from her crotch like the top of a tin can. She lived in a woman's body but—it did not belong to her! It was not hers to offer! With a desperate slingshot thought she hurled her cunt forever into the night. It was not hers to offer to the handsome fellow, though his arms were strong and his own forest magic not inconsiderable. And as she thus disclaimed the ownership of her flesh she sensed a minute knowledge of his innocence, a tiny awareness of the beauty of all the faces circled round the crackling fires of the village. Ah, the pain eased, the torn flesh she finally did not own healed in its freedom, and a new description of herself, so brutally earned, forced itself into her heart: she was Virgin.

—Get the man some food, commanded one beautiful Aunt ferociously.

The ceremony must not be completed, the old magic must not be honored! Catherine Tekakwitha stood up. The hunter smiled, the Aunts smiled, Catherine Tekakwitha smiled sadly, the hunter thought she smiled shyly, the Aunts thought she smiled slyly, the hunter thought the Aunts smiled greedily, the Aunts thought the hunter smiled greedily, the hunter even thought that the little slit in the head of his cock smiled, and maybe Catherine thought her cunt was smiling in its new old home. A strange luminous fish smiled.

—Smack, smack, yum, said the hunter inarticulately.

Catherine Tekakwitha fled the squatting hungry people. Past the fires, the bones, the excrement, she rushed through the door, past the palisade, through the smoky village, into the vaults of the birch trees standing palely in the moonlight.

—After her!

—Don't let her get away!

—Fuck her in the bushes!

—Give her one for me!

—Hoo hoo hoo!

—Eat hair pie!

—All the way!

—Turn her over and do it for me!

—Cover her face with a flag!

—Drive it home!

—Hurry!

—The Shy One flies!

—Screw her in the ass!

—She needs it bad!

—Tcheue! Chireue! Tzeuere!

—Up to the hilt!

—In the armpit!

—. . . walk with me, sit beside me on a mountain. . . .

—Puff! Puff!

—Do her a favor!

—Screw the pimples off her!

—Gobble it!

—Deus non denegat gratiam!

—Piss in it!

—Come back!

—Algonquin hussy!

—Stuck-up Frenchie!

—Shit in her ear!

—Make her say uncle!

—That way!

The hunter entered the woods. He would have no

trouble finding her, the Shy One, the One Who Hobbled. He had followed swifter game than she. He knew every trail. But where was she? He plunged forward. He knew a hundred soft places, beds of pine needle, couches of moss. He stepped on a twig and cracked it, the first time in his life! This was turning into a very expensive fuck. Where are you? I won't hurt you. A branch struck him in the face.

—Ho ho, the voices of the village drifted on the wind.

Above the Mohawk River a fish hovered in a halo of blond mist, a fish that longed for nets and capture and many eaters at the feast, a smiling luminous fish.

—Deus non denegat gratiam.

When Catherine Tekakwitha got home the next morning the Aunts punished her. The young hunter had returned home hours ago, humiliated. His family was enraged.

—Lousy Algonquin! Take that! And that!

—Pow! Sock!

—You'll sleep beside the shit from now on!

—You're not part of the family any more, you're just a slave!

—Your mother was no good!

—You'll do what we say! Slap!

Catherine Tekakwitha smiled cheerfully. It wasn't her body they were kicking around, not her belly the old ladies jumped on in the moccasins she had embroidered. She looked up through the smoke hole while they tormented her. As Le P. Lecompte remarks, Dieu lui avait donné une âme que Tertullien dirait "naturellement chrétienne."

17.

O God, Your Morning Is Perfect. People Are Alive In Your World. I Can Hear The Little Children In The Elevator. The Airplane Is Flying Through The Original Blue Air. Mouths Are Eating Breakfast. The Radio Is Filled With Electricity. The Trees Are Excellent. You Are Listening To The Voices Of The Faithless Who Tarry On The Bridge of Spikes. I Have Let Your Spirit Into The Kitchen. The Westclock Is Also Your Idea. The Government Is Meek. The Dead Do Not Have To Wait. You Comprehend Why Someone Must Drink Blood. O God, This Is Your Morning. There Is Music Even From A Human Thigh-Bone Trumpet. The Ice-Box Will Be Forgiven. I Cannot Think Of Anything Which Is Not Yours. The Hospitals Have Drawers Of Cancer Which They Do Not Own. The Mesozoic Waters Abounded With Marine Reptiles Which Seemed Eternal. You Know The Details Of The Kangaroo. Place Ville Marie Grows And Falls Like A Flower In Your Binoculars. There Are Old Eggs In The Gobi Desert. Nausea Is An Earthquake In Your Eye. Even The World Has A Body. We Are Watched Forever. In The Midst Of Molecular Violence The Yellow Table Clings To Its Shape. I Am Surrounded By Members Of Your Court. I Am Frightened That My Prayer Will Fall Into My Mind. Somewhere This Morning Agony Is Explained. The Newspaper Says That A Human Embryo Was Found Wrapped In A Newspaper And That A Doctor Is Suspected. I Am Trying To Know You In The Kitchen Where I Sit. I Fear My Small Heart. I Cannot Understand Why My Arm Is Not A Lilac Tree. I Am Frightened Because Death Is Your Idea. Now I Do Not Think It Behooves Me To Describe Your World. The Bathroom Door Is Opening By Itself And I Am Shivering With So Much Fear. O God, I Believe Your Morning Is Perfect. Nothing Will Happen Incompletely. O God, I Am Alone In The Desire Of My Education But A Greater Desire Must Be Lodged With You. I Am A Creature In Your Morning Writing A Lot Of Words Beginning With Capitals. Seven-Thirty In The Ruin Of My Prayer. I Sit Still In Your Morning While Cars Drive Away. O God, If There Are Fiery Journeys Be With Edith As She Climbs. Be With F. If He Has Earned Himself Agony. Be With Catherine Who Is Dead Three Hundred Years. Be With Us In Our Ignorance And Our Wretched Doctrines. We Are All Of Us Tormented With Your Glory. You Have Caused Us To Live On The Crust Of A Star. F. Suffered Horribly In His Last Days. Catherine Was Mangled Every Hour In Mysterious Machinery. Edith Cried In Pain. Be With Us This Morning Of Your Time. Be With Us At Eight O'Clock Now. Be With Me As I Lose The Crumbs Of Grace. Be With Me As The Kitchen Comes Back. Please Be With Me Especially While I Poke Around The Radio For Religious Music. Be With Me In The Phases Of My Work Because My Brain Feels Like It Has Been Whipped And I Yearn To Make A Small Perfect Thing Which Will Live In Your Morning Like Curious Static Through A President's Elegy Or A Nude Hunchback Acquiring A Tan On The Crowded Oily Beach.

18.

What is most original in a man's nature is often that which is most desperate. Thus new systems are forced on the world by men who simply cannot bear the pain of living with what is. Creators care nothing for their systems except that they be unique. If Hitler had been born in Nazi Germany he wouldn't have been content to enjoy the atmosphere. If an unpublished poet discovers one of his own images in the work of another writer it gives him no comfort, for his allegiance is not to the image or its progress in the public domain, his allegiance is to the notion that he is not bound to the world as given, that he can escape from the painful arrangement of things as they are. Jesus probably designed his system so that it would fail in the hands of other men, that is the way with the greatest creators: they guarantee the desperate power of their own originality by projecting their systems into an abrasive future. These are F.'s ideas, of course. I don't think he believed them. I wish I knew why he took so much interest in me. Now that I look back he seemed to be training me for something, and he was ready to use any damn method to keep me hysterical. Hysteria is my classroom, F. said once. The occasion of the remark is interesting. We had been to a double feature and had then eaten a huge Greek meal in one of his friends' restaurants. The jukebox was playing a melancholy tune currently on the Athenian Hit Parade. It was snowing on St. Lawrence Boulevard and the two or three customers left in the place were staring out at the weather. F. was eating black olives in a disinterested fashion. A couple of the waiters were drinking coffee, after which they would begin to stack the chairs, leaving our table, as usual, to the very end. If there was an unpressurized place in the whole world, this was it. F. was yawning and playing with his olive pits. He made his remark out of the blue and I could have killed him. As we walked through the rainbow haze of the neon-colored snow he pressed a small book into my hand.

—I received this for an oral favor I happen to have performed for a restaurateur friend. It's a prayer book. Your need is greater than mine.

—You filthy liar! I cried when we had reached the street-lamp and read the cover, ΕΛΛΗΝΟ-ΑΓΓΛΙΚΟΙ ΔΙΑΛΟΓΟΙ. It's an English-Greek phrase book, badly printed in Salonica!

—Prayer is translation. A man translates himself into a child asking for all there is in a language he has barely mastered. Study the book.

—And the English is execrable. F., you torture me purposefully.

—Ah, he said blithely sniffing the night, ah, it's soon Christmas in India. Families gathered round the Christmas curry, carols before the blazing Yule corpse, children waiting for the bells of Bhagavad-Santa.

—You soil everything, don't you?

—Study the book. Comb it for prayers and guidance. It will teach you how to breathe.

—Sniff. Sniff.

—No, that's wrong.

19.

Now it is time for Edith to run, run between the old Canadian trees. But where are the doves today? Where is the smiling luminous fish? Why are the hiding places hiding? Where is Grace today? Why isn't candy being fed to History? Where is the Latin music?

—Help!

Edith ran through the woods, thirteen years old, the men after her. She was wearing a dress made from flour sacks. A certain Flour Company packed their product in sacks printed with flowers. There is a thirteen-

year-old girl running through needle pine. Have you
ever seen such a thing? Follow her young young bum,
Eternal Cock of the Brain. Edith told me this story, or
part of it, years later, and I've been pursuing her little
body through the forest ever since, I confess. Here I am
an old scholar, wild with unspecific grief, compulsive
detective of gonad shadows. Edith, forgive me, it was
the thirteen-year-old victim I always fucked. Forgive
yourself, F. said. Thirteen-year-old skin is very beautiful. What other food besides brandy is good after thirteen years in the world? The Chinese eat old eggs but
that is no comfort. O Catherine Tekakwitha, send me
thirteen-year-olds today! I am not cured. I will never
be cured. I do not want to write this History. I do not
want to mate with Thee. I do not want to be as facile
as F. I do not want to be the leading Canadian authority on the A——s. I do not want a new yellow table.
I do not want astral knowledge. I do not want to do the
Telephone Dance. I do not want to conquer the Plague.
I want thirteen-year-olds in my life. Bible King David
had one to warm his dying bed. Why shouldn't we associate with beautiful people? Tight, tight, tight, oh, I
want to be trapped in a thirteen-year-old life. I know,
I know about war and business. I am aware of shit. Thirteen-year-old electricity is very sweet to suck, and I am
(or let me be) tender as a hummingbird. Don't I have
some hummingbird in my soul? Isn't there something
timeless and unutterably light in my lust hovering over
a young wet crack in a blur of blond air? Oh come,
hardy darlings, there is nothing of King Midas in my
touch, I freeze nothing into money. I merely graze your
hopeless nipples as they grow away from me into business problems. I change nothing as I float and sip under
the first bra.

—Help!

Four men followed Edith. Damn every one of them. I can't blame them. The village was behind them, filled with families and business. These men had watched her for years. French Canadian schoolbooks do not encourage respect for the Indians. Some part of the Canadian Catholic mind is not certain of the Church's victory over the Medicine Man. No wonder the forests of Québec are mutilated and sold to America. Magic trees sawed with a crucifix. Murder the saplings. Bittersweet is the cunt sap of a thirteen-year-old. O Tongue of the Nation! Why don't you speak for yourself? Can't you see what is behind all this teen-age advertising? Is it only money? What does "wooing the teen-age market" really mean? Eh? Look at all the thirteen-year-old legs on the floor spread in front of the tv screen. Is it only to sell them cereals and cosmetics? Madison Avenue is thronged with hummingbirds who want to drink from those little barely haired crevices. Woo them, woo them, suited writers of commercial poems. Dying America wants a thirteen-year-old Abishag to warm its bed. Men who shave want little girls to ravish but sell them high heels instead. The sexual Hit Parade is written by fathers who shave. O suffering child-lust offices of the business world, I feel your blue-balled pain everywhere! There is a thirteen-year-old blonde lying on the back seat of a parked car, one nyloned toe playing with the armrest ashtray, the other foot on the rich interior carpet, dimples on her cheeks and only a hint of innocent acne, and her garter belt is correctly uncomfortable: far away roam the moon and a few police flashlights: her Beethoven panties are damp from the Prom. She alone of all the world believes that fucking is holy, dirty, and beautiful. And who is this making his way through the bushes? It is her Chemistry Teacher, who smiled all night while she danced with the football star because it is the foam rubber of *his* car she lies dreaming upon. Charity begins alone, F. used to say. Many long nights have taught me that the Chemistry Teacher is not merely a sneak. He loves youth truly. Advertising courts lovely things. Nobody wants to make life hell. In the hardest hard sell exists a thirsty love-torn hummingbird. F. wouldn't want me to hate forever the men who pursued Edith.

—Sob. Sob. Whimper. Oh, oh!

They caught up with her in a stone quarry or an abandoned mine, someplace very mineral and hard, owned indirectly by U.S. interests. Edith was a beautiful thirteen-year-old Indian orphan living with foster Indian parents because her father and mother had been killed in an avalanche. She had been abused by schoolmates who didn't think she was Christian. Even at thirteen she had lovely freakishly long nipples, she told me. Perhaps this news had leaked out of the school shower room. Perhaps that was the underground rumor which had inflamed the root of the whole town. Perhaps the business and religion of the town kept operating as usual but every single person is secretly obsessed with this nipple information. The Mass is undermined with nipple dream. The picket line of strikers at the local asbestos factory is not wholly devoted to Labor. There is something absent in the blows and tear gas of the Provincial Police, for all minds are pursing for extraordinary nipple. Daily life cannot tolerate this fantastic intrusion. Edith's nipples are an absolute pearl irritating the workable monotonous protoplasm of village existence. Who can trace the subtle mechanics of the Collective Will to which we all contribute? I believe that in some way the village delegated these four men to pursue Edith into the forest. Get Edith! commanded the Collective Will. Get her magic nipples off Our Mind!

—Help me, Mother Mary!

They ran her to the ground. They ripped off the dress with the Company's raspberry pattern. It was a summer afternoon. Blackflies ate her. The men were drunk on beer. They laughed and called her *sauvagesse*, ha, ha! They pulled off her underwear, rolling it down her long brown legs, and when they tossed it aside they did not notice that it looked like a big pink pretzel. They were surprised that her underwear was so clean: a heathen's underwear should be limp and smeared. They were not frightened by the police, somehow they knew the police wished them well, one of their brothers-in-law was a policeman, and he had balls like everyone. They dragged her into the shadows because each man wanted to be somewhat alone. They turned her over to see if the dragging had scraped her buttocks. Blackflies ate her buttocks, which were dazzlingly round. They twisted her over again and pulled her deeper into the shadows because now they were ready to remove her underwear top. The shadows were so thick and deep at the corner of the quarry that they could hardly see, and this is what they wanted. Edith peed in fear and they heard the noise of it louder than their laughter and hard breathing. It was a steady sound and it seemed to go on forever, steady and forceful, louder than their thoughts, louder than the crickets who were grinding out an elegy for the end of the afternoon. The fall of urine on last year's leaves and pine needles developed to a monolithic tumult in eight ears. It was the pure sound of impregnable nature and it ate like acid at their plot. It was a sound so majestic and simple, a holy symbol of frailty which nothing could violate. They froze, each of them suddenly lonely, their erections collapsing like closed accordions as their blood poured upward like flowers out of a root. But the men refused to cooperate with the miracle (as F. called it). They could not bear to learn that Edith was no longer Other, that she was indeed, Sister. Natural Law they felt, but Collective Law they obeyed. They fell on the child with index fingers, pipe stems, ballpoint pens, and twigs. I would like to know what kind of miracle that is, F. The blood streamed down her legs. The men made coarse jests. Edith screamed.

—Help me, Saint Kateri!

F. urged me to make nothing of this connection. I can't go on with this. Everything has been taken from me. I just had a daydream: I saw the thirteen-year-old Edith suffering under the impotent attack of these four men. As the youngest kneeled down to examine better the progress of his sharp twig, Edith seized his head in her arms and drew him to her bosom, and there he lay weeping like that man on Old Orchard Beach. F., it's too late for the double feature. My stomach is jammed again. I want to begin my fast.

20.

I see it so clearly now! The night of Edith's death, that long night of talk with F., he left a whole side of his chicken and barely touched the barbecue sauce. I see now that it was deliberate. I remember a saying of Kung's he was fond of: When eating beside a man of mourning the Master never ate his fill. Uncles! uncles! how dare any of us eat?

21.

Among the curious items I inherited from F. is a box of
fireworks packed by Rich Brothers Fireworks Co., Sioux
Falls, South Dakota. It contains 64 sparklers, eight 12-
and 8-ball roman candles, large pinwheels, red and
green fire cones, vesuvius fountains, golden jewel, silver
cascade, oriental and radiant fountains, 6 giant parade
sparklers, silver wheels, skyrockets, comets, handle
lawn fountains, snakes, torches, red white and blue
cones. I wept as I unpacked the pieces, wept for the
American boyhood I never had, for my invisible New
England parents, for a long green lawn and an iron
deer, for college romance with Zelda.

22.

I am frightened and alone. I lit one of the snakes. From
the little cone a writhing ribbon of gray ash bubbled in
coils on a corner of the yellow table until all the cone
was consumed in its own extension—a hideous little pile
of skin, gray and black like a blob of birdshit squeezed
like icing. Carcasses! Carcasses! I want to swallow dynamite.

23.

Dear God, It Is Three In The Morning. Aimless Cloudy
Semen Becomes Transparent. Is The Church Mad At Me?
Please Let Me Work. I Lit Five Of The 8-Ball Roman
Candles And Four Of Them Delivered Less Than 8 Balls.
The Firecrackers Are Dying. The Newly Painted Ceiling
Is Burned. Korean Starvation Hurts Me In The Heart. Is
This A Sin To Say? Pain Is Stored In Animal Skins. I
Solemnly Declare That I Renounce Interest In How
Many Times Edith and F. Fucked In Happiness. Are

You So Cruel As To Compel Me To Begin My Fast With
A Stuffed Belly?

24.

Burned my hand badly while holding a red and green
fire cone. The smoldering hull of a skyrocket ignited a
sheaf of Indian notes. The sharp fragrance of gunpowder has cleared my sinuses. Lucky there was butter in
the icebox because I refuse to go into the bathroom. I
never liked my hair but I am not fond of the blisters
bestowed by the silver cascade. Cinders float and stick
like blasted bats in whose torn wings I detect exact
gray-blue replicas of candy-stripe and comet-tail designs. I've handled so much charred cardboard that I
leave my fingerprints on everything. I look around at
this mess of a kitchen and I know that my life is coming
true. I care more about my red watery throbbing thumb
than your whole foul universe of orphans. I salute my
monsterhood. I urinate anywhere on the linoleum and
I am pleased that nothing happens. Every creep for
himself!

25.

Pigskin crackling on my thumb, nummy, nummy, I hate
pain. The way I hate pain is most monumentally extraordinary, much more significant than the way you hate
pain, but my body is so much more central, I am the
Moscow of pain, you are the mere provincial weather
station. Gunpowder and semen is the only research I
intend from now on, and look how harmless I be: no
bullets after hearts, no sperms after destiny: nothing
but the radiance of exhaustion: the gay little cylinders
collapsing in ordinary fire after multiple belches of

shooting stars, rainbows: the viscous blob of come in my palm thinning and clearing, like the end of Creation when all matter returns to water. Gunpowder, ball-sweat, the yellow table starts to look like me, ugh, the kitchen looks like me, me has sneaked outside into furniture, inside smells are outside, bad to be so big, I have occupied the stove, isn't there somewhere fresh where I can tuck my eyes in a clean bed and dream new bodies, oh I've got to get to a movie and take my eyes out for a pee, a movie will put me back in my skin because I've leaked all over the kitchen from all my holes, movie will stuff pores with white splinters and stop my invasion of the world, missed movies will kill me tonight, I am scared of F.'s firecrackers, I hurt too much in my burns, what could you know about burns? All you've ever done is merely burn yourself. Steady, old scholar! I'll turn off the light and write in the dark a résumé of tomorrow's Indian chapter that I must get to work on. Discipline. Click! "Triompher du mal par le bien." St. Paul. That will begin the chapter. I feel better already. Foreign languages are a good corset. Get your hand off yourself. Edith Edith Edith long things forever Edith Edie cuntie Edith where your little Edith Edith Edith Edith Edith stretchy on E E E octopus complexion purse Edith lips lips area thy pant-ies Edith Edith Edith Edith knew you your wet rivulets Eeeeddddiiiittthhhh yug yug sniffle truffle deep bulb bud button sweet soup pea spit rub hood rubber knob girl come head bup bup one bloom pug pig yum one tip tongue lug from end of bed of lips multiple lost sunk gone rise girl head small come knob splash sunk lost-lick search nose help wobble hard once more lurk up girl knob bob bubble sunk in normal skin folds lab drowned lady labia up up appear pea bean brain jewel

where where hurt hiding bruised? come up hard as
brass bubble from hair swamp little leather love pimple
form solid lump for tongue mess mess message oh un-
hood unhide unhair undrown or teeth hounds I warn
you tooth spade teeth dogs unleashed unloved lashed
form form you bead you small blunt boywise girlcock
form command tiny periscope from foreign female lost
sub no man can fathom ever come up come up from
women ocean period mecca egg farm mystery beds
come up come up from where I don't ever go from profound clam stretches from breathless gill yards from
gray broadloom oyster floors of girlsoul far far amazon
sex control rise rise here clity clity clity from amazing
forbidden protoplasmic amoeba fulfilled woman gla gla
galaxy please appear in small helmet of hope lap lap
oh pearl pink precious radio crystal marvelous fruit pit
of whole bumcunt harvest appear form develop unfold unshell unskin look into cocklove lead dykeplug
prickgirl nrrr grrr bridge entre men woman so I can do
you pleasure my lady deliver unto me thy downtown
brain unpuzzled from cunt labyrinth for I may never
join you in the seaweed nets in the sunk hotels in the
spongey jungles passive womb tubed mudlined herbal
cast closet vast as Mrs. God what? you no come up?
splash splash hidden for a newer tongue? for a nobler
tongue? for dirtier tongue? for F. tongue? for stranger?
any stranger doing this to you would be more honored
any stranger how strange therefore therefore I go down
maybe where I meant to go like a snail this automatic
tongue slides down the aquarium moss shoot there is a
ridge tender and yielding as the casting join of a hollow
chocolate bunny I ride it down don't be ashamed all
smells are alchemized tongue goes ring around a rosy
lifesaver flavor mud candy this is a better common but-

ton we both have we must kiss assholes because we
each poor one of us has one we cannot kiss it is ringed
with minnie hills they Bible dance it is ringed with
stunted petals tongue dives petals open shiver petals
tighten in a rubber knot I talk stiff now dig dig dig
bump bump bump thud on hills of petal knot get in
there hands pull cheeks apart pull apart cheeks of
Edith's fabulous private hers hers they give squeeze
they yield like halves of ripe peach like very cooked
chicken perfectly lovely blood balloons this is Edith its
virgin pink brown hairy same as mine same same as
us all poor charmen who flood the world on our knees
this is solid prose this is mystery of everyday thus I
insert cuneiform face mouth to sphinx for my tongue
was only a test game on rosy sphinx hole I focus my
mouth for pure talk gnawing suck adoration shit danger
love bravery open close open close goes the surface
petals closing to feel its own little cliffs of muscle opening in terrible abandon red desperate as baby robin
throat oh Edith ass membrane gasping all my flock of
mouth bathing pruning fluttering in the sunny bird bath
on a pillar of charity bowel where am I now now don't
go way here I am simply with my face between her
buttocks which hands have drawn apart my chin does
automatic good to cunt now I let cheeks go they squeeze
me in I squeeze me in I squash my nose sealing juice
infant shit games in my brain listen Edith listen to me
smother listen darling love it is thy hairy hole I suck
are we not joined Edith are we not proved Edith are
we not breathing Edith are we not awesome lovers
Edith are we not filthy postcards are we not good
meals Edith are we not conversing miraculously darling
pink evil fartrisk terror position darling I swear I loved
you Edith grab grab jumps the little crater kiss kiss kiss

kiss Edith Edith do the same to me do the same to me
pull my withered bum on your face I make it easy do
the same to me do the same to me do the same to me
Edith lilacs Edith Edith Edith Edith Edith Edith turning
in our sleep making spoons of ourselves Edith Edith
Edith Edith please appear as mushrooming dream from
this poor Aladdin cock Edith Edith Edith Edith in your
sweet skin envelope Edith Edith thy lonely husband
Edith thy lonely husband thy lonely husband thy apples
thy run thy creases thy dark lonely husband

26.

Somewhere in my research I learned about *Tekakwitha's
Spring*. It was a Jesuit speaking sweetly of it in a school-
book. Il y a longtemps que je t'aime. I must have paused
in the library. Out of the dust I hummed the old running
tune. I thought of icy streams and clear pools. Christ
spoke through the priest for half a paragraph. He
speaks about a spring called *Tekakwitha's Spring*. The
priest is our Edouard Lecompte, and because of this
half paragraph I know he loved the girl. He died December 20, 1929, le 20 décembre 1929. You died, Father.
This priest I take into my heart whom I did not like at
the beginning because he seemed to write for the
Church and not the Lily How It Grows. The spring re-
freshed me that night as did the snows of another. I
felt its clear crystal. It brought the created world into
my cubicle, the cold and radiant outlines of the things
that be. Entre le village, he writes, Entre le village et
le ruisseau Cayudetta, Between the village and the brook
Cayudetta, au creux d'un bosquet solitaire, in the hollow of a lonely grove, sortant de dessous un vieux tronc
d'arbre couvert de mousse, ensuing from beneath an old
moss-covered tree trunk, chantait et chante encore de

nos jours, sang and in our own day still sings, une petite source limpide, a small clear spring. . . . It was here the girl drew water, each day, for nine years. How much you must know, Katerine Tekakwitha. What a dream of sobriety, glorious sobriety, glorious as the shine of facts, feel of skin, what a hunger for sobriety assaults me here found among ripped firecracker carcasses, selfish burns, spilled personal multitudes. 3285 times you came to this old tree. Long live History for telling us. I want to know you as you knew the path. How tiny the path of your deer shoes. The fragrance of forests is in the world. It clings to our leather clothes wherever we go, even to the whip hidden in our wallet. I believe in Gregory's sky, crowded with saints, yes, Unlettered Pope. The path is crowded with facts. The cold pine river is still there. Let the facts drag me out of the kitchen. Let them keep me from playing myself like a roulette wheel. How good to know something she did.

27.

The twenty-seventh day since I began because of a promise to F. Nothing works. I keep sleeping the wrong times and missing movie schedules. Many more burns. Many less shit. Gone are all the 12-ball roman candles, most of the 64 sparklers, the fraudulent whistling bomb, the so-called cosmic fountains. Come is much dirty underwear, real and dirty underwear, which once, sealed in polyethylene packages, promised me such marble flanks. There is hair under my fingernails.

28.

If Edith saw this room she would vomit. Why did you kill her for me, F.?

29.

I will explain how F. got his extraordinary body. Once again I will explain it to myself. HOW JOE'S BODY BROUGHT HIM *FAME* INSTEAD OF *SHAME*: headline on the back of an American comic which we both read one afternoon when we were thirteen. We were sitting on some trunks in an unused solarium on the third floor of the orphanage, a glass-roofed room dark as any other because of the soot deposited by a badly placed chimney—we often hid here. JOE'S BODY was the concern of an ad for a muscle-building course. His triumph is traced in seven cartoon panels. Can I recall?

1. Joe is skeletal. His legs are piteous sticks. His red bathing suit is the baggy boxer type. His voluptuous girl friend is with him. Her thighs are thicker than his. The calm sea beyond contrasts with Joe's ordeal. A man with a grand physique is humiliating him. We cannot see the torturer's face, but the girl informs Joe that the man is a well-known local nuisance.

2. A tiny sail has appeared on the horizon. We see the bully's face. We appreciate his beery chest. The girl friend has drawn up her knees and is wondering why she ever dated this no-assed weakling. Joe has been pulled to his feet by the bully and now must sustain a further insult.

3. The sail is gone. Some minuscule figures play ball at the edge of the sea. Seagulls appear. An anguished Joe stands beside the girl he is losing. She has put on her white sunhat and has turned her tits from him. She answers him over her right shoulder. Her body is massive and maternal, low-breasted. Somehow we have an impression of stretched muscles in her abdomen.

JOE: The big bully! I'll get even some day.

HER: Oh, don't let it *bother* you, little boy!

4. Joe's room, or the remains of it. A cracked picture hangs askew on the green wall. A broken lamp is in motion. He is kicking a chair over. He wears a blue blazer, tie, white ducks. He clenches his fist, a clawlike articulation from a wrist thin as a bird leg. The girl friend lies in some panel of the imagination snuggling in the bully's armpit, winking out a thousand shameful anecdotes about Joe's body.

JOE: Darn it! I'm sick and tired of being a scarecrow! Charles Axis says he can give me a REAL body. All right! I'll gamble a stamp and get his FREE book.

5. LATER. Could this be Joe? He flexes a whole map of jigsaw muscles before his dresser mirror.

JOE: Boy! It didn't take Axis long to do this for me! What MUSCLES! That bully won't shove me around again!

Is this the same red bathing suit?

6. The beach. The girl has come back. She is having a good time. Her body is relaxed and hips have appeared. Her left hand is raised in a gesture of surprised delight as her vision of Joe undergoes a radical transformation. Joe has just thrown a punch which lands in an electrical blaze on the bully's chin, knocking him off balance, knitting his eyebrows with amazed pain. Beyond we have the same white strand, the same calm sea.

JOE: What! You here again? Here's something I owe you!

7. The girl touches Joe's memorable biceps with her right hand. Her left shoulder and left arm are obscured by Joe's massive chest but we know that she has shoved it down the back of his tight red bathing suit and is

working with his testicles.

HER: Oh, Joe! You ARE a real man after all!

AN ATTRACTIVE GIRL SITTING ON THE SAND NEARBY: GOSH! What a build!

THE ENVIOUS MAN BESIDE HER: He's already famous for it!

Joe stands there in silence, thumbs hooked in the front of his bathing suit, looking at his girl, who leans lasciviously against him. Four thick black words appear in the sky and they radiate spears of light. None of the characters in the panel seems aware of the celestial manifestation exploding in terrific silence above the old marine landscape. HERO OF THE BEACH is the sky's announcement.

F. studied the ad for a long time. I wanted to get on with what we had come for, the scuffling, the dusty caresses, the comparison of hair, the beauty of facing a friend and binding two cocks in my hand, one familiar and hungry, one warm and strange, the flash along the whole length. But F.'s eyes were wet, his lips trembling as he whispered:

—Those words are always in the sky. Sometimes you can see them, like a daytime moon.

The afternoon darkened over the soot-layered glass roof. I waited silently for F.'s mood to change and I suppose I fell asleep, for I started at the sound of scissors.

—What are you clipping out there, F.?

—Charles Axis thing.

—You going to send away?

—Bet your fucking life.

—But it's for thin guys. We're fat.

—Shut your fucking face.

—We're fat, F.

—Smack! Wham! Pow!

—Fat.

—Socko! Sok! Bash!

—Fat fat fat fat fat fat fat!

I lit a stolen match and we both huddled over the comic which had fallen to the floor. At the right-hand side of the ad there is an actual photo of the man who holds the title "The World's Most Flawlessly Formed Man." Oh! I remember! In a flawless bathing suit he stands on the clip-away coupon.

—But look at him, F., the guy's got no hair.

—But *I* have hair. *I* have hair.

His hands are fists, his smile is Florida, he does not look serious, he doesn't really care about us, maybe he is even a little fat.

—Just inspect this photo, F. The guy is soft in the gut.

—He's fat, all right.

—But—

—He's fat. He understands the fat. Use your eyes! Look at his face. Now look at Plastic Man's face. Charles Axis wants to be our uncle. He is one of us slobs who dwells pages behind Plastic Man. But can't you see that he has made his peace with Plastic Man? With Blue Beetle? With Captain Marvel? Can't you see that he believes in the super-world?

—F., I don't like it when your eyes get shiny like that.

—The Fat! The Fat! He's one of us! Charles Axis is on our side! He's with us against Blue Beetle and Ibis and Wonder Woman!

—F., you're talking funny again.

—Charles Axis has an address in New York, look, 405 West 34th St., New York 1! Don't you think he knows about Krypton? Don't you see him suffering on the outer limits of the Bat Cave? Has anyone ever lived so close to fantastic imaginary muscles?

—F.!

—Charles Axis is all compassion, he's our sacrifice! He calls the thin but he means both the fat and the thin; he calls the thin because it is worse to be fat than thin; he calls the thin so that the fat can hear and come and not be named!

—Get away from that window!

—Charles! Charles! Charlie! I'm coming, I'm coming to be with you at the sad edge of the spirit world!

—F.! Uppercut! Sok! Thud!

—Puff! °#! Sob! Thank you, my friend, I guess you kinda saved my life.

That was the last time I ever equaled F. in a physical contest. He gave Charles Axis fifteen minutes a day in the privacy of his room. Fat fell away or turned to muscle, he increased his chest measurement, he was not ashamed to strip for sports. Once on the beach a huge man in a very white bathing suit kicked sand in his face as we sat sunbathing on a small towel. F. merely smiled. The huge man stood there, hands on hips, then he performed a little hop and jump, like a soccer kickoff, and kicked sand in his face once again.

—Hey! I cried: Quit kicking that sand in our faces! F., I whispered: That man is the worst nuisance on the beach.

The bully ignored me completely. He seized F.'s thick hard wrist in his own massive fist and yanked F. to a standing position.

—Listen here, he snarled, I'd smash your face . . . only you're so skinny you might dry up and blow away.

—Why did you let him shove you around?

F. sat down meekly as the man strode away.

—That was Charles Axis.

—But that man is the worst nuisance on the beach.

30.

A note! At the bottom of the box of firecrackers I find
a note.

> Dear Friend
> > Turn on the radio
> > > your dear dead friend
> > > F.

At the *bottom*. How well he knew me. I held the message (written on a telegraph form) against my cheek.
Oh, F., help me, for a grave divides me from all that I
love.

RADIO: . . . . to Mrs. T. R. Voubouski, 56784 Clanranald,
to the three nurses in the Barclay dormi-
tory from you-know-who, a real climbing
disk by Gavin Gate and the Goddesses—
and don't forget, during this hour of the
Early Morning Record Gal you can
phone your dedications in—

DRUMS SHUFFLING: SHNN shnn shnn SHNN shnn

ELECTRIC INSTRUMENTS: Zunga zunga zunga (a promise
of incessant regular sex pumping)

GAVIN GATE: *I could have left* zunga zunga zunga
(he's got all the time in the world—
he's traveled a long path to tell this
cruel story)
and said (electric pulse breathing)
I told you so

GODDESSES: *told you so* (a battalion of black girls,
his officers recruited from bombed
gospel altars, they ambush me with

unspecific hatred and white teeth)

GAVIN GATE: *I could have told*
the whole wide world
he leave you sad and blue

GODDESSES: *sad and blue*

GAVIN GATE: *Shaid I coov ran*

       GODDESSES: Ahhhhhhhh

and said   ahhhhhhhh

it good for you   ahhhhhhhh

to geh now   ahhhhhhhh (STOP!)

GAVIN GATE: *But I know when it hurt you*

   DRUM: Smack!

GAVIN GATE: *don't you know it hurt me too?*

GODDESSES: *hurt me too* (they had soared away into
universal love suffering but now they
are back in uniform, more precise now,
as if they had vowed to guard themselves against a fatal emotional excess,
chop/chop/chop/)

DRUMS CLIMB FIVE STEPS. GAVIN GATE WHEELS OUT OF
HIS CORNER FOR THE SECOND ROUND. THIS WILL BE TO THE
DEATH. THE GODDESSES ARE READY TO SUCK-MURDER THE
VICTOR.

GAVIN GATE: *I could have said*
that you had
it coming to you (Who are you Gavin
Gate? You have a strange command.
I think you have been through some
ordeal and have learned too much.
You are the king of some slum block
and you have handed down Laws)

GODDESSES: *coming to you* (they take off their
luminous bras and drive to fearful
heart like a squadron of kamikaze)

GAVIN GATE: *When you walked out*
               and turned
               your back on me

GODDESSES: *back on me*

GAVIN GATE: *I pleaded Baby* (his strength is estab-
               lished, his troops are in razor order,
               now he can weep over us)
               Ohh No!
               Please Plea Please!
                        GODDESSES: Ahhhhhhhhhhh
               Baby don't go!
               Cause I knew he would hurt you (back
               to superior narrative style)

DIDACTIC DRUM THUMP

               Don't you know it hurt me too?

GODDESSES: *hurt me too*
               Ah
                    Ah
                        Ah (step down the marble
               stairs to lift his head)

GAVIN GATE: *He said he had you*
               dancing on a string (in some sad locker-
               room where all male lovers recreate,
               Gavin has heard the details of the
               lay)

GODDESSES: *Ahhhhhhhh* (Revenge! revenge! but
               don't we still bleed, Sisters?)

GAVIN GATE: *As far as love goes*
               you were

GODDESSES: *Hah!* (they purge their hatred with this
               exclamation)

GAVIN GATE: *just another fling*
               Oh I oh oh oh
               may be a fool (but we know you're not,

nor am I, for we deal with sacred material. Oh, God! All states of love give power!)
to love you the way I do

GODDESSES: *the way I do* (a sweet punctuation. Now they are women waiting for their men, soft and wet they squat on balconies looking for our smoke signals, touching themselves)

GAVIN GATE: *Don't you realize*
even fools have feelings too?
So baby

GODDESSES: *Ahhhhhhhhh*

GAVIN GATE: *C'mon back* (a command)
and let me dry (a hope)
the tears (the real life of pity)
from your eye (one eye, darling, one eye at a time)

GAVIN AND THE GODDESSES WHIP THEMSELVES WITH ELECTRIC BRAIDS

Cause I would never hurt you

GODDESSES: *I would never hurt you*

GAVIN GATE: *No no I would never hurt you*

GODDESSES: *I would never hurt you*

GAVIN GATE: *Cause Baby when it hurt you*

DRUM: Swak!

GAVIN GATE: *Don't you know it hurts me too?*

GODDESSES: *hurt me too*

GAVIN GATE: *It hurts me so bad*

GODDESSES: *hurt me too*

GAVIN GATE: *I never desert you*

GODDESSES: *hurt me too*

THEY FADE, THE ELECTRIC OPERATORS, GAVIN, THE GODDESSES, THEIR BACKS BLEEDING, THEIR GENITALIA RED AND

SORE. THE GREAT STORY HAS BEEN TOLD, IN THE DICTATOR-
SHIP OF TIME, A COME HAS RENT THE FLAG, TROOPS ARE MAS-
TURBATING WITH 1948 PIN-UPS IN THEIR TEARS, A PROMISE
HAS BEEN RENEWED.

RADIO: That was Gavin Gate and the Goddesses. . . .

I ran for the telephone. I called the station. Is that
the Early Morning Record Gal, I shouted into the mouthpiece. Is it? Is it really you? Thank you, thank you. A
dedication? Oh, my love. Don't you understand how
long I've been in the kitchen alone? I'm irregular. I
suffer from irregularity. I'm burnt bad in the thumb.
Don't Sir me, you Early Morning Record Gal. I have to
talk to someone such as you because—

TELEPHONE: Click click.

What are you doing? Hey! Hey! Hello, hello, oh, no.
I remembered that there was a telephone booth a few
blocks down. I had to talk to her. My shoes stuck in
the semen as I walked across the linoleum. I gained the
door. I commanded the elevator. I had so much to tell
her, her with her blue voice and city knowledge. Then
I was out on the street, 4 a.m. in the morning, the
streets damp and dark as newly poured cement, the
streetlamps nearly merely decoration, the moon given
speed by flying scarves of cloud, the thick walled ware-
houses with gold family names, the cold blue air filled
with smells of burlap and the river, the sound of trucks
with country vegetables, the creaks of a train unload-
ing skinned animals from beds of ice, and men in over-
alls with great armfuls of traveling food, great wrestling
embraces in the front-line war of survival, and men
would win, and men would tell the grief in victory—I
was outside in the cold ordinary world, F. had led me
here by many compassionate tricks, a gasp in praise of
existence blasted my chest and unfolded my lungs like

a newspaper in the wind.

31.

The King of France was a man. I was a man. Therefore I was the King of France. F.! I'm sinking again.

32.

Canada became a royal colony of France in 1663. Here come the troops led by le marquis de Tracy, lieutenant-general of the armies of the king, here they come marching through the snow, twelve hundred tall men, the famous régiment de Carignan. The news travels down the icy banks of the Mohawk: the King of France has touched the map with his white finger. The Intendant Talon, the Governor M. de Courcelle, and Tracy, they gaze over the infested wilderness. My brothers, let us be masters of the Richelieu! Voices spoken over maps, voices spoken into windows, and the forts rise along shore, Sorel, Chambly, Sainte-Thérèse, Saint-Jean, Sainte-Anne on an island in Lake Champlain. My brothers, the Iroquois live in too many trees. January 1666, M. de Courcelle led a column of men deep into Mohawk country, a Napoleonic blunder. He went without his Algonquin scouts, who did not happen to show up on time. The Indians marked the aimless trail of his retreat with many bristling corpses. Tracy waited until September of the same year. Out of Québec, into the scarlet forests, marched six hundred of the Carignan, another six hundred of the Militia, and one hundred friendly Indians. Four priests accompanied the expedition. After a three-week march they reached the first Mohawk village, Gandaouagué. The fires were cold, the village was deserted, as were all the villages they would come to. Tracy planted a Cross, a Mass was celebrated, and over the empty long houses rose the solemn music of the Te Deum. Then they burned the village to the ground, Gandaouagué and all those they came to, they devastated the countryside, destroyed provisions of corn and bean, into the fire went every harvest. The Iroquois sued for peace, and as in 1653 priests were dispatched to every village. The truce of 1666 lasted eighteen years. Mgr. de Laval blessed his Fathers before they left Québec in the search for souls. The priests entered the rebuilt village of Gandaouagué in the summer of 1667. The Mohawks sounded their great shell trumpets as the Robes-Noires, they of the long black dresses, settled among them. They stayed three days at the village we have studied, but here we may note a delicate attention of Providence. They were billeted in the cabin of Catherine Tekakwitha, and she served them, she followed them as they visited the captives of the village, Christian Hurons and Algonquins, watched as they baptized their young, wondered as they isolated the old in far-off cabins. After three days the priests moved on to Gandarago, then to Tionnontoguen, where they were greeted by two hundred braves, a chief's eloquent welcome, and the cheers of the people who preferred the intrusion of foreign magic to the wrath of the Carignan. Five missions were established throughout the Iroquois confederation: Sainte-Marie at Tionnontoguen, Saint-François-Xavier at Onneyout, Saint-Jean-Baptiste at Onnontagué, Saint-Joseph at Tsonnontouan—from lac Saint-Sacrement to Erie, the work of only six evangelists, but a story of fire behind them. In 1668 our village Gandaouagué moved again. From the south bank of the Mohawk they crossed the river, built their long houses once again a few miles to the west, where the Mohawk meets the Cayudetta. They called the new village Kahnawaké, which means at the rapids. Close by was a small clear spring where she came each day for water. She kneeled on the moss. The water sang in her ears. The fountain rose from the heart of the forest, crystal and green were the tiny orchards of the moss. She drew a wet hand across her forehead. She longed for a deep brotherhood with the water, she longed for the spring to guarantee the gift she had made of her body, she longed to kneel wet before black robes. She swooned, collapsed beside the upturned bucket, weeping like Jill.

33.

Be with me, religious medals of all kinds, those suspended on silver chains, those pinned to the underwear with a safety pin, those nestling in black chest hair, those which run like tram cars on the creases between the breasts of old happy women, those that by mistake dig into the skin while love is made, those that lie abandoned with cufflinks, those that are fingered like coins and inspected for silver hallmark, those that are lost in clothes by necking fifteen-year-olds, those that are put in the mouth while thinking, those very expensive ones that only thin small girl children are permitted to wear, those hanging in a junk closet along with unknotted neckties, those that are kissed for luck, those that are torn from the neck in anger, those that are stamped, those that are engraved, those that are placed on streetcar tracks for curious alterations, those that are fastened to the felt on the roofs of taxis, be with me as I witness the ordeal of Catherine Tekakwitha.

34.

—Take your fingers out of your ears, said le P. Jean Pierron, first permanent missionary at Kahnawaké. You won't be able to hear me if you keep your fingers in your ears.

—Ha, ha, chuckled the ancient members of the village, who were too old to learn new tricks. You can lead us to water but you can't make us drink, us old dogs and horses.

—Remove those fingers immediately!

—Dribble, dribble, went the foam and spit between toothless jaws as the old ones squatted around the priest.

The priest went back to his cabin and took out his paints, for he was a skilled artist. A few days later he emerged with his picture, a bright mandala of the torments of hell. All the damned had been portrayed as Mohawk Indians. The mocking aged Indians squatted around him, finger-eared still, as he uncovered his work. Gasps escaped from their rotting mouths.

—Now, my children, this is what awaits you. Oh, you can keep your fingers where they are. See. A demon will place round your neck a rope and drag you along. A demon will cut off your head, extract your heart, pull out your intestines, lick up your brain, drink your blood, eat your flesh, and nibble your bones. But you will be incapable of dying. Though your body be hacked to pieces it will revive again. The repeated hacking will cause intense pain and torture.

—Arghhh!

The colors of the picture were red, white, black, orange, green, yellow, and blue. In the very center was the representation of a very old Iroquois woman, bent and wrinkled. She was enclosed in her own personal frame of finely drawn skulls. Leaning over the oval skulls is a Jesuit priest who is trying to instruct her. Her arthritic fingers are stuffed in her ears. A demon twists corkscrews of fire into her ears, perhaps jamming the fingers in there forever. A demon hurls a javelin of flame at her deplorable breasts. Two demons apply a fiery two-handled saw to her crotch. A demon encourages several burning snakes to twist around her bleeding ankles. Her mouth is a burnt black hole seared in an eternal screech for attention. As Marie de l'Incarnation wrote her son, On ne peut pas les voir sans frémir.

—Arghhh!

Il a baptisé un grand nombre de personnes, writes Marie de l'Incarnation.

—That's right, pull them right out, the priest invited them. And don't put them back. You must never put them back again. Old as you are, you must forget forever the Telephone Dance.

—Pop! Pop! Pop! Pop!

—That's better, isn't it?

As those waxy digits were withdrawn a wall of silence was thrown up between the forest and the hearth, and the old people gathered at the priest's hem shivered with a new kind of loneliness. They could not hear the raspberries breaking into domes, they could not smell the numberless pine needles combing out the wind, they could not remember the last moment of a trout as it lived between a flat white pebble on the streaked bed of a stream and the fast shadow of a bear claw. Like children who listen in vain to the sea in plastic sea shells they sat bewildered. Like children at the end of a long bedtime story they were suddenly thirsty.

35.

Catherine's uncle was happy to see le P. Pierron leave in 1670 for a post at the Iroquois mission on the St. Lawrence. Many of his brethren had been converted to the new faith, and many had left the village to live and worship at the new missions. The new priest, le P. Boniface, was not any less effective than his predecessor. He spoke the language. Perceiving how the Indians loved music, he formed a choir of seven- and eight-year-olds. Their pure rough voices drifted through the village like the news of a good meal, and many were lured to the little wooden chapel. In 1673 this village of less than four hundred souls witnessed the salvation of thirty of them. These were adult souls—the number does not include infant souls or moribund souls. Kryn, the chief of the Mohawks, converted and established himself as a preacher at the new mission. Of all the Iroquois, the Mohawks were the most susceptible to the new doctrines, they who had been most ferocious in their original resistance. Le P. Dablon, Superior General of the Missions of Canada, could write in 1673: La foi y a été plus constamment embrassée qu'en aucun autre pays d'Agniers. In 1674 le P. Boniface led a group of neophytes to the mission at Saint-François-Xavier. Shortly after he returned to Kahnawaké he died during a December snowfall. Le P. Jacques de Lamberville replaced him.

36.

The cabins of the village were empty. It was spring. It was 1675. Somewhere Spinoza was making sunglasses. In England, Hugh Chamberlen was pulling babies out with a secret instrument, obstetrical forceps, the only man in Europe to deliver women with this revolutionary technique which had been developed by his grandfather. Marquis de Laplace was looking at the sun prior to his assumption that the sun rotated at the very beginning of existence, which he would develop in his book, *Exposition du Système du Monde*. The fifth reincarnation of Tsong Khapa achieved temporal supremacy: the regency of Tibet was handed to him by Mongolia, with the title Dalai Lama. There were Jesuits in Korea. A group of colonial doctors interested in anatomy but frustrated by the laws against human dissection managed to obtain "the middle-most part of an Indian executed the day before." Thirty years before the Jews reentered France. Twenty years before we remark the first outbreak of syphilis in Boston. Frederick William was the Great Elector. Friars of the Order of Minims, according to a regulation of 1668, should not be excommunicated if, "when about to yield to the temptations of the flesh . . . they prudently laid aside the monastic habit." Corelli, the forerunner of Alessandro Scarlatti, Handel, Couperin, and J. S. Bach, was, in 1675, the third violin in the church orchestra of St. Louis of France, which was in Rome in 1675. Thus the moon of the seventeenth century waned into its last quarter. In the next century 60,000,000 Europeans would die of smallpox. F. often said: Think of the world without Bach. Think of the Hittites without Christ. To discover the truth in anything that is alien, first dispense with the indispensable in your own vision. Thank you, F. Thank you, my lover. When will I be able to see the world without you, my dear? O Death, we are your Court Angels, hospitals are your Church! My friends have died. People I know have died. O Death, why do you make Halloween out of every night? I am scared. If it's not one thing it's another: if I'm not constipated I'm scared. O Death, let the firecracker burns heal once more. The trees around F.'s treehouse (where I am writing this), they are dark. I can't smell the apples. O Death, why do you do so much acting and so little talking? The cocoons are soft and creepy. I am afraid of worms with a butterfly heaven. Is Catherine a flower in the sky? Is F. an orchid? Is Edith a branch of hay? Does Death chase the cobwebs? Has Death anything to do with Pain, or is Pain working on the other side? O F., how I loved this treehouse when you lent it to me and Edith for our honeymoon!

37.

The cabins of Kahnawaké were empty. The fields around were filled with workers, men and women with handfuls of kernels. They were planting the corn in the spring of 1675.

—Yuh yuh, went the strains of the Corn-Planting Song.

Catherine's uncle squeezed his fist over the heap of yellow cradled in his palm. He could feel the powers of the seeds, their longing to be covered with earth and explode. They seemed to force his fingers open. He tipped his hand like a cup and one kernel dropped into a hole.

—Ah, he mused, in such a way did Our Female Ancestress fall from heaven into the waste of primeval waters. Some are of the opinion that various amphibious animals, such as the otter, beaver, and muskrat, noticed her fall, and hastened to break it by shoveling up earth from the mud beneath the waters.

Suddenly he stiffened. In his mind's heart he felt the sinister presence of le P. Jacques de Lamberville. Yes, he could feel the priest as he walked through the village,

more than a mile away. Catherine's uncle released a
Shadow to greet the priest.

Le P. Jacques de Lamberville paused outside
Tekakwitha's cabin. They were all in the fields, he
thought, so there's no point trying even if they let me
in this time.

—La ha la ha, came a tinkle of laughter from within.

The priest wheeled around and made toward the
door. The Shadow greeted him and they wrestled. The
Shadow was naked and easily tripped his heavily robed
opponent. The Shadow threw himself on the priest, who
was struggling to extricate himself from the coils of his
robe. The Shadow in his ferocity managed to entangle
himself in the very same robes. The priest quickly per-
ceived his advantage. He lay perfectly still while the
Shadow suffocated in the prison of a fortunate pocket.
He got up and threw the door open.

—Catherine!

—At last!

—What are you doing inside, Catherine? All of your
family is in the field planting corn.

—I stubbed my toe.

—Let me look.

—No. Let it go on hurting.

—What a lovely thing to say, child.

—I'm nineteen. Everyone hates me here, but I don't
mind. My aunts kick me all the time, not that I hold
anything against them. I have to carry the shit, well,
someone has to do it. But, Father, they want me to
fuck—but I have given my fuck away.

—Don't be an Indian Giver.

—What should I do, Father?

—Let me have a look at that toe.

—Yes!

—I'll have to take off your moccasin.

—Yes!

—Here?

—Yes!

—What about here?

—Yes!

—Your toes are cold, Catherine. I'll have to rub them between my palms.

—Yes!

—Now I'll blow them, you know, as one blows one's fingers in the winter.

—Yes!

The priest breathed heavily on her tiny brown toes. What a lovely little cushion her big toe had. The bottoms of her five toes looked like the faces of small children sleeping tucked up under a blanket up to their chins. He started to kiss them good night.

—Tosy rosy tosy rosy.

—Yes!

He nibbled at a cushion, which felt like a rubber grape. He was kneeling as Jesus had kneeled before a naked foot. In an orderly fashion, he inserted his tongue between each toe, four thrusts, so smooth the skin between, and white! He gave his attention to each toe, mouthing it, covering it with saliva, evaporating the saliva by blowing, biting it playfully. It was a shame that four toes should always suffer from loneliness. He forced all her tiny toes into his mouth, his tongue going like a windshield wiper. Francis had done the same for lepers.

—Father!

—Libalobaglobawoganummynummy.

—Father!

—Gobblegobblegogglewoggle. Slurp.

—Baptize me!

—Although some find our reluctance excessive we Jesuits do not rush Indian adults along the path to Baptism.

—I have two feet.

—Indians are fickle. We must protect ourselves from the catastrophe of producing more apostates than Christians.

—Wiggle.

—Comme nous nous défions de l'inconstance des Iroquois, j'en ai peu baptisé hors du danger de mort.

The girl slipped her foot into the moccasin and sat on it.

—Baptize me.

—Il n'y a pas grand nombre d'adultes, parce qu'on ne les baptise qu'avec beaucoup de précautions.

Thus the argument progressed in the shadows on the long house. A mile away Uncle sank to his knees, exhausted. *There would be no harvest!* But he was not thinking of the kernels he had just sown, he was thinking about the life of his people. All the years, all the hunts, all the wars—it would all come to nothing. *There would be no harvest!* Even his soul when it ripened would not be gathered to the warm southwest, whence blows the wind which brings sunny days and the bursting corn. *The world was unfinished!* A deep pain seized his chest. The great wrestling match between Ioskeha, the White one, and Tawiscara, the Dark one, the eternal fight would fizzle out like two passionate lovers falling asleep in a tight embrace. *There would be no harvest!* Each day the village was growing smaller as more of his brethren left for the new missions. He fumbled for a small wolf he had carved of wood. In the autumn past he had placed the whittled nostrils to his own, inhaling the animal's courage. Then he had breathed out deeply in order to spread the breath of the animal over a wide area in the forest, and so paralyze all the game in the neighborhood. When he had killed his deer that day he cut out the liver and smeared blood on the mouth of the carved wood wolf. And he prayed: Great Deer, First and Perfect Deer, ancestor of the carcass at my feet, we are hungry. Please do not seek vengeance against me for taking the life of one of your children. Uncle collapsed on the cornfield, gasping for breath. The Great Deer was dancing on his chest, crushing his ribs. They carried him back to the cabin. His niece wept when she saw his face. After a while, when they were alone, the old man spoke.

—He came in, the Black Dress?

—Yes, Father Tekakwitha.

—And you want to be baptized?

—Yes, Father Tekakwitha.

—I will allow you to on one condition: that you promise never to leave Kahnawaké.

—I promise.

—There will be no harvest, my daughter. Our heaven is dying. From every hill, a spirit cries out in pain, for it is being forgotten.

—Sleep.

—Bring me my pipe and open the door.

—What are you doing?

—I am blowing the breath of the tobacco at them, at all of them.

It was F.'s theory that White America has been punished by lung cancer for having destroyed the Red Man and stolen his pleasures.

—Try to forgive them, Father Tekakwitha.

—I can't.

As he blew the smoke weakly at the open door Uncle told himself the story he had heard as a little boy, how Kuloskap had abandoned the world because of the evil in it. He made a great feast to say good-by, then he paddled off in his great canoe. Now he lives in a splendid long house, making arrows. When the cabin is filled with them he will make war on all mankind.

38.

Is All The World A Prayer To Some Star? Are All The Years Of The World A Catalogue Of The Events Of Some Holiday? Do All Things Happen At Once? Is There A Needle In The Haystack? Do We Perform In The Twilight Before A Vast Theater Of Empty Stone Benches? Do We Hold Hands With Our Grandfathers? Are They Warm And Royal, The Rags Of Death? Are All The People Living At This Very Second Fingerprinted? Is Beauty The Pulley? How Are The Dead Received In The Expanding Army? Is It True That There Are No Wallflowers At The Dance? May I Suck Cunts For My Gift? May I Love The Forms Of Girls Instead Of Licking Labels? May I Die A Little At The Uncovering Of Unfamiliar Breasts? May I Raise A Path Of Goosepimples With My Tongue? May I Hug My Friend Instead Of Working? Are Sailors Naturally Religious? May I Squeeze A Golden-Haired Thigh Between My Legs And Feel Blood Flowing And Hear The Holy Tick Of The Fainting Clock? May I See If Someone Is Alive By Gobbling His Come? Could It Be Recorded In The Books Of Some Law That Shit Is Kosher? Is There A Difference In Dreaming Geometry And Bizarre Sex Positions? Is The Epileptic Always Graceful? Is There Such

A Thing As Waste? Is It Wonderful To Think About An Eighteen-Year-Old Girl Wearing Tight Jelly Underwear? Does Love Visit Me When I Pump Myself? O God, There Is A Scream, All The Systems Are Screaming. I Am Locked In A Fur Store But I Believe You Want To Steal Me. Does Gabriel Trip A Burglar Alarm? Why Was I Sewn Into Bed With The Nymphomaniac? Am I As Easy To Pluck As A Spear Of Grass? Can I Be Torn Away From The Roulette Wheel? By How Many Billion Cables Is The Zeppelin Secured? O God, I Love So Many Things It Will Need Years To Take Them Away One By One. I Adore Thy Details. Why Have You Let Me See The Bare Ankle Tonight In The Treehouse? Why Did You Vouchsafe Unto Me A Minute Flash Of Desire? May I Unfasten My Loneliness And Collide Once Again With A Beautiful Greedy Body? May I Fall Asleep After A Soft Happy Kiss? May I Have A Dog For A Pet? May I Teach Myself To Be Handsome? May I Pray At All?

39.

I remember one night with F. as he drove down the highway to Ottawa where he was to make his Maiden Speech in Parliament the next day. There was no moon. The headlights flowed over the white posts like a perfect liquid eraser, and behind us we abandoned a blank blueprint of vanished roads and fields. He had pushed it up to eighty. The St. Christopher's medal pinned to the felt above the windshield was involved in a tiny orbit lately initiated by a sharp curve.

—Take it easy, F.

—It's my night! My night!

—Yes it is, F. You finally made it: you're a Member of Parliament.

—I'm in the world of men.

—F., put it back. Enough is enough.

—Never put it back when it gets like this.

—My God! I've never seen you so big! What's going on in your mind? What are you thinking of? Please teach me how to do it. Can I hold it?

—No! This is between me and God.

—Let's stop the car. F., I love you, I love your power. Teach me everything.

—Shut up. There is a tube of sun cream in the glove compartment. Open the glove compartment by depressing the button with your thumb. Dig into the tangle of maps and gloves and string and extract the tube. Screw off the cap and squeeze a couple of inches of cream into my palm.

—Like this, F.?

—Yeah.

—Don't shut your eyes, F. Do you want me to drive?

Oh, what a greasy tower he there massaged! I might as well have addressed myself to the missing landscape we flung in our wake, farm houses and oil signs bouncing like sparks off our fenders as we cut open the painted white line at ninety, fast as an acetylene saw. His right hand beneath the steering wheel, urging, urging, he seemed to be pulling himself into the far black harbor like a reflexive stevedore. What beautiful hair poked out of his underwear. His cufflink gleamed in the maplight, which I had switched on the better to witness the delicious operation. As his cupped hand bobbed faster the needle tickled ninety-eight. How I was torn between the fear for my safety and the hunger to jam my head between his knees and the dashboard! Whish! went an orchard. A Main Street flared up in our headlights—we left it in cinders. I longed for the little wrinkles of his tightening scrotum to trap the tatters of my lips. F.'s eyes closed suddenly as if they had been squirted with lemon. His fist closed hard around the pale slippery shaft and he commenced to throttle himself madly. I feared for the organ, feared and coveted it, so hard it gleamed, streamlined as a Brancusi, the swelled head red and hot as a radioactive fireman's helmet. I wanted an anteater's tongue to whip off the wet pearl which F. himself now noticed and with a happy violent motion incorporated into the general lubrication. I could bear my loneliness no longer. I ripped the buttons of my old-fashioned European trousers in my frenzy to touch myself as a lover. What a handful of blood I was. Zoom! A parking lot blazed and expired. The warmth spread through leather gloves which I had not time to remove. Kamikaze insects splashed against the glass. My life was in my hands, all the messages I longed to deliver to the Zodiac gathered to begin their journey and I moaned with the intolerable pressure of pleasure. F. was screaming gibberish, his spit flying in all directions.

—Face me, face me, face me, suck bright, suck bright, F. wailed (if I remember the sounds correctly).

Thus we existed in some eye for a second: two men in a hurtling steel shell aimed at Ottawa, blinded by a mechanical mounting ecstasy, the old Indian land sunk in soot behind us, two swelling pricks pointing at eternity, two naked capsules filled with lonely tear gas to stop the riot in our brains, two fierce cocks separate as the gargoyles on different corners of a tower, two sacrificial lollipops (orange in the map light) offered to the ruptured highway.

—Ay ay ay ay ay! cried F. from the very top of his ladder.

—Slof tlif, sounded the geysers of his semen as they hit the dashboard (surely the sound of upstream salmon smashing their skulls on underwater cliffs).

As for me, I knew that one more stroke would deliver me—I hovered on the edge of my orgasm like a parachutist in the whistling doorway—I was suddenly forlorn—I was suddenly without desire—I was suddenly more awake (for this fraction of a second) than ever before in my whole life—

—The wall!

The wall occupied the whole windshield, first as a blur, then focused precisely as if an expert had adjusted the microscope—every pimple of the concrete three-dimensional—bright! precise!—fast film of the moon's hide—then the windshield blurred again as the wall rushed into the glass of the headlights—I saw F.'s cufflink skimming the edge of the steering wheel like a surfboard—

—Darling! Ehhhffff. . . .

—Rrrrriiiippppp, went the wall.

We passed through the wall because the wall was made of a scrim of painted silk. The car bumped over an empty field, the torn fabric clinging to the chrome Mercedes hood emblem. The undamaged headlights illumined a boarded-up hot-dog stand as F. applied the brake. On the wood counter I noticed an empty bottle with a perforated cap. I stared blankly at it.

—Did you come? asked F.

My prick hung out of my fly like a stray thread.

—Too bad, said F.

I started to shiver.

—You missed a great come.

I placed my clenched fists on the top of the dashboard and laid my forehead on them, weeping in spasms.

—We went to a lot of trouble rigging the thing up, renting the parking lot and all.

I jerked my face toward him.

—We? What do you mean "we"?

—Edith and I.

—Edith was in on it?

—How about that second just before you were about to shoot? Did you sense the emptiness? Did you get the freedom?

—Edith knows about our filthy activities?

—You should have kept on with it, my friend. You weren't driving. There was nothing you could do. The wall was on top of you. You missed a great come.

—Edith knows we're fairies?

I threw my hands at his neck with a murderous intention. F. smiled. How thin and puny my wrists looked in the dim orange light. F. removed my fingers like a necklace.

—Easy. Easy. Dry your eyes.

—F., why do you torture me?

—O my friend, you are so lonely. Each day you get lonelier. What will happen when we are gone?

—None of your fucking business! How dare you presume to teach me anything? You're a fake. You're a menace! You're a disgrace to Canada! You've ruined my life!

—All these things may be true.

—You filthy bastard! How dare you admit they're true?

He leaned forward to switch on the ignition and looked at my lap.

—Button up. It's a long cold drive to Parliament.

40.

I have been writing these true happenings for some time now. Am I any closer to Kateri Tekakwitha? The sky is very foreign. I do not think I will ever tarry with the stars. I do not think I will ever have a garland. I do not think ghosts will whisper erotic messages in my warm hair. I will never find a graceful way to carry a brown lunch bag on a bus ride. I'll go to funerals and they won't remind me of anything. It was years and years ago that F. said: Each day you get lonelier. That was years and years ago. What did F. mean by advising me to go down on a saint? What is a saint? A saint is someone who has achieved a remote human possibility. It is impossible to say what that possibility is. I think it has something to do with the energy of love. Contact with this energy results in the exercise of a kind of balance in the chaos of existence. A saint does not dissolve the chaos; if he did the world would have changed long ago. I do not think that a saint dissolves the chaos even for himself, for there is something arrogant and warlike in the notion of a man setting the universe in order. It is a kind of balance that is his glory. He rides the drifts like an escaped ski. His course is a caress of the hill. His track is a drawing of the snow in a moment of its particular arrangement with wind and rock. Something in him so loves the world that he gives himself to the laws of gravity and chance. Far from flying with the angels, he traces with the fidelity of a seismograph needle the state of the solid bloody landscape. His house is dangerous and finite, but he is at home in the world. He can love the shapes of human beings, the fine and twisted shapes of the heart. It is good to have among us such men, such balancing monsters of love. It makes me think that the numbers in the bag actually correspond to the numbers on the raffles we have bought so dearly, and so the prize is not an illusion. But why fuck one? I remember once slobbering over Edith's thigh. I sucked, I kissed the long brown thing, and it was Thigh, Thigh, Thigh—Thigh softening and spreading as it flowed in a perfume of bacon to the mound of Cunt—Thigh sharpening and hardening as I followed the direction of its tiny hairs and bounced into Kneecap. I don't know what Edith did (maybe one of her magnificent lubrication squirts) or what I did (maybe one of my mysterious sprays of salivation) but all at once my face was wet and my mouth slid on skin; it wasn't Thigh or Cunt or any chalk schoolboy slogan (nor was I Fucking): it was just a shape of Edith: then it was just a humanoid shape: then it was just a shape—and for a blessed second truly I was not alone, I was part of a family. That was the first time we made love. It never happened again. Is that what you will cause me to feel, Catherine Tekakwitha? But aren't you dead? How do I get close to a dead saint? The pursuit seems like such nonsense. I'm not happy here in F.'s old treehouse. It's long past the end of summer. My brain is ruined. My career is in tatters. O F., is this the training you planned for me?

41.

Catherine Tekakwitha was baptized on the eighteenth of April (the Month of Bright Leaves) in the year 1676.

Please come back to me, Edith. Kiss me, darling. I love you, Edith. Come back to life. I can't be alone any more. I think I have wrinkles and bad breath. Edith!

42.

A few days after her baptism Catherine Tekakwitha was
invited to a great feast in Québec. Present were the
Marquis de Tracy, the intendant Talon, the Governor
M. de Courcelle, the Mohawk Chief Kryn, who was
one of the fiercest converts Christianity has ever commanded, and many handsome ladies and gentlemen.
Perfume rose out of their hair. They were elegant in
the manner only citizens two thousand miles from Paris
can be. Wit flourished in every conversation. Butter was
not passed without an aphorism. They discussed the
activities of the French Academy of Sciences, which
was only ten years old. Some of the guests had spring
pocket watches, a new timepiece invention which was
sweeping Europe. Someone explained another recently
developed device used to regulate clocks, the pendulum.
Catherine Tekakwitha listened quietly to everything
that was said. With a bowed head she received the
compliments which the quillwork on her deerskin gown
evoked. The long white table shone with the pride of
silver and crystal and early spring flowers, and for a
minor second her eyes swam in the splendor of the
occasion. Handsome servants poured wine into glasses
that resembled long-stem roses. A hundred candle
flames echoed and re-echoed in a hundred pieces of
silver cutlery as the fragrant guests worked over their
slabs of meat, and for a minor second the flashing multiple suns hurt her eyes, burned away her appetite.
With a tiny abrupt movement which she did not command, she knocked over her glass of wine. She stared
at the whale-shaped stain, frozen with shame.

—It is nothing, said the Marquis. It is nothing, child.

Catherine Tekakwitha sat motionless. The Marquis
returned to his conversation. It concerned a new mili-

tary invention which was being developed in France, the bayonet. The stain spread quickly.

—Even the tablecloth is thirsty for this good wine, joked the Marquis. Don't be frightened, child. There are no punishments for spilling a glass of wine.

Despite the suave activity of several servants the stain continued to discolor larger and larger areas of the tablecloth. Conversation dwindled as the diners directed their attention to its remarkable progress. It now claimed the entire tablecloth. Talk ceased altogether as a silver vase turned purple and the pink flowers it contained succumbed to the same influence. A beautiful lady gave out a cry of pain as her fine hand turned purple. A total chromatic metamorphosis took place in a matter of minutes. Wails and oaths resounded through the purple hall as faces, clothes, tapestries, and furniture displayed the same deep shade. Beyond the high windows there were islands of snow glinting in the moonlight. The entire company, servants and masters, had directed its gaze outside, as if to find beyond the contaminated hall some reassurance of a multicolored universe. Before their eyes these drifts of spring snow darkened into shades of spilled wine, and the moon itself absorbed the imperial hue. Catherine stood up slowly.

—I guess I owe you all an apology.

43.

It is my impression that the above is apocalyptic. The word apocalyptic has interesting origins. It comes from the Greek *apokalupsis*, which means revelation. This derives from the Greek *apokaluptein*, meaning uncover or disclose. *Apo* is a Greek prefix meaning from, derived from. *Kaluptein* means to cover. This is cognate with *kalube* which is cabin, and *kalumma* which means woman's veil. Therefore apocalyptic describes that which is revealed when the woman's veil is lifted. What have I done, what have I not done, to lift your veil, to get under your blanket, Kateri Tekakwitha? I find no mention of this feast in any of the standard biographers. The two principal sources of her life are the Jesuit Fathers Pierre Cholenec and Claude Chauchetière. Both were her confessors at the mission Sault Saint-Louis, to which Catherine Tekakwitha came in the autumn of 1677 (breaking her promise to Uncle). Of P. Cholenec we have *Vie de Catherine Tegakouita, Première Vierge Irokoise*, in manuscript. Another *Vie*, written in Latin, was sent to P. Général de la Compagnie de Jésus in 1715. Of P. Chauchetière we have *La Vie de la B. Catherine Tekakouita, dite à présent la Saincte Sauvegesse*, written in 1695, the manuscript of which is at present preserved in the archives of Collège Sainte-Marie. In those archives rests another important document written by Remy (Abbé, P.S.S.), intitled *Certificat de M. Remy, curé de la Chine, des miracles faits en sa paroisse par l'intercession de la B. Cath. Tekakwita*, written in 1696. I love the Jesuits because they saw miracles. Homage to the Jesuit who has done so much to conquer the frontier between the natural and the supernatural. Under countless disguises, now as a Cabinet Minister, now as a Christian priest, now as a soldier, a Brahmin, an astrologer, now as the Confessor to a monarch, now as a mathematician, now as a Mandarin—by a thousand arts, luring, persuading, compelling men to acknowledge, under the weight of recorded miracles, that the earth is a province of Eternity. Homage to Ignatius Loyola, struck down by a French Protestant bullet in the breach of Pampeluna, for in his sick room, in the cave of Manresa, this proud soldier saw the Mysteries of heaven, and these visions brought forth the mighty Society of Jesus. This Society has made bold to assert that the marble face of Caesar is only a mask of God, and in the imperial appetite for worldly power the Jesuit has understood the divine thirst for souls. Homage to my teachers in the orphanage of downtown Montréal who smelled of semen and incense. Homage to the priests of crutch-filled rooms who have penetrated an illusion, who know that lameness is only an aspect of perfection, just as weeds are flowers which no one collects. Homage to the walls of crutches which are weed museums. Homage to the alchemical stench of burning wax which bespeaks an intimacy with ghouls. Homage to the vaulted halls where we knelt face to face with the shit-enhaloed Accuser of the World. Homage to those who prepared me for the freezing vigil tonight, the only material sardine in a can of ghosts. Homage to those old torturers who did not doubt the souls of their victims, and, like the Indians, allowed the power of the Enemy to nourish the strength of the community. Homage to those who believed in the Adversary and could therefore flourish in the manly style of the warrior. Homage to desks in our old classroom, that little brave armada which, year after year, attempts the Flood with a green crew. Homage to our soiled books which were municipal gifts, especially the Catechism which invited marginal obscenity and contributed to the maintenance of the lavatory as a thrilling temple of the Profane. Homage to the great slabs of marble with which the cubicles were constructed, to which no smear of shit could ever adhere. Here was enshrined the anti-Lutheran possibility of matter which succumbed easily to washing. Homage to marble in the Halls of Excrement, Maginot Line against the invasion of Papal Fallibility. Homage to the parables of the orphans' lavatory, the yellow failure of the porcelain proving a single drop of water was as powerful as the Ice Age. Oh somewhere, let something remember us strong orphans lined up in single file to use one cake of soap for our finger warts on sixty hands in order to appease Inspection. Homage to the brave boy who bit off his warts who was my friend F. Homage to the one who couldn't sink his teeth into himself who was the coward me, who was the author of this history, and who is frightened at this moment in his booth above the drifts of Canada, whose digit wart has been distorted by years of pencil erosion. May I get warm with homage? I have offended everyone, and I see that I am frozen by everyone's automatic magic.

—F.! Don't eat your warts!

—I will eat my warts in front of the whole world. You better too.

—I'm waiting for mine to clear up.

—What?

—Waiting for them to clear up.

—Clear up?

F. struck his forehead and ran from cubicle to cubicle like a man waking up a village, opening each door and addressing each squatting machine.

—Come out, come out, F. shouted. He's waiting for them to clear up. Come and see the poor fish who's waiting for them to clear up.

Stumbling over their lowered ankle-chain trousers my classmates poured out of the cubicles, shuffling awkwardly in the rubberless loci of their underwear. Out they rushed, some in the midst of masturbation, comics sliding from their kneecaps, romantic information scratched in the varnished door half-read. They closed around us in a circle, pressing in to see F.'s freak. F. swung my hand into the air like a boxing gesture, and I dangled beneath his grip, my whole body withering like a sheaf of tobacco to be auctioned off by the Liggett and Myers midget bellboy.

—Don't humiliate me, F., I pleaded.

—Step right up, folks. Look at the man who can wait. Look at the man who has a thousand years on his hands.

They shook their clustered faces in disbelief.

—I wouldn't have missed this for anything, one of them said.

—Ha ha ha.

F. flung down my hand without letting go and I fell in a heap at his feet. He placed his Charity Shoe heel on my thumb with just enough pressure to make me give up any notion of escape.

—Under my foot is the hand that will merely wave good-by to a number of warts.

—Ho ho.

—That's rich.

O Reader, do you know that a man is writing this? A man like you who longed for a hero's heart. In arctic isolation a man is writing this, a man who hates his memory and remembers everything, who was once as proud as you, who loved society as only an orphan can, who loved it as a spy in the milk and honey. A man like you writes this most daring passage, who dreamed like you of leadership and gratitude. No no please, not the cramps, not the cramps. Take away the cramps and I promise never to interrupt, I swear, O you Gods and Goddesses of the Pure Event.

—Ho ho.

—Priceless.

Early morning as this takes place. There wasn't much sun behind the barred opaque windows of the lavatory but we weren't allowed to use the lights in the morning except during winter. Dirty aquarium light in which things supposed to sparkle only gleam like a half-dollar hidden in a small jar of petroleum jelly. Each white sink, every spike on the walls between the cubicles (so you couldn't climb) had its jar of Vaseline. Shiniest of all were the bare kneecaps of my scornful audience, whitest of all were the slum-white shins of the older pituitary boys who were beginning to hair. With an intake of breath F. hushed their derision. I tried to catch his eye so I could beg him. I lay waiting for punishment on the Vaseline-colored marble tiles. He began his harangue in an objective tone, but I knew what was to follow.

—Some believe that the wart will clear up. Some are of the opinion that the wart will vanish with time. Some are reluctant to consider the wart at all. There are even those who deny the existence of warts. There are those who claim that the wart is beautiful and encourage it wherever it occurs. Some argue that warts are useful, are susceptible to education, and can learn to speak. Experts have arisen on this question. Theories developed concerning techniques. At first the methods were brutal. A school arose around the idea that the wart should not be coerced. A radical wing believes that the wart can master only languages of the Sinotic group. A lunatic fringe holds it error to force any human language on the wart since there is a unique wart tongue which the instructors themselves must first comprehend. A very few certifiable individuals insist that the wart is already voluble, has been so forever, and we have only to learn the way to listen.

—Get to the point, F.

—So what?

—How long before the torture?

Having bored them with great daring, F. now launched the dramatic phase of the credo. He drove down on his heel to get a shriek from me. Suddenly it was used Vaseline, and the light was like the holes in dead floating minnows, and one had a sensation that all the toilets were blocked and the teachers would have to come now and learn too much about us.

—I do not believe that the wart will "clear up." To me the wart is ugly. I'm a simple man. There's enough talking as it is, far as *I* see. To me a wart is a secret I don't *want* to keep. When I see wart I think scalpel.

—Ahhh!

As he said his last word he had shot his hand out in a salute. The salute ended in a penknife, just as a bayonet illumines unmistakenly the use of a rifle. The orphans gasped.

—When I see wart I think Speedy Removal. I think Before and After. I think Miracle Drugs. I think In Just Ten Days.

—Go. Go.

—I think Yours For Only. I think Try This SCIENTIFIC HOME Method. I think RUSH ME MY FREE. Grab him, men!

They swarmed over me and pulled me to my feet. My arm was seized and stretched out straight. They lined up along my arm like sailors hauling a rope. Their backs were in the way and I could not see my hand. Someone flattened my palm against the porcelain and spread my fingers.

—Yes, F. cried above the clamor, I think Act Now. I think Don't Delay. I think This Offer Expires.

—Help!

—Stuff his mouth.

—Mmmmmm. Mmmmmmm.

—Now! Slice! R-i-i-i-p!

I tried to imagine that I was just one of those backs tugging at the arm, just one of the sailors, and that a long way off they were carving butter.

44.

The story of Catherine Tekakwitha's feast is apocalyptic, as I started to say. In fact, it was my wife Edith who told me the story. I remember the evening perfectly. I had just returned from a weekend in Ottawa, where F. had arranged for me to have access to the Archives. The three of us were using the sunlamp in our basement apartment. F. said that I was the only one who could lie naked because both he and Edith had already seen my prick, but they had not seen each other's parts (a lie). F.'s logic was infallible but still I felt queer about taking down my pants in front of them, and it was true I would never have let Edith get nude or let F. strut around.

—But I'd rather not, I said weakly.

—Nonsense, darling.

—At least one of us should get a proper tan.

They stared at me as I rolled them down over my knees, worried that I had wiped myself imperfectly maybe and there was tell-tale. Truth was, I felt that F. was using me like an advertisement for his own body. I was the tattered billboard for his reality. His expression seemed to say to Edith: If a thing like that can breathe and get up every morning, think of the fuck you can get off of me.

—Lie between us.

—Uncross your legs.

—Take your hands away.

And when Edith rubbed on the Sun and Ski I didn't know whether to get an erection. On Sunday nights, such as this was, Edith and F. used to inject themselves with a little heroin, which is harmless and safer than alcohol. I was still of the old school in those days and considered it a killer drug, so I always passed up their offers to include me. That night it struck me that they were extremely ritualistic while preparing the hypodermic syringe and "toasting" the "horse."

—Why are you both so solemn?

—Oh, nothing.

Edith rushed over to me and hugged tight, and then F. joined her, and I felt like some Maidenform dream in an airport for Kamikaze pilots saying farewell.

—Get off! You don't have to suck up to me. I won't squeal.

—Good-by, my darling.

—Good-by, old friend.

—Oh, get on with it, both of you. Go on, you degenerates, fly off to your crutch-supported Paradise.

—Good-by, Edith said sadly once more, and I should have known that this was not an ordinary Sunday night.

They rustled among their veins for one that still carried blood, tapped the needles under the flesh, waited for the red signal of a "hit," and then squirted the solution into circulation. Withdrawing the needles abruptly, they fell back onto the couch. After minutes of stupor Edith said:

—Darling?

—What is it?

—Don't answer so quickly.

—Yes, F. added. Do us a favor.

—I can't watch this, my wife and my friend.

Angrily I stalked into the bedroom, slamming the door. I suppose they saw my buttocks in a blur as I left. One of the reasons I had left was because watching them use the needles always gives me a hard-on and, since I had chosen not to get one when the Sun and Ski was rubbed, I considered that getting one now would put me in an abnormal light. Secondly I wanted to sneak in Edith's drawers which I did every Sunday night while they were senseless in their narcotic world, and this illegal inspection, because of many failures which this chronicle has made clear, had become my chief amusement. But this was not your usual Sunday night. I loved her cosmetic drawer best of all, because it was bright and fragrant, and little bottles fell over when you pulled it out, and a solitary white-root woman's whisker might still adhere to the tweezers, or her thumbprint on an oily pancake cap—it was strange, but with this evidence I somehow got closer to her beauty, just as a thousand pilgrims cherish a relic, a formaldehyde organ of a saint few of them would have acclaimed in the flesh. I pulled the drawer knob, anticipating the lovely tinkle, when! There was nothing in the drawer but smashed glass, two cheap-looking rosaries, several ampules of colorless liquid, and some scraps of paper. The wooden bottom of the drawer was wet. Carefully I extracted one of the scraps of paper which turned out to be a coupon.

But Edith's legs were beautiful! And here was another:

What was going on here? What could Edith want with these pathetic invitations? What went on at 134 East 92nd Street? Was it an amputated-leg pool? In a corner of the drawer, half-soaked, was the beginning of the explanation. I can still see it. I can still reproduce it in my brain, word for word.

The paper in my fist, I ran from the bedroom. Edith and F. were asleep on the couch, respectably apart. On the coffee table were strewn the gruesome appliances of their habit, the needles, the eyedroppers, the belt, and —a dozen empty Perpetual Lourdes Water Ampules. I shook them both by their clothes.

—How long has this been going on?

I visited each of them with a close-up of the ad.

—How long have you been putting this into your bodies?

—Tell him, Edith, F. whispered.

—This is the first time we've used it.

—Tell him everything, Edith.

—Yes, I demand to know everything.

—We made a mixture.

—We mixed two different types of water.

—I'm listening.

—Well, some of the water was from the Lourdes Ampules and some of it was from—

—Yes?

—Tell him, Edith.

—Was from Tekakwitha's Spring.

—So you're not drug addicts any more?

—Is that all you want to ask? F. said wearily.

—Leave him alone, F. Come sit between us.

—I don't like sitting between you naked.

—We won't look.

—All right.

I checked their eyes with a match, I threw punches that didn't land, and when I was sure they weren't peeking I sat down.

—Well, what does it do?

—We don't know.

—Tell him the truth, Edith.

—We do know.

And, as if she were about to begin an explanation with an anecdote, Edith fumbled for my hand and told me the story of Catherine Tekakwitha's Feast long ago in Québec. F. took my other hand as she spoke. I think they were both weeping, for there was mucus in her voice, and F. seemed to tremble like someone falling off to sleep. That night in the bedroom Edith did whatever I wanted. I used not one radio command for her busy mouth. A week later she was under the elevator, a "suicide."

45.

I'm freezing to death in this damn treehouse. I thought Nature would be better than my little semen basement kitchen. I thought the noise of bird would be more sweet than the noise of elevator. Experts with tape recorders say that what we hear as a single bird note is really ten or twelve tones with which the animal weaves many various beautiful liquid harmonies. This he proves by slowing down his tape. I demand National Health! I demand an operation! I want a slow transistor machine sewn in my head. Otherwise let Science keep its insights out of the newspapers. The Canadian summer passed like a Halloween mask, now the cold countryside day after day. Is this all the candies we get? Where is the science-fiction world of tomorrow they promised us today? I demand a change of climate. What bravado impelled me to come here without my radio? Three months without my radio, humming the obsolete Top Ten, my Top Ten removed so abruptly from history, cut off from the dynamic changes of jukebox stock market, my poor Top Ten that no thirteen-year-olds energize by slippery necking on the carpet beside the hi-fi, my over-serious Top Ten goose-stepping through my head like the generals of a junta who do not know the coup d'état has been staged the very night of the formal ball, my dear old Top Ten like a battalion of gold-sleeved tramway conductors patiently steering for seniority and retirement while the subway has been decreed in a board room and all the streetcars are in museums, my awkward Top Ten of electric echoes and longing puberty voices crying down my heart like a squad of bare-thighed cheer-leaderettes turning cartwheels before the empty benches, their delicate bra-straps bunching the skin ever so sweetly, their shiny fluorescent underwear flashing out of little upside-down pleated skirts as they pivot on their friendship fingers, their school-spirit satin-clad gym-trained firm little rah-rah bums describing unutterably lovely and brief rainbow-shaped streaks of mauve and orange, the round metal mouthpieces of their megaphones warm with Alma Maters and smelling of white lipstick, and for whom these moist Technicolor acrobatics? for whom these inflammatory arcs of unskirted exhibition panties gleaming through the cheers like so many expertly peeled fresh figs, yes, a million seedy secrets in each sealed purse, wheeling down the damp sidelines into the stumpy mouth of time? for whom do you sail, little bums of the Top Ten? The Leader of the Pack lies mangled under his Honda in a wreck of job prospects, the ghostly Negro fullback floats down the wintry gridiron into Law School prizes, and the lucky football you autographed takes pictures of the moon. Oh, my poor Top Ten, longing to perish in popularity, I have forgotten my radio, so you languish with the other zombies in my memory, you whose only honor is hara-kiri with the blunt edge of returned identification bracelets, my weary Top Ten hoping to be forgotten like escaped balloons and kites, like theater stubs, like dry ball pens, like old batteries, like coiled sardine keys, like bent aluminum partitioned eaten tv dinner plates—I hoard you like the stuff of my chronic disease, I sentence you to National Anthem hard labor, I deny you martyrdom in tomorrow's Hit Parade, I turn you into boomerangs, my little Kamikazes, you long to be the Lost Tribes but I burn arm numbers, I pour miracle drugs in the Death House, from bridges I hang suicide nets. Saints and friends, help me out of History and Constipation. Make the birds sing slower, make me listen faster. Remove yourself from this treehouse, Pain, you tree-climbing frog, large as industry.

46.

—I am sick, but I am not too sick, said Catherine Tekak-witha's uncle.

—Let me baptize you, said the Black-Robe.

—Do not let any of your water fall on me. I have seen many die after you have touched them with your water.

—They are in Heaven now.

—Heaven is a good place for Frenchmen, but I wish to be among Indians, for the French will give me nothing to eat when I get there, and the French women will not lie with us under the shadowy firs.

—We are all of the same Father.

—Ah, Black-Robe, were we of one Father we should know how to make knives and coats as well as you.

—Listen, old man, in the hollow of my hand I hold a mystic drop which can snatch you from an eternity of woe.

—Do they hunt in Heaven, or make war, or go to feasts?

—Oh, no!

—Then I will not go. It is not good to be lazy.

—Infernal fire and torturing demons await you.

—Why did you baptize our enemy the Huron? He will get to Heaven before us and drive us out when we come.

—There is room for all in Heaven.

—If there is so much room, Black-Robe, why do you guard the entrance so jealously?

—There is little time left. You will surely go to Hell.

—There is much time, Black-Robe. If you and I should talk until the weasel befriends the rabbit, we would not break the rope of days.

—Your eloquence is diabolic. Fire waits for you, old man.

—Yes, Black-Robe, a small shadowy fire, about which sit the shades of my relatives and ancestors.

When the Jesuit left him he called for Catherine Tekakwitha.

—Sit beside me.

—Yes, Uncle.

—Remove the blanket which covers me.

—Yes, Uncle.

—Look at this body. This is an old Mohawk body. Look closely.

—I am looking, Uncle.

—Do not weep, Kateri. We do not see well through tears, and although that which we see through tears is bright it is also bent.

—I will look at you without tears, Uncle.

—Remove all my garments and look at me closely.

—Yes, Uncle.

—Look for a long time. Look closely. Look and look.

—I will do as you say, Uncle.

—There is much time.

—Yes, Uncle.

—Your Aunts are spying through the spaces between the bark but do not distract yourself. Look and look.

—Yes, Uncle.

—What do you see, Kateri?

—I see an old Mohawk body.

—Look and look and I will tell you what will happen when the spirit begins to leave my body.

—I cannot listen, Uncle. I am a Christian now. Oh, do

not hurt my hand.

—Listen and look. What I tell you cannot offend any god, yours or mine, the Mother of the Beard or the Great Hare.

—I will listen.

—When the wind is no longer in my nostrils my spirit body will begin a long journey homeward. Look at this wrinkled, scarred body as I speak to you. My beautiful spirit body will begin a hard, dangerous journey. Many do not complete this journey, but I will. I will cross a treacherous river standing on a log. Wild rapids will try to throw me against sharp rocks. A huge dog will bite my heels. Then I will follow a narrow path between dancing boulders which crash together, and many will be crushed, but I will dance with the boulders. Look at this old Mohawk body as I speak to you, Catherine. Beside the path there is a bark hut. In the hut lives Oscotarach, the Head-Piercer. I will stand beneath him and he will remove the brain from my skull. This he does to all the skulls which pass by. It is the necessary preparation for the Eternal Hunt. Look at this body and listen.

—Yes, Uncle.

—What do you see?

—An old Mohawk body.

—Good. Cover me now. Do not weep. I will not die now. I will dream my cure.

—Oh, Uncle, I am so happy.

As soon as smiling Catherine Tekakwitha left the long house her cruel Aunts fell on her with fists and curses. She fell beneath their blows. "Ce fut en cette occasion," writes P. Cholenec, "qu'elle déclara ce qu'on aurait peut-être ignoré, si elle n'avait pas été mise à cette épreuve, que, par la miséricorde du Seigneur, elle ne se souvenait pas d'avoir jamais terni la pureté de son corps, et qu'elle n'appréhendait point de recevoir aucun reproche sur cet article au jour du jugement."

—You fucked your Uncle! they cried.

—You uncovered his nakedness!

—You peeked at his tool!

They dragged her to the priest, le P. de Lamberville.

—Here's a little Christian for you. Fucked her Uncle!

The priest sent away the howling savages and examined the young girl stretched bleeding on the ground before him. When he was satisfied he drew her up.

—You live here like a flower among poison thorns.

—Thank you, my father.

47.

Long ago (it seems) I awakened in my bed with F. pulling my hairs.

—Come with me, my friend.

—What time is it, F.?

—It is the summer of 1964.

He wore a curious smile on his face which I had not seen before. I cannot explain it, but it made me shy, and I crossed my legs.

—Get up. We're going for a walk.

—Turn around while I get dressed.

—No.

—Please.

He pulled the sheet from my body, still heavy with sleep and the dreams of a lost wife. He shook his head slowly.

—Why didn't you listen to Charles Axis?

—Please, F.

—Why didn't you listen to Charles Axis?

I squeezed my thighs tighter and laid the nightcap

across my pubic hair. F. stared at me relentlessly.

—Confess. Why didn't you listen to Charles Axis? Why didn't you send away the coupon on that distant afternoon in the orphanage?

—Leave me alone.

—Just look at your body.

—Edith had no complaints about my body.

—Ha!

—Did she ever say anything to you about my body?

—Plenty.

—Such as?

—She said you have an arrogant body.

—What the hell is that supposed to mean?

—Confess, my friend. Confess about Charles Axis. Confess your sin of pride.

—I have nothing to confess. Now turn around and I'll get dressed. It's too early for your cheap koans.

With a lightning flash he twisted my arm in a half-nelson, twisted me off the nostalgic bed, and forced me to confront the full-length mirror in the bathroom. Miraculously the nightcap had adhered to the wiry growth of my pubic hair. I shut my eyes.

—Ouch!

—Look. Look and confess. Confess why you ignored Charles Axis.

—No.

He tightened his expert grip.

—Oh, oh, oh, please! Help!

—The truth! You disdained the coupon because of the sin of pride, didn't you. Charles Axis wasn't enough for you. In your greedy brain you cherished an unspeakable desire. You wanted to be Blue Beetle. You wanted to be Captain Marvel. You wanted to be Plastic Man. Robin wasn't even good enough for you, you wanted to be Batman.

—You're breaking my back!

—You wanted to be the Superman who was never Clark Kent. You wanted to live at the front of the comic. You wanted to be Ibis the Invincible who never lost his Ibistick. You wanted SOCK! POW! SLAM! UGG! OOF! YULP! written in the air between you and all the world. To become a New Man in just fifteen minutes a day meant absolutely nothing to you. Confess!

—The pain! The pain! Yes, yes, I confess. I wanted miracles! I didn't want to climb to success on a ladder of coupons! I wanted to wake up suddenly with X-ray Vision! I confess!

—Good.

He turned the half-nelson into an embrace and drew me to him. My fingers were very skillful there in the porcelain gloom of my prison bathroom. As I undid the top clasp of his beltless Slim Jim slacks, I flicked away the nightcap. It fell between my toes and his shoes like an autumn figleaf in a utopia of nudists. The curious smile hadn't left his luscious mouth.

—Ah, my friend, I have waited a long time for that confession.

Arm in arm, we walked through the narrow harbor streets of Montréal. We watched great showers of wheat fall into the holds of Chinese cargo boats. We saw the geometry of the gulls as they drifted in perfect circles over center points of garbage. We watched great liners shrink as they hooted down the widening St. Lawrence, shrink into shining birch-bark canoes, then into white-caps, then into the mauve haze of distant hills.

—Why do you smile like that all the time? Doesn't your face get sore?

—I'm smiling because I think I've taught you enough.

Arm in arm, we climbed the streets that led to the mountain, Mont Royal, which gives its name to our city. Never before had the shops of Ste. Catherine Street bloomed so brightly, or the noon crowds thronged so gaily. I seemed to see it for the first time, the colors wild as those first splashes of paint on the white skin of the reindeer.

—Let's buy steamed hot dogs in Woolworth's.

—Let's eat them with our arms crossed, taking risks with mustard.

We walked along Sherbrooke Street, west, toward the English section of the city. We felt the tension immediately. At the corner of Parc Lafontaine Park we heard the shouted slogans of a demonstration.

—Québec Libre!

—Québec Oui, Ottawa Non!

—Merde à la reine d'angleterre!

—Elizabeth Go Home!

The newspapers had just announced the intention of Queen Elizabeth to visit Canada, a state visit planned for October.

—This is an ugly crowd, F. Let's walk faster.

—No, it is a beautiful crowd.

—Why?

—Because they think they are Negroes, and that is the best feeling a man can have in this century.

Arm in arm, F. pulled me to the scene of commotion. Many of the demonstrators wore sweatshirts inscribed with QUEBEC LIBRE. I noticed that everyone had a hard-on, including the women. From the base of a monument, a well-known young film maker addressed the cheering assembly. He wore the scholarly thin beard and violent leather jacket so commonly seen in the corridors of L'Office National du Film. His voice rang out clearly. F.'s judo pressure cautioned me to listen carefully.

—History! the young man called over our heads. What have we to do with History?

The question inflamed them.

—History! they shouted. Give us back our History! The English have stolen our History!

F. pressed deeper into the mass of bodies. They received us automatically, like quicksand swallowing up the laboratory monster. The echoes of the young man's clear voice hung above us like skywriting.

—History! he continued. History decreed that in the battle for a continent the Indian should lose to the Frenchman. In 1760 History decreed that the Frenchman should lose to the Englishman!

—Booo! Hang the English!

I felt a pleasant sensation at the base of my spine and jiggled ever so slightly against the thin nylon dress of a fanatic, who cheered behind me.

—In 1964 History decrees, no, History commands that the English surrender this land, which they have loved so imperfectly, surrender it to the Frenchman, surrender it to us!

—Bravo! Mon pays malheureux! Québec Libre!

I felt a hand slip down the back of my baggy trousers, a female hand because it had long fingernails smooth and tapered as a fuselage.

—Fuck the English! I shouted unexpectedly.

—That's it, F. whispered.

—History decrees that there are Losers and Winners. History cares nothing for cases, History cares only whose Turn it is. I ask you, my friends, I ask you a simple question: whose Turn is it today?

—Our Turn! rose in one deafening answer.

The crowd, of which I was now a joyful particle, pressed even closer about the monument, as if we were a nut on a screw to which the whole city we longed to possess wound us tighter and tighter like a wrench. I loosed my belt to let her hand go deeper. I did not dare turn around to face her. I did not want to know who she was—that seemed to me the highest irrelevance. I could feel her nylon-sheathed breasts squash against my back, making damp sweat circles on my shirt.

—Yesterday it was the Turn of the Anglo-Scottish banker to leave his name on the hills of Montréal. To-day it is the Turn of the Québec Nationalist to leave his name on the passport of a new Laurentian Republic!

—Vive la République!

This was too much for us. Almost wordlessly we roared our approval. The cool hand turned so now her palm was cupped around me and had easy access to the hairy creases. Hats were jumping above us like popping corn, and no one cared whose hat he got back because we all owned each other's hats.

—Yesterday it was the Turn of the English to have French maids from our villages in Gaspé. Yesterday it was the Turn of the French to have Aristotle and bad teeth.

—Booo! Shame! To the wall!

I smelled the perfume of her sweat and birthday presents, and that was more thrillingly personal than any exchange of names could be. She herself thrust her pelvic region hard against her own trouser-covered hand to reap, as it were, the by-products of her erotic entry. With my free hand I reached behind the both of us to grab like a football her flowery left cheek, and so we were locked together.

—Today it is the Turn of the English to have dirty houses and French bombs in their mailboxes!

F. had detached himself to get closer to the speaker. I snaked my other hand behind and fastened it on the right cheek. I swear that we were Plastic Man and Plastic Woman, because I seemed to be able to reach her everywhere, and she traveled through my underwear effortlessly. We began our rhythmical movements which corresponded to the very breathing of the mob, which was our family and the incubator of our desire.

—Kant said: If someone makes himself into an earthworm, can he complain if he is stepped on? Sekou Touré said: No matter what you say, Nationalism is psychologically inevitable and we all are nationalists! Napoleon said: A nation has lost everything if it has lost its independence. History chooses whether Napoleon shall speak these words from a throne to a throng, or from the window of a hut to a desolate sea!

This academic virtuosity was a little problematical for the crowd and provoked only a few exclamations. However, at that moment, out of the corner of my eye, I saw F. lifted on the shoulders of some young men. A wildcat cheer went up as he was recognized, and the speaker hastened to incorporate the spontaneous outburst into the intense orthodoxy of the whole crowd.

—We have among us a Patriot! A man the English could not disgrace even in their own Parliament!

F. slid back into the reverent knot which had hoisted him, his clenched fist raised above him like the periscope of a diving sub. And now, as if the presence of this veteran conferred a new mystic urgency, the speaker began to speak, almost to chant. His voice caressed us, just as my fingers her, just as her fingers me, his voice fell over our desire like a stream over a moaning water wheel, and I knew that all of us, not just the girl and me, all of us were going to come together. Our arms were tangled and squashed, and I did not know if it was I who held the root of my cock or she who greased the stiffening of her labia! Every one of us there had the arms of Plastic Man, and we held each other, all naked from the waist, all sealed in a frog jelly of sweat and juice, all bound in the sweetest bursting daisy chain!

—Blood! What does Blood mean to us?

—Blood! Give us back our Blood!

—Rub harder! I shouted, but some angry faces shushed me.

—From the earliest dawn of our race, this Blood, this shadowy stream of life, has been our nourishment and our destiny. Blood is the builder of the body, and Blood is the source of the spirit of the race. In Blood lurks our ancestral inheritance, in Blood is embodied the shape of our History, from Blood blooms the flower of our Glory, and Blood is the undercurrent which they can never divert, and which all their stolen money cannot dry up!

—Give us our Blood!

—We demand our History!

—Vive la République!

—Don't stop! I shouted.

—Elizabeth Go Home!

—More! I pleaded. Bis! Bis! Encore!

The meeting began to break up, the daisy chain began to fray. The speaker had disappeared from the pedestal. Suddenly I was facing everyone. They were leaving. I grabbed lapels and hems.

—Don't go! Get him to speak more!

—Patience, citoyen, the Revolution has begun.

—No! Make him speak more! Nobody leave this park!

The throng pushed past me, apparently satisfied. At first the men smiled when I seized their lapels, attributing my imprecations to revolutionary ardor. At first the women laughed when I took their hands and checked them for traces of my pubic hair, because I wanted her, the girl I'd come to the dance with, the girl whose round sweat fossils I still wore on the back of my shirt.

—Don't go. Don't leave! Seal the park!

—Let go of my hand!

—Stop hanging on my lapels!

—We've got to go back to work!

I implored three big men wearing QUEBEC LIBRE sweatshirts to hoist me on their shoulders. I tried to get my foot hooked on the top of a pair of trousers so I could scramble up their sweaters and address the disintegrating family from the height of a shoulder.

—Get this creep off me!

—He looks English!

—He looks Jewish!

—But you can't leave! I haven't come yet!

—This man is a sex pervert!

—Let's beat the shit out of him. He's probably a sex pervert.

—He's smelling girls' hands.

—He's smelling his own hands!

—He's an odd one.

Then F. was beside me, big F., certifying my pedigree, and he led me away from the park which was now nothing but an ordinary park with swans and candy wrappers. Arm in arm, he led me down the sunny street.

—F., I cried. I didn't come. I failed again.

—No, darling, you passed.

—Passed what?

—The test.

—What test?

—The second-to-last test.

48.

"Let the cold wind blow, as long as you love me, East
or West, I can stand the test, as long as you love me."
That was number seven on the Western Hit Parade
long, long ago. I think it was seven. There are six
words in the title. 6 is ruled by Venus, planet of love
and beauty. According to Iroquois astrology, the sixth
day should be devoted to grooming, having your hair
done, wearing ornate shell-woven robes, seeking romance, and games of chance and wrestling. "What's
the reason I'm not pleasing you?" Somewhere on the
charts. Tonight is the freezing 6th of March. That is not
spring in the Canadian forest. The moon has been in
Aries for two days. Tomorrow the moon enters Taurus.
The Iroquois would hate me right now if they saw me
because I have a beard. When they captured Jogues,
the missionary back in 16-something, one of the minor
tortures (after having an Algonquin slave sever his
thumb with a clam-shell) was to let the children pull
out his beard with their hands. "Send me a picture of
Christ without a beard," wrote the Jesuit Garnier to a
friend in France, showing an excellent knowledge of
Indian peculiarities. F. once told me about a girl who
was favored with such a luxuriant growth of pubic hair
that, with daily brush training, she taught it to descend
nearly six inches down her thighs. Just below the navel
she painted (with black liquid eye liner) two eyes and

nostrils. Separating the hair just above the clitoris she drew it apart in two symmetrical arcs, creating the impression of a mustache above pursed pink lips, from which the remaining growth appended like a beard. A piece of costume jewelry squeezed in the navel like a caste mark completed the comic picture of an exotic fortune teller or mystic. Hiding her body under sheets except for this section, she amused F. with humorous renditions of Eastern sayings so popular at the time, casting her voice from beneath the linen with the skill of a ventriloquist. Why can't I have memories like that? What good are all your gifts, F., the soap collection, the phrase books, if I can't inherit your memories, too, which would confer some meaning on your rusty bequests, just as tin cans and automobile crashes achieve high value when placed in the context of a plush art gallery? What use all your esoteric teaching without your particular experience? You were too exotique for me, you and all the other masters, with your special breathing and success disciplines. What about us with asthma? What about us failures? What about us who can't shit properly? What about us who have no orgies and excessive fucking to become detached about? What about us who are broken when our friends fuck our wives? What about us such as me? What about us who aren't in Parliament? What about us who are cold on March 6 for no apparent reason? You did the Telephone Dance. You heard the inside of Edith. What about us who poke in dead tissue? What about us Historians who have to read the dirty parts? What about us who have smelled up a treehouse? Why did you make everything so baffling? Why couldn't you comfort me like St. Augustine, who sang: "Behold the ignorant arise and snatch heaven beneath our eyes"? Why couldn't you say to me what the Blessed Virgin said to the peasant girl Catherine Labouré on an ordinary street, Rue du Bac, in 18-something: "Grace will be showered on all who ask for it with faith and fervor." Why do I have to explore the pock marks on Catherine Tekakwitha's face like the lens of a moon missile? What did you mean when you lay bleeding in my arms and said: "Now it's up to you"? People who say that always imply that that which *they* have done is so much more the major part of the ordeal. Who wants to just tidy up? Who wants to slide into a warm empty driver's seat? I want cool leather, too. I loved Montréal, too. I wasn't always the Freak of the Forest. I was a citizen. I had a wife and books. On May 17, 1642, Maisonneuve's little armada—a pinnace, a flat-bottomed sailboat, and two rowboats— approached Montréal. The next day they glided past the green, solitary shores, and landed at the spot which Champlain, thirty-one years before, had chosen for the site of a settlement. Early spring flowers were riding the young grass. Maisonneuve sprang ashore. Tents, baggage, arms, and stores followed him. An altar was raised on a pleasant spot. Now all the company stood before the shrine, tall Maisonneuve, his men clustering around him, rough men, and Mlle. Mance, M. de la Peltrie, her servant, and the artisans and laborers. And here stood le P. Vimont, Superior of the Missions, in the rich vesture of his office. They knelt in hush as the Host was raised aloft. Then the priest turned to the little band and said:

—You are a grain of mustard seed, that shall rise and grow till its branches overshadow the earth. You are few, but your work is the work of God. His smile is on you, and your children shall fill the land.

The afternoon darkened. The sun was lost in the western forest. Fireflies were twinkling over the darkened meadow. They caught them, tied them with threads into shining bouquets, and hung them before the altar, where the Host remained exposed. Then they pitched their tents, built their bivouac fires, stationed guards, and lay down to rest. Such was the first Mass sung in Montréal. And, oh, from this shack I can see the lights of the great city prophesied, the city foretold to cast its shadow across the earth, I see them twinkling in great soft garlands, the fireflies of downtown Montréal. This is my mental comfort in the snow of March the 6th. And I recall a line from the Jew Cabala (Sixth Part of the Beard of Macroprosopus), "that every work existeth in order that it may procure increase for Mercy. . . ." Move closer, corpse of Catherine Tekakwitha, it is 20 below, I do not know how to hug you. Do you smell in this refrigerator? St. Angela Merici died in 1540. She was dug up in 1672 (you were a child of six, Kateri Tekakwitha), and the body had a sweet scent, and in 1876 it was still intact. St. John Nepomucene was martyred in Prague in 1393 for refusing to reveal a secret of the confessional. His tongue has been entirely preserved. Experts examined it 332 years later in 1725, and testified that it was the shape, color, and length of the tongue of a living person, and that it was also soft and flexible. The body of St. Catherine of Bologna (1413-1463) was dug up three months after her burial and it gave off a sweet fragrant scent. Four years after the death of St. Pacificus di San Severino in 1721, his body was exhumed and found to be sweet and incorrupt. While the body was being moved, someone slipped, and the head of the corpse smashed against the stairway and the head fell off;

fresh blood gushed from the neck! St. John Vianney was buried in 1859. His body was intact at the disinterment of 1905. Intact: but can intact support a love affair? St. Francis Xavier was dug up four years after his burial in 1552 and it still had its natural color. Is natural color enough? St. John of the Cross looked all right nine months after his death in 1591. When his fingers were cut they bled. Three hundred years later (almost), in 1859, the body was incorrupt. Merely incorrupt. St. Joseph Calasanticus died in 1649 (the same year that the Iroquois burned Lalemant across an ocean). His insides were removed although not embalmed. His heart and tongue are intact up to this day, but no news of the rest. My basement kitchen was very stuffy and the oven timer sometimes switched it on because of faulty mechanism. F., is this why you led me up the frozen trunk? I am frightened of no perfume. The Indians ascribed disease to an ungratified wish. Pots, skins, pipes, wampum, fishhooks, weapons were piled in front of the sick person, "in the hope that in their multiplicity the desideratum might be supplied." It often happened that the patient dreamed his own cure, and his demands were never refused, "however extravagant, idle, nauseous, or abominable." O sky, let me be sick Indian. World, let me be dreaming Mohawk. No wet dream died in laundry. I know sexual information about Indians which is heavenly psychiatry, and I would like to sell it to the part of my mind which buys solutions. If I sold this to Hollywood it would end Hollywood. I am angry now, and cold. I threaten to end Hollywood if I do not receive instantaneous ghost love, not merely incorrupt but overwhelmingly fragrant. I'm going to end Movies if I don't feel better very soon. I will destroy your neighborhood theater in the near future.

I will draw a billion blinds over the Late Show. I don't like my predicament. Why do I have to be the one who cuts fingers? Must I do the Wassermann on skeletons? I want to be the only-child stiff carried by clumsy doctors, my young 300-yr. blood flushing away the concrete stairway. I want to be the light in the morgue. Why must I dissect F.'s old tongue? The Indians invented the steam bath. That is just a tidbit.

49.

Catherine Tekakwitha's uncle dreamed his cure. The village hastened to fulfill his specifications. His cure was not an unusual one, it was one of the recognized remedies, and both Sagard and our Lalemant describe the treatment in various Indian villages. Uncle said:

—Bring me all the young girls of the town.

The village hastened to obey. All the young girls stood around his bearskin, the starlets of the cornfields, the sweet weavers, girls in leisure, their hair half braided. "Toutes les filles d'vn bourg auprès d'vne malade, tant à sa prière."

—Are you all here?

—Yes.

—Yes.

—Sure.

—Uh-huh.

—Yes.

—Here.

—Yes.

—I'm here.

—Yes.

—Of course.

—Here.

—Here.

—Yes.

—Present.

—Yes.

—I guess so.

—Yes.

—Looks like it.

—Yes.

Uncle smiled with satisfaction. Then to each one he asked an old question: "On leur demand à toute, les vnes apres les autres, celuy qu'elles veulent des ieunes hommes du bourg pour dormir auec elles la nuict prochaine." I give the documentation out of duty, for I fear that sometimes my sorrow does violence to the facts, and I do not wish to alienate the fact, for the fact is one of the possibilities I cannot afford to ignore. The fact is a crude spade but my fingernails are blue and bleeding. The fact is like a bright new coin, and you do not want to spend it until it has picked up scratches in your jewelry box, and it is always the final nostalgic gesture of bankruptcy. My fortune is gone.

—What young brave will you sleep with tonight?

Each girl gave the name of the that evening's lover.

—What about you, Catherine?

—A thorn.

—That will be something to see, they all chuckled.

O God, help me get through this. I am corrupt in stomach. I am cold and ignorant. I am sick in window. I have taunted Hollywood which I love. Do you imagine what servant writes this? Old fashioned Cave-Jew yell of supplication, trembling with fear vomit at his first moon eclipse. Ara ara ara arrrooowwww. Fashion this prayer to Thee. I don't know to get it with 1000-voice choir effect like "consider the lily." Fashion this heap with gleaming snow-shovel facets, for I meant to build an altar. I meant to light a curious little highway shrine, but I drown in the ancient snake cistern. I meant to harness plastic butterflies with rubber-band motors and whisper: "Consider the plastic butterfly": but I shiver under the shadow of the diving archaeopteryx.

The Masters of the Ceremony (les Maistres de la ceremonie) summoned the young men whom the girls had named, and, hand in hand, they came to the long house in the evening. The mats were spread. From one end of the cabin to the other they lay, two by two, "d'vn bout à l'autre de la Cabane," and they began to kiss and fuck and suck and hug and moan and take off their skins and squeeze each other and nibble tits and tickle cocks with eagle feathers and turn over for other holes and lick the creases of each other and laugh when others were fucking funny or stop and clap when two screaming bodies went into a climax trance. At either end of the cabin two captains sang and rang their turtleshell rattles, "deux Capitaines aux deux bouts du logis chantent de leur Tortue." Uncle felt better toward midnight and got off his mat and crawled slowly down the length of the cabin, stopping here and there to rest his head on a free buttock or leave his fingers in a dripping hole, taking chances with his nose between "bouncers" for the sake of microscopic perspectives, always with an eye for the unusual or a joke for the grotesque. From one sprawl to another he dragged himself, red-eyed as a movie addict on 42nd Street, now flicking a quivering cock with his thumb and forefinger, now slapping a stray brown flank. Each fuck was the same and each fuck was different, that is the glory of an old man's cure. All his girls came back to him, all his ferny intercourse, all the feathery holes and gleaming dials, and as he crawled from pair to pair, from these lovers to those lovers, from sweet position to sweet position, from pump to pump, from gobble to gobble, from embrace to embrace—he suddenly knew the meaning of the greatest prayer he had ever learned, the first prayer in which Manitou had manifest himself, the greatest and truest sacred formula. As he crawled he began to sing the prayer:

> —I change
> I am the same
> I change
> I am the same
> I change
> I am the same
> I change
> I am the same
> I change
> I am the same
> I change
> I am the same

He did not miss a syllable and he loved the words he sang because as he sang each sound he saw it change and every change was a return and every return was a change.

> —I change
> I am the same
> I change
> I am the same
> I change
> I am the same
> I change
> I am the same
> I change
> I am the same
> I change

> I am the same
> I change
> I am the same

It was a dance of masks and every mask was perfect because every mask was a real face and every face was a real mask so there was no mask and there was no face for there was but one dance in which there was but one mask but one true face which was the same and which was a thing without a name which changed and changed into itself over and over. When the morning came the captains shook their rattles slower. The clothes were gathered up as the dawn came on. The old man was on his knees proclaiming his faith, declaring his cure complete, as into the misty green morning all the lovers sauntered, arms about each other's waists and shoulders, the end of night shift in a factory of lovers. *Catherine had lain among them and left with them unnoticed*. As she walked out in the sun the priest came running.

—How was it?

—It was acceptable, my father.

—Dieu veuille abolir vne si damnable et malheureuse ceremonie.

That last remark is from the letter of Sagard. This unique mode of cure was called Andacwandet by the Hurons.

50.

And I listen for answers in the cold wind, for instruction, for comfort, but all I hear is the infallible promise of winter. Night after night I cry out for Edith.

—Edith! Edith!

—Ara ara ara arrrooooowwww, cries the wolf silhouette on the hill.

—Help me, F. Explain the bombs!

—Ara ara ara arrooooowwww. . . .

Dream after dream we all lie in each other's arms. Morning after morning the winter finds me alone among the frayed leaves, frozen snot and tears in my eyebrows.

—F.! Why did you lead me here?

And do I hear an answer? Is this treehouse the hut of Oscotarach? F., are you the Head-Piercer? I did not know the operation was so long and clumsy. Raise the blunt tomahawk and try once more. Poke the stone spoon among the cerebral porridge. Does the moonlight want to get into my skull? Do the sparkling alleys of the icy sky want to stream through my eyeholes? F., were you the Head-Piercer, who left his hut and applied to the public ward in pursuit of his own operation? Or are you still with me, and is the surgery deep in progress?

—F., you lousy wife-fucker, explain yourself!

I cry that question out tonight, as I cried it out many times before. I remember your annoying habit of looking over my shoulders as I studied, just on the off chance that you might pick up a phrase of cocktail information. You noticed a line from a letter le P. Lalemant wrote in 1640, "que le sang des Martyrs est la semence des Chrestiens." Le P. Lalemant regretting that no priest had yet been put to death in Canada, and that this was a bad augury for the young Indian missions, for the blood of Martyrs is the seed of the Church.

—The Revolution in Québec needs the lubrication of a little blood.

—Why are you looking at me that way, F.?

—I'm wondering if I've taught you enough.

—I don't want any of your filthy politics, F. You're a thorn in the side of Parliament. You've smuggled dynamite into Québec disguised as firecrackers. You've turned Canada into a vast analyst's couch from which we dream and redream nightmares of identity, and all your solutions are as dull as psychiatry. And you subjected Edith to many irregular fucks which broke her mind and body and left me the lonely bookworm whom you now torment.

—Oh my darling, what a hunchback History and the Past have made of your body, what a pitiful hunchback.

We stood close together, as we'd stood in so many rooms, this time in the sepia gloom of the library stacks, our hands in each other's pockets. I always resented his superior expression.

—Hunchback! Edith had no complaints about my body.

—Edith! Ha! Don't make me laugh. You know nothing about Edith.

—Keep your tongue off her, F.

—I cured Edith's acne.

—Edith's acne indeed! She had perfect skin.

—Ho ho.

—It was lovable to kiss and touch.

—Thanks to my famous soap collection. Listen, friend, when I first met Edith she was in an ugly mess.

—No more, F. I don't want to hear any more.

—The time has come for you to learn just who it was whom you married, just who that girl was whom you discovered performing extraordinary manicures in the barber shop of the Mount Royal Hotel.

—No, F., please. Don't destroy anything more. Leave me with her body. F! What is happening to your eyes?

What is happening to your cheeks? Are those tears? Are you weeping?

—I am wondering what will happen to you when I leave you alone.

—Where are you going?

—The Revolution needs a little blood. It will be my blood.

—Oh no!

—London has announced the Queen's intention to visit French Canada in October 1964. It is not enough that she and Prince Philip will be greeted by police cordons, riot tanks, and the proud backs of hostile crowds. We must not make the mistake the Indians made. Her advisers in London must be made to understand that our dignity is fed with the same food as anyone's: the happy exercise of the arbitrary.

—What do you intend to do, F.?

—There is a statue of Queen Victoria on the north side of Sherbrooke Street. We have passed it many times on our way to the darkness of the System Theatre. It is a pleasant statue of Queen Victoria in early womanhood before pain and loss had made her fat. It is cast in copper which is now green with age. Tomorrow night I will place a charge of dynamite on her metal lap. It is only the copper effigy of a dead Queen (who knew, incidentally, the meaning of love), it is only a symbol, but the State deals in symbols. Tomorrow night I will blow that symbol to smithereens—and myself with it.

—Don't do it, F. Please.

—Why not?

I know nothing about love, but something like love tore the following words from my throat with a thousand fishhooks:

—BECAUSE I NEED YOU, F.

A sad smile spread on my friend's face. He extracted his left hand from my warm pocket, and extending his arms as if in a benediction he crushed me to his Egyptian shirt in a warm bear hug.

—Thank you. Now I know that I have taught you enough.

—BECAUSE I NEED YOU, F.

—Stop whimpering.

—BECAUSE I NEED YOU, F.

—Hush.

—BECAUSE I NEED THEE, F.

—Good-by.

I felt lonely and cold as he walked away, the brown books along the steel shelves rustling like windy heaps of fallen leaves, each with the same message of exhaustion and death. As I set this down I have a clear impression of F's pain. His *pain!* Oh yes, as I peel off this old scab of history, gleaming like one pure triumphant drop of red blood—his pain.

—Good-by, he called to me over his muscular shoulder. Listen for the explosion tomorrow night. Keep your ear next to the ventilation shaft.

Like the frozen moonlight through the windows of this shack, his pain floods my recognition, altering the edge, color, and weight of each possession in my heart.

51.

Kateri Tekakwitha

calling you, calling you, calling you, testing 9 8 7 6 5 4 3 2 1 my poor unelectric head calling you loud and torn 1 2 3 4 5 6 7 8 9 lost in needles of pine, tenant of meat freezer, fallen on squeezed knees searching hair for antennae, rubbing blue Aladdin prick, calling you, testing sky cables, poking blood buttons, finger fucks in star porridge, dentist drill in forehead bone, broken like convict stone, calling you calling you, frightened of stew, signals filthy laundry of this mind rubber girls aside, wafer banana skins of vaudeville, black air filled with pies of humiliation, no AC outlet beneath scalped hair, testing, testing the last dance, rubber scorpion on pillow of tit, handfuls of milk flung at doctors, calling you to call me, calling you to pull me if only once, fake proof accepted, plastic birchbark accepted, calling, artificial limb accepted, Hong Kong sex auxiliaries accepted, money confessions accepted, wigs of celanese acetate accepted, come pills, postcards of old-fashioned uncle sucking accepted even as ideal brown Plato, movie seat rubbing accepted, fat stage tease accepted and lap hats hiding hairy windows of underwear accepted, gratefully accepted, astrology boredom accepted, wife limit accepted, cop-gun deaths, urban voodoo accepted, false harem smells accepted, dimes accepted, seance feels up lonely old lady thighs, criminal bridge sales accepted, Zabbatai vote buttons worn in stigmata places, market Moses horns, square earth theories accepted, microscope girdles for Tom that failed, cunt dictionaries illustrated deceptively in vellum fuzz, calling you now, all reasons accepted, rope buttock creases, luminous highway Mary houses, pharmacy visions unrevoked, Zen Ph.D. tolerated, unpolished enemas, no references required, academic fashion ecstasy believed, dirty cars, all my baffled unbelief calling you with bowed physical brain terror, testing 9 8 7 6 5 4 3 2 1 2 3 4 5 6 7 8 9, unelectric head calling.

52.

Phrase-book on my knees, I beseech the Virgin everywhere.

KATERI TEKAKWITHA AT THE WASH HOUSE
(hers the lovely italics)

I bring you linens for washing

I need them until to-morrow

what do you think? Can you get them ready until tomorrow?

they are absolutely necessary to me

especially my shirts

as for the others, I must have them the most late until
the day after tomorrow

I want them entirely new and clear

a shirt is missing for me, a handkerchief and a pair of
stockings, too

I want this back

I want this costume to be cleared

when can I get it?

I have, too, a dress, a coat, trousers, a tressed waist-
coat, a blouse, underclothes, stockings, so forth.

I shall come back again after three days to get them

please, iron them for me

yes, sir. Come to get them

what do you think about the trousers?

I like it. That's what I want

when will my suit be ready?

after a week

it takes a lot of work

I shall make you a wonderful suit

I shall come to take it myself

no, don't come!
we shall send it ourselves to your house, sir
good. Then I shall be waiting for it on next Saturday
the suit is dear
the suit is cheap
you are a good tailor
thank you
goodbye
later I shall get another one
as you like, sir
we shall satisfy you very much

KATERI TEKAKWITHA AT THE TOBACCONIST'S
    (hers the lovely italics)
Can you, please, tell me where is a tovacconist-shop?
at the corner of the road on the right, sir
in front of you, sir
give me, please, a box of cigarettes
what kind of cigarettes have you?
We have excellent cigarettes
I want some tobacco for pipe
I want heavy cigarettes
I want light cigarettes
Give me a box of matches, too
I want a cigarette-case, a good lighter, cigarettes
how much do all these cost?
twenty shillings, sir
thank-you. Goot-bye

KATERI TEKAKWITHA AT THE BARBER'S SHOP
    (hers the lovely italics)
the hair-dresser

the hair
the beard
the moustache
the soap
the cold water
the comb
the brush
I want to shave myself
please, sit down!
please, come in!
please, shave me!
please, cut my hair very short behind
not very short
wash my hair!
please, brush me
I shall come back
I'm pleased
until when is the barber's shop open?
until 8 o'clock in the evening
I shall come to shave myself regularly
thank-you, good bye
we will treat you as well as we can, because you are
    our client

KATERI TEKAKWITHA AT THE POST-OFFICE
    (hers the lovely italics)
where is the Post-Office, sir?
I'm a foreign here, excuse me
ask that sir
he knows French, German
he will help you
please, show me the Post-Office

it's there on the opposite side
I want to send a letter
give me some postage-stamps
I want to send something
I want to send a telegram
I want to send a package
I want to send an urgent letter
have you your passport?
have you your identity?
yes, sir
I want to send a check
give me a post card
how much will I pay for sending a package?
15 shillings, sir
thank-you good-bye

KATERI TEKAKWITHA AT THE TELEGRAPHIC-
    OFFICE   (hers the lovely italics)
what do you want, sir?
I want to send a telegram
with a paid answer?
how much does the word cost?
fifty pence a word
a telegram for
it's dear, but never mind
will the telegram be late to go?
how long does it take to go?
two days, sir
It isn't a long time
I shall send a telegram to my parents to
I hope that they will take it tomorrow
there is a long time and I didn't get any news from

them
I think they will answer to me telegraphically
take, please, the money for the telegram
goodbye. Thanks.

KATERI TEKAKWITHA AT THE BOOKSELLER'S
(hers the lovely italics)

goodmornig, sir
may I choose any books?
with pleasure. What do you want? Choose!
I want to buy a journey book
I want to know England and Ireland
Do you want anything else?
I want a lot of books, but, as I see, they are dear
*we shall do a little decline of prices for you if you get
    many books*
we have books of every kind. Cleap and dear
do you want them bound or not bound?
I want bound books
those they aren't destroyed
here they are
How much does it cost?
four dollars
have you any dictionary?
I have
please, envelop them
I shall take them with me
thank you very much
good-bye!

O God, O God, I have asked for too much, I have asked
for everything! I hear myself asking for everything in

every sound I make. I did not know, in my coldest terror, I did not know how much I needed. O God, I grow silent as I hear myself begin to pray:

ΣΤΟ ΦΑΡΜΑΚΕΙΟ	AT THE DRUG - SHOP
Παρακαλῶ, ἑτοιμάστε μου αὐτὴ τὴ συνταγή	Please, get this mebical prescription ready for me
παρακαλῶ, περάστε σὲ εἴκοσι λεπτά. Θὰ εἶναι ἕτοιμη	please, call after twenty minutes. It will be ready
θὰ περιμένω. Δὲν πειράζει!	I shall be waiting. Never mind!
πῶς πρέπει νὰ παίρνω αὐτὸ τὸ φάρμακο;	How must I take this medicine?
πρωΐ, μεσημέρι καὶ βράδυ	In the morning, at noon and in the evening
πρὶν ἀπὸ τὸ φαγητό	before the meal
μετὰ ἀπὸ τὸ φαγητό	after the meal
αὐτὸ τὸ φάρμακο εἶναι πολὺ ἀκριβό	this medicine is very dear
εἶμαι κρυωμένος. Δῶστε μου κάτι γιὰ τὸ κρύο	I caught cold. Give me sommething for the cold
κάτι γιὰ τὸν πονοκέφαλο	something for the headache
κάτι γιὰ τὸν λαιμό	something for the throat
κάτι γιὰ τὸ στομάχι μου	something for my stomach
τὸ στομάχι μου μὲ πονεῖ	my stomach aches me
ἔχω ἕνα τραῦμα στὸ πόδι	I have a wound on the foot
παρακαλῶ, περιποιηθῆτε αὐτὸ τὸ τραῦμα	please, nurse this wound
πόσο κοστίζουν ὅλα;	how much does all cost?
δέκα σελλίνια. Εὐχαριστῶ	ten shillings. Thanks.

Book Two

A Long Letter

from F.

M

Y DEAR FRIEND,

Five years with the length of five years. I do not know exactly where this letter finds you. I suppose you have thought often of me. You were always my favorite male orphan. Oh, much more than that, much more, but I do not choose, for this last *written* communication, to expend myself in easy affection.

If my lawyers have performed according to my instructions, you are now in possession of my worldly estate, my soap collection, my factory, my Masonic aprons, my treehouse. I imagine you have already appropriated my style. I wonder where my style has led you. As I stand on this last springy diving board I wonder where my style has led me.

I am writing this last letter in the Occupational Therapy Room. I have let women lead me anywhere, and I am not sorry. Convents, kitchens, perfumed telephone booths, poetry courses—I followed women anywhere. I followed women into Parliament because I know how they love power. I followed women into the beds of men so that I could learn what they found there. The air is streaked with the smoke of their perfume. The world is clawed with their amorous laughter. I followed women into the world, because I loved the world. Breasts, buttocks, everywhere I followed the soft balloons. When women hissed at me from brothel windows, when they softly hissed at me over the shoulders of their dancing husbands, I followed them and I sank down with them, and sometimes when I listened to their hissing I knew it was nothing but the sound of the withering and collapse of their soft balloons.

This is the sound, this hissing, which hovers over every woman. There is one exception. I knew one woman who surrounded herself with a very different noise, maybe it was music, maybe it was silence. I am speaking, of course, about our Edith. It is five years now that I have been buried. Surely you know by now that Edith could not belong to you alone.

I followed the young nurses to Occupational Therapy. They have covered the soft balloons with starched linen, a pleasant tantalizing cover which my old lust breaks as easily as an eggshell. I have followed their dusty white legs.

Men also give off a sound. Do you know what our sound is, dear frayed friend? It is the sound you hear in male sea shells. Guess what it is. I will give you three guesses. You must fill in the lines. The nurses like to see me use my ruler.

1._____

2._____

3.

The nurses like to lean over my shoulder and watch me use my red plastic ruler. They hiss through my hair and their hisses have the aroma of alcohol and sandalwood, and their starched clothes crackle like the white tissue paper and artificial straw which creamy chocolate Easter eggs come in.

Oh, I am happy today. I know that these pages will be filled with happiness. Surely you did not think that I would leave you with a melancholy gift.

Well, what are your answers? Isn't it remarkable that I have extended your training over this wide gulf?

It is the very opposite of a hiss, the sound men make. It is Shhh, the sound made around the index finger raised to the lips. Shhh, and the roofs are raised against the storm. Shhh, the forests are cleared so the wind will not rattle the trees. Shhh, the hydrogen rockets go off to silence dissent and variety. It is not an unpleasant noise. It is indeed a perky tune, like the bubbles above a clam. Shhh, will everybody listen, please. Will the animals stop howling, please. Will the belly stop rumbling, please. Will Time call off its ultrasonic dogs, please.

It is the sound my ball pen makes on the hospital paper as I run it down the edge of the red ruler. Shhh, it says to the billion unlines of whiteness. Shhh, it whispers to the white chaos, lie down in dormitory rows. Shhh, it implores the dancing molecules, I love dances but I do not love foreign dances, I love dances that have rules, my rules.

Did you fill in the lines, old friend? Are you sitting in a restaurant or a monastery as I lie underground? Did you fill in the lines? You didn't have to, you know. Did I trick you again?

Now what about this silence we are so desperate to

clear in the wilderness? Have we labored, plowed, muzzled, fenced so that we might hear a Voice? Fat chance. The Voice comes out of the whirlwind, and long ago we hushed the whirlwind. I wish that you would remember that the Voice comes out of the whirlwind. Some men, some of the time, have remembered. Was I one?

I will tell you why we nailed up the cork. I am a born teacher and it is not my nature to keep things to myself. Surely five years have tortured and tickled you into that understanding. I always intended to tell you everything, the complete gift. How is your constipation, darling?

I imagine they are about twenty-four years old, these soft balloons that are floating beside me this very second, these Easter candies swaddled in official laundry. Twenty-four years of journey, almost a quarter of a century, but still youth for breasts. They have come a long way to graze shyly at my shoulder as I gaily wield my ruler to serve someone's definition of sanity. They are still young, they are barely young, but they hiss fiercely, and they dispense a heady perfume of alcohol and sandalwood. Her face gives nothing away, it is a scrubbed nurse's face, family lines mercifully washed away, a face prepared to be a screen for our blue home movies as we sink in disease. A compassionate sphinx's face to drip our riddles on, and, like paws buried in the sand, her round breasts claw and scratch against the uniform. Familiar? Yes, it is a face such as Edith often wore, our perfect nurse.

—Those are very nice lines you've drawn.

—I'm quite fond of them.

Hiss, hiss, run for your lives, the bombs are dying.

—Would you like some colored pencils?

—As long as they don't marry our erasers.

Wit, invention, shhh, shhh, now do you see why we've soundproofed the forest, carved benches round the wild arena? To hear the hissing, to hear wrinkles squeezing out the bounce, to attend the death of our worlds. Memorize this and forget it. It deserves a circuit, but a very tiny circuit, in the brain. I might as well tell you that I exempt myself, as of now, from all these categories.

Play with me, old friend.

Take my spirit hand. You have been dipped in the air of our planet, you have been baptized with fire, shit, history, love, and loss. Memorize this. It explains the Golden Rule.

See me at this moment of my curious little history, nurse leaning over my work, my prick rotten and black, you saw my worldly prick decayed, but now see my visionary prick, cover your head and see my visionary prick which I do not own and never owned, which owned me, which was me, which bore me as a broom bears a witch, bore me from world to world, from sky to sky. Forget this.

Like many teachers, a lot of the stuff I gave away was simply a burden I couldn't carry any longer. I feel my store of garbage giving out. Soon I'll have nothing left to leave around but stories. Maybe I'll attain the plane of spreading gossip, and thus finish my prayers to the world.

Edith was a promoter of sex orgies and a purveyor of narcotics. Once she had lice. Twice she had crabs. I've written crabs very small because there is a time and a place for everything, and a young nurse is standing close behind me wondering whether she is being drawn by my power or her charity. I appear to be engrossed in my therapeutic exercises, she in the duties of supervision, but shhh, hiss, the noise of steam spreads through O.T., it mixes with the sunlight, it bestows a rainbow halo on each bowed head of sufferer, doctor, nurse, volunteer. You ought to look up this nurse sometime. She will be twenty-nine when my lawyers locate you and complete my material bequest.

Down some green corridor, in a large closet among pails, squeegees, antiseptic mops, Mary Voolnd from Nova Scotia will peel down her dusty white stockings and present an old man with the freedom of her knees, and we will leave nothing behind us but our false ears with which to pick up the steps of the approaching orderly.

Steam coming off the planet, clouds of fleecy steam as boy and girl populations clash in religious riots, hot and whistling like a graveyard sodomist our little planet embraces its fragile yo-yo destiny, tuned in the secular mind like a dying engine. But some do not hear it this way, some flying successful moon-shot eyes do not see it this way. They do not hear the individual noises shhh, hiss, they hear the sound of the sounds together, they behold the interstices flashing up and down the cone of the flowering whirlwind.

Do I listen to the Rolling Stones? Ceaselessly.

Am I hurt enough?

The old hat evades me. I don't know if I can wait. The river that I'll walk beside—I seem to miss it by a coin toss every year. Did I have to buy that factory? Was I obliged to run for Parliament? Was Edith such a good lay? My café table, my small room, my drugged true friends from whom I don't expect too much—I seem to abandon them almost by mistake, for promises, phone calls casually made. The old hat, the rosy ugly old face

that won't waste time in mirrors, the uncombed face
that will laugh amazed at the manifold traffic. Where
is my old hat? I tell myself I can wait. I argue that my
path was correct. Is it only the argument that is incorrect? Is it Pride that tempts me with intimations of
a new style? Is it Cowardice that keeps me from an
old ordeal? I tell myself: wait. I listen to the rain, to
the scientific noises of the hospital. I get happy because
of many small things. I go to sleep with the earplug of
the transistor stuck in. Even my Parliamentary disgrace
begins to evade me. My name appears more and more
frequently among the nationalist heroes. Even my hospitalization has been described as an English trick to
muzzle me. I fear I will lead a government yet, rotten
prick and all. I lead men too easily: my fatal facility.

My dear friend, go beyond my style.

Something in your eyes, old lover, described me as
the man I wanted to be. Only you and Edith extended
that generosity to me, perhaps only you. Your baffled
cries as I tormented you, you were the good animal I
wanted to be, or failing that, the good animal I wanted
to exist. It was I who feared the rational mind, therefore I tried to make you a little mad. I was desperate to
learn from your bewilderment. You were the wall which
I, batlike, bounced my screams off of, so I might have
direction in this long nocturnal flight.

I cannot stop teaching. Have I taught you anything?

I must smell better with this confession, because
Mary Voolnd has just awarded me a distinct signal of
cooperation.

—Would you like to touch my cunt with one of your
old hands?

—Which hand are you thinking of?

—Would you like to depress a nipple with a forefinger

and make it disappear?

—And make it reappear too?

—If it reappears I will hate you forever. I will inscribe you in the Book of Fumblers.

_____

—That's better.

_____
_____

—Ummmm.

___ _____ ____ _____ ____ _____ ____

—I'm dripping.

Do you see how I cannot stop teaching? All my arabesques are for publication. Can you imagine how I envied you, whose suffering was so traditional?

From time to time, I will confess, I hated you. The teacher of composition is not always gratified to listen to the Valedictorian Address delivered in his own style, especially if he has never been Valedictorian himself. Times I felt depleted: you with all that torment, me with nothing but a System.

When I worked among the Jews (you own the factory), regularly I saw a curious expression of pain cross the boss's Levantine face. This I observed as he ushered out a filthy coreligionist, bearded, shifty, and smelling of low Romanian cuisine, who visited the factory every second month begging on behalf of an obscure Yiddish physical-therapy university. Our boss always gave the creature a few groschen and hurried him through the shipping exit with awkward haste, as if his presence there might start something far worse than a strike. I was always kinder to the boss on those days, for he was strangely vulnerable and comfortless. We walked slowly between the great rolls of cashmere and Harris tweed and I let him have his way with me. (He, for one, did not resent my new muscles, achieved through Dynamic Tension. Why did you drive me away?)

—What is my factory today? A pile of rags and labels, a distraction, an insult to my spirit.

—A tomb of your ambition, sir?

—That's right, boy.

—Dust in the mouth, cinders in the eye, sir?

—I don't want that bum in here again, do you hear me? One of these days they're going to walk out of here with him. And I'll be at the head of the line. That poor wretch is happier than the whole caboodle.

But, of course, he never turned the loathesome beggar away, and suffered for it, regular as menstruation pain, which is how the female regrets life beyond the pale of lunar jurisdiction.

You plagued me like the moon. I knew you were bound by old laws of suffering and obscurity. I am fearful of the cripple's wisdom. A pair of crutches, a grotesque limp can ruin a stroll which I begin in a new suit, clean-shaven, whistling. I envied you the certainty that you would amount to nothing. I coveted the magic of torn clothes. I was jealous of the terrors I constructed for you but could not tremble before myself. I was never drunk enough, never poor enough, never rich enough. All this hurts, perhaps it hurts enough. It makes me want to cry out for comfort. It makes me stretch my hands out horizontally. Yes, I long to be President of the new Republic. I love to hear the armed teen-agers chant my name outside the hospital gates. Long live the Revolution! Let me be President for my last thirty days.

Where are you walking tonight, dear friend? Did you give up meat? Are you disarmed and empty, an instrument of Grace? Can you stop talking? Has loneliness led you into ecstasy?

There was a deep charity in your suck. I hated it, I abused it. But I dare to hope that you embody the best of my longings. I dare to hope that you will produce the pearl and justify these poor secreted irritations.

This letter is written in the old language, and it has caused me no little discomfort to recall the obsolete usages. I've had to stretch my mind back into areas bordered with barbed wire, from which I spent a lifetime removing myself. However, I do not regret the effort.

Our love will never die, that I can promise you, I, who launch this letter like a kite among the winds of your desire. We were born together, and in our kisses we confessed our longing to be born again. We lay in each other's arms, each of us the other's teacher. We sought the peculiar tone of each peculiar night. We tried to clear away the static, suffering under the hint that the static was part of the tone. I was your adventure and you were my adventure. I was your journey and you were my journey, and Edith was our holy star. This letter rises out of our love like the sparks between dueling swords, like the shower of needles from flapping cymbals, like the bright seeds of sweat sliding through the center of our tight embrace, like the white feathers hung in the air by razored bushido cocks, like the shriek between two approaching puddles of mercury, like the atmosphere of secrets which twin children exude. I was your mystery and you were my mystery, and we rejoiced to learn that mystery was our home. Our love cannot die. Out of history I come to tell you this. Like two mammoths, tusk-locked in earnest sport at the edge of the advancing age of ice, we preserve each other. Our queer love keeps the lines of our manhood hard and clean, so that we bring nobody but our own self to our separate marriage beds, and our women finally know us.

Mary Voolnd has finally admitted my left hand into the creases of her uniform. She watched me compose the above paragraph, so I let it run on rather extravagantly. Women love excess in a man because it separates him from his fellows and makes him lonely. All that women know of the male world has been revealed to them by lonely, excessive refugees from it. Raging fairies they cannot resist because of their highly specialized intelligence.

—Keep writing, she hisses.

Mary has turned her back to me. The balloons are shrieking like whistles signaling the end of every labor. Mary pretends to inspect a large rug some patient wove, thus shielding our precious play. Slow as a snail I push my hand, palm down, up the tight rough stocking on the back of her thigh. The linen of her skirt is crisp and cool against my knuckles and nails, the stockinged thigh is warm, curved, a little damp like a loaf of fresh white bread.

—Higher, she hisses.

I am in no hurry. Old friend, I am in no hurry. I feel I shall be doing this throughout eternity. Her buttocks contract impatiently, like two boxing gloves touching before the match. My hand pauses to ride the quiver on the thigh.

—Hurry, she hisses.

Yes, I can tell by the tension in the stocking that I am approaching the peninsula which is hitched to the garter device. I will travel the whole peninsula, hot skin on either side, then I will leap off the nipple-shaped garter device. The threads of the stocking tighten. I bunch my fingers together so as not to make premature contact. Mary is jiggling, endangering the journey. My forefinger scouts out the garter device. It is warm. The little metal loop, the rubber button—warm right through.

—Please, please, she hisses.

Like angels on the head of a pin, my fingers dance on the rubber button. Which way shall I leap? Toward the outside thigh, hard, warm as the shell of a beached tropical turtle? Or toward the swampy mess in the middle? Or fasten like a bat on the huge soft overhanging boulder of her right buttock? It is very humid up her white starched skirt. It is like one of those airplane hangars wherein clouds form and it actually rains indoors. Mary is bouncing her bum like a piggy bank which is withholding a gold coin. The inundations are about to begin. I choose the middle.

—Yesssss.

Delicious soup stews my hand. Viscous geysers shower my wrist. Magnetic rain tests my Bulova. She jiggles for position, then drops over my fist like a gorilla net. I had been snaking through her wet hair, compressing it between my fingers like cotton candy. Now I am surrounded by artesian exuberance, nipply frills, numberless bulby brains, pumping constellations of mucous hearts. Moist Morse messages move up my arm, master my intellectual head, more, more, message dormant portions of dark brain, elect happy new kings for the exhausted pretenders of the mind. I am a seal inventing undulations in a vast electric aquacade, I am wires of tungsten burning in the seas of bulb, I am creature of Mary cave, I am froth of Mary wave, bums of nurse Mary applaud greedily as she maneuvers to plow her asshole on the edge of my arm bone, rose of rectum sliding up and down like the dream of banister fiend.

—Slish slosh slish slosh.

Are we not happy? Loud as we are, no one hears us, but this is a tiny miracle in the midst of all this bounty, so are the rainbow crowns hovering over every skull but tiny miracles. Mary looks at me over her shoulder, greeting me with rolled-up eyes white as eggshells, and an open goldfish mouth amazed smile. In the gold sunshine of O.T. everyone believes he is a stinking genius, offering baskets, ceramic ashtrays, thong-sewn wallets on the radiant altars of their perfect health.

Old friend, you may kneel as you read this, for now I come to the sweet burden of my argument. I did not know what I had to tell you, but now I know. I did not know what I wanted to proclaim, but now I am sure. All my speeches were preface to this, all my exercises but a clearing of my throat. I confess I tortured you but only to draw your attention to this. I confess I betrayed you but only to tap your shoulder. In our kisses and sucks, this, ancient darling, I meant to whisper.

God is alive. Magic is afoot. God is alive. Magic is afoot. God is afoot. Magic is alive. Alive is afoot. Magic never died. God never sickened. Many poor men lied. Many sick men lied. Magic never weakened. Magic never hid. Magic always ruled. God is afoot. God never died. God was ruler though his funeral lengthened. Though his mourners thickened Magic never fled. Though his shrouds were hoisted the naked God did live. Though his words were twisted the naked Magic thrived. Though his death was published round and round the world the heart did not believe. Many hurt men wondered. Many struck men bled. Magic never faltered. Magic always led. Many stones were rolled but God would not lie down. Many wild men lied. Many fat men listened. Though they offered stones Magic still was fed. Though they locked their coffers God was always served. Magic is afoot. God rules. Alive is afoot. Alive is in command. Many weak men hungered. Many strong men thrived. Though they boasted solitude God was at their side. Nor the dreamer in his cell, nor the captain on the hill. Magic is alive. Though his death was pardoned round and round the world the heart would not believe. Though laws were carved in marble they could not shelter men. Though altars built in parliaments they could not order men. Police arrested Magic and Magic went with them for Magic loves the hungry. But Magic would not tarry. It moves from arm to arm. It would not stay with them. Magic is afoot. It cannot come to harm. It rests in an empty palm. It spawns in an empty mind. But Magic is no instrument. Magic is the end. Many men drove Magic but Magic stayed behind. Many strong men lied. They only passed through Magic and out the other side. Many weak men lied. They came to God in secret and though they left him nourished they would not tell who healed. Though mountains danced before them they said that God was dead. Though his shrouds were hoisted the naked God did live. This I mean to whisper to my mind. This I mean to laugh with in my mind. This I mean my mind to serve till service is but Magic moving through the world, and mind itself is Magic coursing through the flesh, and flesh itself is Magic dancing on a clock, and time itself the Magic Length of God.

Old friend, aren't you happy? You and Edith alone know how long I've waited for this instruction.

—Damn you, Mary Voolnd spits at me.

—What?

—Your hand's gone limp. Grab!

How many times must I be slain, old friend? I do not understand the mystery, after all. I am an old man with one hand on a letter and one hand up a juicy cunt, and I understand nothing. If my instruction were gospel, would it wither up my hand? Certainly not. It doesn't figure. I'm picking lies out of the air. They're aiming lies at me. The truth should make me strong. I pray you, dear friend, interpret me, go beyond me. I know now that I am a hopeless case. Go forth, teach the world what I meant to be.

—Grab.

Mary wiggles and the hand comes to life, like those ancestral sea ferns which turned animal. Now the soft elbows of her cunt are nudging me somewhere. Now her asshole is rubbing the ridge of my arm, not like rosy banister reverie as before, but like an eraser removing dream evidence, and now, alas, the secular message appears.

—Grab, please, please. They'll start to notice at any second.

That is true. The air in O.T. is restless, no longer golden sunshine, merely sunny and warm. Yes, I've let the magic die. The doctors remember that they are at work and refuse to yawn. A fat little lady issues a duchess command, poor thing. A teen-ager weeps because he has wet himself again. A former school principal farts hysterically, threatening us all with no gym. Lord of Life, is my pain sufficient?

—Hurry.

Mary bears down. My fingers brush something. It is not part of Mary. It is foreign matter.

—Grab it. Pull it out. It's from our friends.

—Soon.

Dear Friend,

It comes back to me.

I sent you the wrong box of fireworks. I did not include the Pimple Cure in my famous soap and cosmetic collection. I cured Edith's acne with it, you know. But of course you do not know, because you have no reason to believe that Edith's complexion was ever anything but lovable to kiss and touch. When I found her her complexion was not lovable to kiss and touch, nor even to look at. She was in an ugly mess. In another part of this long letter I will tell you how we, Edith and I, constructed the lovely wife whom you discovered performing extraordinary manicures in the barber shop of the Mount Royal Hotel. Begin to prepare yourself.

The soap collection, though it includes transparent bars, ghosts of pine, lemon and sandalwood, Willy jelly, is useless without the Pimple Cure. All you will achieve is scrubbed, fragrant pimples. Perhaps that is enough for you—a demoralizing speculation.

You always resisted me. I had a body waiting for you, but you turned it down. I had a vision of you with 19-inch arms, but you walked away. I saw you with massive lower pecs and horseshoe triceps, with bulk and definition simultaneously. In certain intimate embraces I saw exactly how low your buttocks should descend. In no case, when you were squatting in front of me, should your buttocks have been lowered so far down that they sat on your heels, for once this occurs the thigh muscles are no longer engaged *but the buttocks muscles are*, ergo your rocky cheeks, a very selfish development that gave me no happiness and is a factor in your bowel predicament. I saw you oiled and shining, a classic midsection of washboard abdominals fluted with razor-edged obliques and serratus. I had a way to cut up the serratus. I had access to a Professional Greek Chair. I had the straps and stirrups to blitz your knob into a veritable sledgehammer, mouthful for a pelican. I had a Sphincter Kit that worked off the tap like washing machines and bosom aggrandizers. Had you a notion of my Yoga? Call it ruin, or call it creation, have you a notion of my work on Edith? Are you aware of the Ganges you insulted with a million mean portages?

Perhaps it is my own fault. I withheld certain vital items, an apparatus here, a fact there—but only because (yes, this is closer to truth) I dreamed you would be greater than me. I saw a king without dominion. I saw a gun bleeding. I saw the prince of Paradise Forgotten. I saw a pimpled movie star. I saw a racing hearse. I saw the New Jew. I saw popular lame storm troopers. I wanted you to bring pain to heaven. I saw fire curing headaches. I saw the triumph of election over discipline. I wanted your confusion to be a butterfly net for magic. I saw ecstasy without fun and vice versa. I saw all things change their nature by mere intensification of their properties. I wanted to discredit training for the sake of purer prayer. I held things back from you because I wished you greater than my Systems conceived. I saw wounds pulling oars without becoming muscles.

Who is the New Jew?

The New Jew loses his mind gracefully. He applies finance to abstraction resulting in successful messianic politics, colorful showers of meteorites and other symbolic weather. He has induced amnesia by a repetitious study of history, his very forgetfulness caressed by facts which he accepts with visible enthusiasm. He changes for a thousand years the value of stigma, causing men of all nations to pursue it as superior sexual talisman.

The New Jew is the founder of Magic Canada, Magic French Québec, and Magic America. He demonstrates that yearning brings surprises. He uses regret as a bulwark of originality. He confuses nostalgic theories of Negro supremacy which were tending to the monolithic. He confirms tradition through amnesia, tempting the whole world with rebirth. He dissolves history and ritual by accepting unconditionally the complete heritage. He travels without passport because powers consider him harmless. His penetration into jails enforces his supranationality, and flatters his legalistic disposition. Sometimes he is Jewish but always he is American, and now and then, Québecois.

These were my dreams for you and me, vieux copain —New Jews, the two of us, queer, militant, invisible, part of a possible new tribe bound by gossip and rumors of divine evidence.

I sent you the wrong box of fireworks, and this was not entirely by mistake. You got the Rich Brothers' All-American Assortment, which claims to be the largest selection offered at the price, over 550 pieces. Let us be charitable and say that I didn't know exactly how long the ordeal should last. I could have sent you the Famous Banner Fireworks Display, same price as the other, with over a *thousand* pieces of noise and beauty. I denied you the rocking Electric Cannon Salutes, the good old-fashioned Cherry Bombs, the Silver Rain Torch, the 16-report Battle in Clouds, the suicidal Jap Pop-Bottle Night Rockets. Let charity record that I did this out of charity. The explosions might have drawn malicious attention. But how can I justify withholding the Big Colorful Family Lawn Display, a special package made up for those tuned to a minimum of noise? Musical Vesuvius Flitter Fountains I hid from you, Comet Star

Shells, Flower Pots with Handles, Large Floral Shells, Triangle Spinning Wheels, Patriotic Colored Fire Flag. Stretch your heart, darling. Let charity argue that I spared you a domestic extravagance.

I am going to set you straight on everything: Edith, me, you, Tekakwitha, the A——s, the firecrackers.

I didn't want you to burn yourself to suicide. On the other hand, I didn't want the exodus to be too easy. This last from professional teacher's pride, and also a subtle envy which I have previously exposed.

What is more sinister is the possibility that I may have contrived to immunize you against the ravages of ecstasy by regular inoculations of homeopathic doses of it. A diet of paradox fattens the ironist not the psalmist.

Perhaps I should have gone all the way and sent you the sub-machine guns which the firecrackers concealed in my brilliant smuggling operation. I suffer from the Virgo disease: nothing I did was pure enough. I was never sure whether I wanted disciples or partisans. I was never sure whether I wanted Parliament or a hermitage.

I will confess that I never saw the Québec Revolution clearly, even at the time of my parliamentary disgrace. I simply refused to support the War, not because I was French, or a pacifist (which of course I'm not), but because I was tired. I knew what they were doing to the Gypsies, I had a whiff of Zyklon B, but I was very, very tired. Do you remember the world at that time? A huge jukebox played a sleepy tune. The tune was a couple of thousand years old and we danced to it with our eyes closed. The tune was called History and we loved it, Nazis, Jews, everybody. We loved it because we made it up, because, like Thucydides, we knew that whatever happened to us was the most im-

portant thing that ever happened in the world. History
made us feel good so we played it over and over, deep
into the night. We smiled as our uncles went to bed,
and we were glad to get rid of them, because they
didn't know how to do the H. in spite of all their
boasts and old newspaper clippings. Good night, old
frauds. Someone worked the rheostat and we squeezed
the body in our arms, we inhaled the perfumed hair,
we bumped into each other's genitals. History was our
song, History chose us to make History. We gave ourselves to it, caressed by events.

In perfect drowsy battalions we moved through the
moonlight. Its will be done. In perfect sleep we took
the soap and waited for the showers.

Never mind, never mind. I've gone too deep into the
old language. It may trap me there.

I was tired. I was sick of the inevitable. I tried to slip
out of History. Never mind, never mind. Just say I was
tired. I said no.

—Leave Parliament this instant!
—Frogs!
—They can't be trusted!
—Vote him dead!

I ran off with heavy heart. I loved the red chairs of
Parliament. I cherished the fucks under the monument.
I had cream in National Library. Too impure for empty
future, I wept old jackpots.

Now my fat confession. I loved the magic of guns. I
sneaked them in under the skin of firecrackers. My old
monkey made me do it. I planted guns in Québec for I
was hung between free and coward. Guns suck magic.
I buried guns for future History. If History rule let me
be Mr. History. The guns are green. The flowers poke. I
let History back because I was lonely. Do not follow. Go

beyond my style. I am nothing but a rotten hero.

Among the bars in my soap collection. Never mind.

Among the bars in my soap collection. I paid big cash for it. Argentine vacation hotel week-end shack-up with Edith. Never mind that. I paid equivalent U.S. $635. Waiter giving me the eye for days. He not cute little recent immigrant. Former Lord of few miserable European acres. Transaction beside swimming pool. I wanted it. I wanted it. My lust for secular gray magic. Human soap. A full bar, minus the wear of one bath in which I plunged myself, for better or for worse.

Mary, Mary, where are you, my little Abishag?

My dear friend, take my spirit hand.

I am going to show you everything *happening*. That is as far as I can take you. I cannot bring you into the middle of action. My hope is that I have prepared *you* for this pilgrimage. I didn't suspect the pettiness of my dream. I believed that I had conceived the vastest dream of my generation: I wanted to be a magician. That was my idea of glory. Here is a plea based on my whole experience: do not be a magician, be magic.

That week end when I arranged for you to work in the Archives, Edith and I flew down to Argentine for a little sun and experiments. Edith was having trouble with her body: it kept changing sizes, she even feared that it might be dying.

We took a large air-conditioned room overlooking the sea, double-locking the door as soon as the porter had left with his hand full of tip.

Edith spread a large rubber sheet over the double bed, carefully moving from corner to corner to smooth it out. I loved to watch her bend over. Her buttocks were my masterpiece. Call her nipples an eccentric extravagance, but the bum was perfect. It's true that from year to year it required electronic massage and applications of hormone mold, but the conception was perfect.

Edith took off her clothes and lay down on the rubber sheet. I stood over her. Her eyes blazed.

—I hate you, F. I hate you for what you've done to me and my husband. I was a fool to get mixed up with you. I wish he'd known me before you—

—Hush, Edith. We don't want to go over all that again. You wanted to be beautiful.

—I can't remember anything now. I'm all confused. Perhaps I was beautiful before.

—Perhaps, I echoed in a voice as sad as hers.

Edith shifted her brown hips to make herself comfortable, and a shaft of sunlight infiltrated her pubic hair, giving it a rust-coloured tint. Yes, that was beauty beyond my craft.

> Sun on Her Cunt
> Wispy Rusty Hair
> Her Tunnels Sunk in Animal
> Her Kneecaps Round and Bare

I knelt beside the bed and lay one of my thin ears on the little sunlit orchard, listening to the tiny swamp machinery.

—You've meddled, F. You've gone against God.

—Hush, my little chicken. There is some cruelty even I cannot bear.

—You should have left me like you found me. I'm no good to anyone now.

—I could suck you forever, Edith.

She made the shaved hairs on the back of my neck tingle with the grazing of her lovely brown fingers.

—Sometimes I feel sorry for you, F. You might have been a great man.

—Stop talking, I bubbled.

—Stand up, F. Get your mouth off me. I'm pretending that you are someone else.

—Who?

—The waiter.

—Which one? I demanded.

—With the mustache and the raincoat.

—I thought so, I thought so.

—You noticed him, too, didn't you, F.?

—Yes.

I stood up too suddenly. Dizziness twirled my brain like a dial and formerly happy chewed food in my stomach turned into vomit. I hated my life, I hated my meddling, I hated my ambition. For a second I wanted to be an ordinary bloke cloistered in a tropical hotel room with an Indian orphan.

> Take from me my Camera
> Take from me my Glass
> The Sun the Wet Forever
> Let the Doctors Pass

—Don't cry, F. You knew it had to happen. You wanted me to go all the way. Now I'm no good to anyone and I'll try anything.

I stumbled to the window but it was hermetically sealed. The ocean was deep green. The beach was polka-dotted with beach umbrellas. How I longed for my old teacher, Charles Axis. I strained my eyes for an immaculate white bathing suit, unshadowed by topography of genitalia.

—Oh, come here, F. I can't stand watching a man vomit and cry.

She cradled my head between her bare breasts, stuffing a nipple into each ear.

—There now.

—Thankyou, thankyou, thankyou, thankyou.

—Listen, F. Listen the way you wanted us all to listen.

—I'm listening, Edith.

> Let me let me follow
> Down the Sticky Caves
> Where embryonic Cities
> Form Scum upon the Waves

—You're not listening, F.

—I'm trying.

—I feel sorry for you, F.

—Help me, Edith.

—Then get back to work. That's the only thing that can help you. Try to finish the work you began on all of us.

She was right. I was the Moses of our little exodus. I would never cross. My mountain might be very high but it rises from the desert. Let it suffice me.

I recovered my professional attitude. Her lower perfume was still in my nostrils but that was my business. I surveyed the nude girl from my Pisgah. Her soft lips smiled.

—That's better, F. Your tongue was nice but you do better as a doctor.

—All right, Edith. What seems to be the trouble now?

—I can't make myself come any more.

—Of course you can't. If we're going to perfect the pan-orgasmic body, extend the erogenous zone over the whole fleshy envelope, popularize the Telephone Dance, then we've got to begin by diminishing the tyranny of the nipples, lips, clitoris, and asshole.

—You're going against God, F. You say dirty words.

—I'll take my chances.

—I feel so lost since I can't make myself come any more. I'm not ready for the other stuff yet. It makes me too lonely. I feel blurred. Sometimes I forget where my cunt is.

—You make me weary, Edith. To think I've pinned all my hopes on you and your wretched husband.

—Give it back to me, F.

—All right, Edith. It's a very simple matter. We do it with books. I thought this might happen, so I brought the appropriate ones along. I also have in this trunk a number of artificial phalli (used by women), Vaginal Vibrators, the Rin-No-Tam and Godemiche or Dildo.

—Now you're talking.

—Just lie back and listen. Sink into the rubber sheet. Spread your legs and let the air-conditioning do its filthy work.

—O.K., shoot.

I cleared my famous throat. I chose a swollen book, frankly written, which describes various Auto-Erotic practices as indulged in by humans and animals, flowers, children and adults, and women of all ages and cultures. The areas covered included: Why Wives Masturbate, What We Can Learn From the Anteater, Unsatisfied Women, Abnormalities and Eroticism, Techniques of Masturbation, Latitude of Females, Genital Shaving, Clitoral Discovery, Club Masturbation, Female Metal, Nine Rubber, Frame Caress, Urethral Masturbation, Individual Experiments, Masturbation in and of Children, Thigh-Friction Technique, Mammary Stimulation, Auto-Eroticism in Windows.

—Don't stop, F. I feel it coming back.

Her lovely brown fingers inched down her silky rounded belly. I continued reading in my slow, tantalizing, weather-reporting tones. I read to my deep-breathing protégée of the unusual sex practices, when Sex Becomes "Different." An "Unusual" sex practice is one where there is some greater pleasure than orgasm through intercourse. Most of these bizarre practices involve a measure of mutilation, shock, voyeurism, pain, or torture. The sex habits of the average person are relatively free of such sadistic or masochistic traits. NEVERTHELESS, the reader will be shocked to see how abnormal are the tastes of the so-called normal person. CASE HISTORIES and intensive field work. Filled with chapters detailing ALL ASPECTS of the sex act. SAMPLE HEADINGS: Rubbing, Seeing, Silk Rings, Satyriasis, Bestiality in Others. The average reader will be surprised to learn how "Unusual" practices are passed along by seemingly innocent, normal sex partners.

—It's so good, F. It's been so long.

Now it was late afternoon. The sky had darkened somewhat. Edith was touching herself everywhere, smelling herself shamelessly. I could hardly keep still myself. The texts had got to me. Goose pimples rose on her young form. I stared dumbly at Original drawings: male and female organs, both external and internal, drawings indicating correct and incorrect methods of penetration. Wives will benefit from seeing how the penis is received.

—Please, F. Don't leave me like this.

My throat was burning with the hunger of it. Love fondled. Edith writhed under her squeezes. She flipped over on her stomach, wielding her small beautiful fists in anal stimulation. I threw myself into a Handbook of Semi-Impotence. There were important pieces woven into the theme: how to enlarge the erect penis, penis darkness, use of lubricants, satisfaction during menstruation, abusing the menopause, a wife's manual assistance in overcoming semi-impotence.

—Don't touch me, F. I'll die.

I blurted out a piece on Fellatio and Cunnilingus Between Brother and Sister, and others. My hands were almost out of control. I stumbled through a new concept for an exciting sex life. I didn't miss the section on longevity. Thrilling culminations possible for all. Lesbians by the hundreds interviewed and bluntly questioned. Some tortured for coy answers. Speak up, you cheap dyke. An outstanding work showing the sex offender at work. Chemicals to get hair off palms. Not models! Actual Photos of Male and Female Sex Organs and Excrement. Explored Kissing. The pages flew. Edith mumbling bad words through froth. Her fingers were bright and glistening, her tongue bruised from the taste of her waters. I spoke the books in everyday terms, the most sensitivity, cause of erection, Husband-Above 1-17, Wife-Above 18-29, Seated 30-34, On-The-Side 35-38, Standing & Kneeling Positions 39-53, Miscellaneous Squats 54-109, Coital Movement In All Directions, both for Husband and Wife.

—Edith! I cried. Let me have Foreplay.

—Never.

I sped through a glossary of Sexual Terms. In 1852, Richard Burton (d. aet. 69) submitted calmly to circumcision at the age of 31. "Milkers." Detailed Library of Consummated Incest. Ten Steps on Miscegenation. Techniques of Notorious Photographers. The Evidence of Extreme Acts. Sadism, Mutilation, Cannibalism, Cannibalism of Oralists, How To Match Disproportionate Organs. See the vivid birth of the new American woman. I shouted the recorded facts. She will not be denied the pleasures of sex. CASE HISTORIES show the changing trends. Filled with accounts of college girls eager to be propositioned. Women no longer inhibited by oral intimacy. Men masturbated to death. Cannibalism during Foreplay. Skull Coition. Secrets of "Timing" the Climax. Foreskin, Pro, Con, and Indifferent. The Intimate Kiss. What are the benefits of sexual experimentation? Own and other's sexual make-up. Sin has to be taught. Kissing Negroes on their Mouths. Thigh Documents. Styles of Manual Pressure in Volutary Indulgence. Death Rides a Camel. I gave her everything. My voice cried the Latex. I hid no laces, nor a pair of exciting open-front pants, nor soft elasticized bra instead of sagging, heavy wide bust, therefore youthful separation. O'er Edith's separate nipples I blabbed the full record, Santa Pants, Fire Alarm Snow, Glamor Tip, plain wrapper Thick Bust Jelly, washable leather Kinsey Doll, Smegma Discipline, the LITTLE SQUIRT ash-tray, "SEND ME ANOTHER Rupture-Easer so I will have one to change off with. It is enabling me to work top speed at my press machine 8 hrs a day," this I threw in for sadness, for melancholy soft flat groin pad which might lurk in Edith's memory swamp as soiled lever, as stretched switch to bumpy apotheosis wet rocket come out of the fine print slum where the only trumpet solo is grandfather's stringy cough and underwear money problems.

Edith was wiggling her saliva-covered kneecaps, bouncing on the rivulets of lubrication. Her thighs were aglow with froth, and her pale anus was excavated by cruel false fingernails. She screamed for deliverance, the flight her imagination commanded denied by a half-enlightened cunt.

—Do something, F. I beg you. But don't touch me.

—Edith, darling! What have I done to you?

—Stand back, F!

—What can I do?

—Try.

—Torture story?

—Anything, F. Hurry.

—The Jews?

—No. Too foreign.

—1649? Brébeuf and Lalemant?

—Anything.

So I began to recite my schoolboy lesson of how the Iroquois killed the Jesuits Brébeuf and Lalemant, whose scorched and mangled relics were discovered the morning of the twentieth by a member of the Society and seven armed Frenchmen. "Ils y trouuerent vn spectacle d'horreur. . . ."

On the afternoon of the sixteenth the Iroquois had bound Brébeuf to a stake. They commenced to scorch him from head to foot.

—Everlasting flames for those who persecute the worshipers of God, Brébeuf threatened them in the tone of a master.

As the priest spoke the Indians cut away his lower lip and forced a red-hot iron down his throat. He made no sign or sound of discomfort.

Then they led out Lalemant. Around his naked body they had fastened strips of bark, smeared with pitch. When Lalemant saw his Superior, the bleeding unnatural aperture exposing his teeth, the handle of the heated implement still protruding from the seared and ruined mouth, he cried out in the words of St. Paul:

—We are made a spectacle to the world, to angels, and to men.

Lalemant flung himself at Brébeuf's feet. The Iroquois took him, bound him to a stake, and ignited the vegetation in which he was trussed. He screamed for heaven's help, but he was not to die so quickly.

They brought a collar made of hatchets heated red-hot and conferred it on Brébeuf. He did not flinch.

An ex-convert, who had backslid, now shouldered forward and demanded that hot water be poured on their heads, since the missionaries had poured so much cold water on them. A kettle was slung, water boiled, and then poured slowly on the heads of the captive priests.

—We baptize you, they laughed, that you may be happy in heaven. You told us that the more one suffers on earth, the happier he is in heaven.

Brébeuf stood like a rock. After a number of revolting tortures they scalped him. He was still alive when they laid open his breast. A crowd came forward to drink the blood of so courageous an enemy and to devour his heart. His death astonished his murderers. His ordeal lasted four hours.

Lalemant, physically weak from childhood, was taken back to the house. There he was tortured all night, until, sometime after dawn, one Indian wearied of the extended entertainment and administered a fatal blow with his hatchet. There was no part of his body which was not burned, "even to his eyes, in the sockets of which these wretches had placed live coals." His ordeal lasted seventeen hours.

—How do you feel, Edith?

There was no need for me to ask. My recitals had served only to bring her closer to a summit she could not achieve. She moaned in terrible hunger, her goose-flesh shining in supplication that she might be freed from the unbearable coils of secular pleasure, and soar into that blind realm, so like sleep, so like death, that journey of pleasure beyond pleasure, where each man travels as an orphan toward an atomic ancestry, more anonymous, more nourishing than the arms of blood or foster family.

I knew she would never make it.

—F., get me out of this, she moaned pitifully.

I plugged in the Danish Vibrator. A degrading spectacle followed. As soon as those delicious electric oscillations occupied my hand like an army of trained seaweed, weaving, swathing, caressing—I was reluctant to surrender the instrument to Edith. Somehow, in the midst of her juicy ordeal, she noticed me trying to slip the Perfected Suction Bracers down into the shadows of my underwear.

She lifted herself out of her pools and lunged at me.

—Give me that. You rat!

Bearlike (some ancestral memory?) she swung at me. I had not had the opportunity to fasten the Improved Wonder Straps, and the Vibrator flew out of my embrace. Thus the bear, with a swipe of his clawed paw, scoops the fish from the bosom of the stream. Crablike, the D.V. scuttled across the polished floor, humming like an overturned locomotive.

—You're selfish, F., Edith snarled.

—That's the observation of a liar and an ingrate, I said as gently as possible.

—Get out of my way.

—I love you, I said as I inched my way toward the D.V. I love you, Edith. My methods may have been wrong, but I never stopped loving you. Was it selfish of me to try to end your pain, yours and his (you, dear old comrade)? I saw pain everywhere. I could not bear to look into your eyes, so maggoty were they with pain and desire. I could not bear to kiss either of you, for each of your embraces disclosed a hopeless, mordant plea. In your laughter, though it were for money or for sunsets, I heard your throats ripped with greed. In the midst of the high jump, I saw the body wither. Between the spurts of come, you launched your tidings of regret. Thousands built, thousands lay squashed beneath tubes of highway. You were not happy to brush your teeth. I gave you breasts with nipples: could you nourish anyone? I gave you prick with separate memory: could you train a race? I took you to a complete movie of the Second World War: did you feel any lighter when we walked out? No, you threw yourselves upon the thorns of research. I sucked you, and you howled to dispense me something more than poison. With every handshake you wept for a lost garden. You found a cutting edge for every object. I couldn't stand the racket of your pain. You were smeared with blood and tortured scabs. You needed bandages—there was no time to boil the germs out of them—I grabbed what was at hand. Caution was a luxury. There was no time for me to examine my motives. Self-purification would have been an alibi. Beholding such a spectacle of misery, I was free to try anything. I can't answer for my own erection. I have no explanation for my own vile ambitions. Confronted with your pus, I could not stop to examine my direction, whether or not I was aimed at a star. As I limped down the street every window broadcast a command: Change! Purify! Experiment! Cauterize! Reverse! Burn! Preserve! Teach! Believe me, Edith, I had to act, and act fast. That was my nature. Call me Dr. Frankenstein with a deadline. I seemed to wake up in the middle of a car accident, limbs strewn everywhere, detached voices screaming for comfort, severed fingers pointing homeward, all the debris withering like sliced cheese out of Cellophane—and all I had in the wrecked world was a needle and thread, so I got down on my

knees, I pulled pieces out of the mess and I started to
stitch them together. I had an idea of what a man
should look like, but it kept changing. I couldn't devote
a lifetime to discovering the ideal physique. All I heard
was pain, all I saw was mutilation. My needle going so
madly, sometimes I found I'd run the thread right
through my own flesh and I was joined to one of my
own grotesque creations—I'd rip us apart—and then I
heard my own voice howling with the others, and I
knew that I was also truly part of the disaster. But I
also realized that I was not the only one on my knees
sewing frantically. There were others like me, making
the same monstrous mistakes, driven by the same impure urgency, stitching themselves into the ruined heap,
painfully extracting themselves—

—F., you're weeping.

—Forgive me.

—Stop blubbering. See, you've lost your hard-on.

—It's all breaking down now. My discipline is collapsing. Have you any idea how much discipline I had to
use in training the two of you?

We both leaped for the Vibrator at the same instant.
Her fluids made her slippery. For a second in our strug-
gle I wished we were making love, for all her nozzles
were stiff and fragrant. I grabbed her around the waist,
before I knew it her bum popped out of my bear hug
like a wet watermelon seed, her thighs went by like a
missed train, and there I was with empty lubricated
arms, nose squashed against the expensive mahogany
floor.

Old friend, are you still with me? Do not despair. I
promised you that this would end in ecstasy. Yes, your
wife was naked during this story. Somewhere in the
dark room, draped over the back of a chair like a

huge exhausted butterfly, her Gal panties, stiffened by
the slightest masonry of sweat, dreamed of ragged fingernails, and I dreamed with them—large, fluttering, descending dreams crisscrossed with vertical scratches.
For me it was the end of Action. I would keep on trying, but I knew I had failed the both of you, and that
both of you had failed me. I had one trick left, but it
was a dangerous one, and I'd never used it. Events, as
I will show, would force me into it, and it would end
with Edith's suicide, my hospitalization, your cruel ordeal in the treehouse. How many times did I warn you
that you would be whipped by loneliness?

So I lay there in Argentine. The Danish Vibrator
hummed like a whittler as it rose and fell over Edith's
young contours. It was cold and black in the room.
Occasionally one of her glistening kneecaps would catch
a glint of moonlight as she jerked her box up and
down in desperate supplication. She had stopped moaning; I assumed she had approached the area of intense
breathless silence which the orgasm loves to flood with
ventriloquist gasps and cosmic puppet plots.

—Thank God, she whispered at last.

—I'm glad you could come, Edith. I'm very happy for
you.

—Thank God it's off me. I had to blow it. It made me
do oral intimacy.

—Wha—?

Before I could question her further it was upon my
buttocks, its idiot hum revved up to a psychotic whine.
The detachable crotch piece inserted itself between my
hairy thighs, ingeniously providing soft support for my
frightened testicles. I had heard of these things happening before, and I knew it would leave me bitter and
full of self-loathing. Like a cyanide egg dropped into the

gas chamber the D.V. released a glob of Formula Cream at the top of the muscular cleavage I had labored so hard to define. As my body heat melted it to the trickle which would grease its shameful entry, several comfortable Latex cups assumed exciting holds here and there. The elastic Developer seemed to have a life of its own, and the Fortune Straps spread everything apart, and I felt the air-conditioning coolly evaporating sweat and cream *from tiny surfaces I hardly knew existed*. I was ready to lie there for ten days. I was not even surprised. I knew it would be insatiable but I was ready to submit. I heard Edith faintly calling to me just as the Foam Pad rose the full length. After that I heard nothing. It was like a thousand Sex Philosophers working over me with perfect cooperation. I may have screamed at the first thrust of the White Club, but the Formula Cream kept coming, and I think a cup was converted to handle excreta. It hummed in my ears like alabaster lips.

I don't know how long it swarmed among my private pieces.

Edith made it to a light switch. She couldn't bear to look at me.

—Are you happy, F.?

I did not answer.

—Should I do something, F.?

Perhaps the D.V. answered with a sated whir. It pulled in the American Laces fast as an Italian eater, the suck went out of the cups, my scrotum dropped unceremoniously, and the machine slipped off my quivering body meat. I think I was happy. . . .

—Should I pull out the plug, F.?

—Do what you want, Edith. I'm washed up.

Edith yanked at the electric cord. The D.V. shuddered,

fell silent, and stopped. Edith sighed with relief, but too soon. The D.V. began to produce a shattering sonic whistle.

—Does it have batteries?

—No, Edith. It doesn't have batteries.

She covered her breasts with crossed arms.

—You mean—?

—Yes. It's learned to feed itself.

Edith backed into a corner as the Danish Vibrator advanced toward her. She stooped queerly, as if she were trying to hide her cunt behind her thighs. I could not stir from the puddle of jelly in which I had been buggered by countless improvements. It made its way across the hotel room in a leisurely fashion, straps and cups flowing behind it, like a Hawaiian skirt made of grass and brassières.

It had learned to feed itself.

(O Father, Nameless and Free of Description, lead me from the Desert of the Possible. Too long I have dealt with Events. Too long I labored to become an Angel. I chased Miracles with a bag of Power to salt their wild Tails. I tried to dominate Insanity so I could steal its Information. I tried to program the Computers with Insanity. I tried to create Grace to prove that Grace existed. Do not punish Charles Axis. We could not see the Evidence so we stretched our Memories. Dear Father, accept this confession: we did not train ourselves to Receive because we believed there wasn't Anything to Receive and we could not endure with this Belief.)

—Help, help me, F.

But I was fastened to the floor with a tingling nail, the head of which was my anus.

It took its time getting to her. Edith, meanwhile, her back squeezed into the right angle, had sunk to a defenseless sitting position, her lovely legs spread apart. Numbed by horror and the prospect of disgusting thrills, she was ready to submit. I have stared at many orifices, but never have I seen one wear such an expression. The soft hairs were thrown back from the dripping lips like a Louis Quatorze sunburst. The layers of lip spread and gathered like someone playing with a lens opening. The Danish Vibrator mounted her slowly, and soon the child (Edith was twenty) was doing things with her mouth and fingers that no one, believe me, old friend, no one has ever done to you. Perhaps this was what you wanted from her. But you did not know how to encourage her, and this was not your fault. No one could. That is why I tried to lead the fuck away from mutual dialing.

The whole assault lasted maybe twenty-five minutes. Before the tenth minute passed she was begging the thing to perform in her armpits, specifying which nipple was hungriest, twisting her torso to offer it hidden pink terrain—until the Danish Vibrator began to command. Then Edith, quite happily, become nothing but a buffet of juice, flesh, excrement, muscle to serve its appetite.

Of course, the implications of her pleasure are enormous.

The Danish Vibrator slipped off her face, uncovering a bruised soft smile.

—Stay, she whispered.

It climbed onto the window sill, purring deeply, revved up to a sharp moan, and launched itself through the glass, which broke and fell over its exit like a fancy stage curtain.

—Make it stay.

—It's gone.

We dragged our strange bodies to the window. The

perfumed sticky tropical night wafted into the room as we leaned out to watch the Danish Vibrator move down the marble stories of the hotel. When it reached the ground it crossed the parking lot and soon achieved the beach.

—Oh, God, F., it was beautiful. Feel this.

—I know, Edith. Feel this.

A curious drama began to unfold beneath us on the deserted moonlit sand. As the D.V. made slowly toward the waves breaking in dark flowers on the bright shore, a figure emerged from a grove of ghostly palms. It was a man wearing an immaculate white bathing suit. I do not know whether he was running to intercept the Danish Vibrator with the intention of violently disabling it, or merely wished to observe at closer range its curiously graceful progress toward the Atlantic.

How soft the night seemed, like the last verse of a lullaby. With one hand on his hip and the other scratching his head, the tiny figure beneath us watched, as did we, the descent of the apparatus into the huge rolling sea, which closed over its luminous cups like the end of a civilization.

—Will it come back, F.? To us?

—It doesn't matter. It's in the world.

We stood close to each other in the window, two figures on a rung of a high marble ladder built into the vast cloudless night, leaning on nothing.

A small breeze detached a wisp of her hair and I felt its tiny fall across my cheek.

—I love you, Edith.

—I love you, F.

—And I love your husband.

—So do I.

—Nothing is as I planned it, but now I know what will happen.

—So do I, F.

—Oh, Edith, something is beginning in my heart, a whisper of rare love, but I will never be able to fulfill it. It is my prayer that your husband will.

—He will, F.

—But he will do it alone. He can only do it alone.

—I know, she said. We must not be with him.

A great sadness overtook us as we looked out over the miles of sea, an egoless sadness that we did not own or claim. Here and there the restless water kept an image of the shattered moon. We said good-by to you, old lover. We did not know when or how the parting would be completed, but it began that moment.

There was a professional knock on the blond door.

—It must be him, I said.

—Should we put our clothes on?

—Why bother.

We did not even have to open the door. The waiter had a passkey. He was wearing the old raincoat and mustache, but underneath he was perfectly nude. We turned toward him.

—Do you like Argentine? I asked for the sake of civil conversation.

—I miss the newsreels, he said.

—And the parades? I offered.

—And the parades. But I can get everything else here. Ah!

He noticed our reddened organs and began to fondle them with great interest.

—Wonderful! Wonderful! I see you have been well prepared.

What followed was old hat. I have no intention of

adding to any pain which might be remaindered to you, by a minute description of the excesses we performed with him. Lest you should worry for us, let me say that we had, indeed, been well prepared, and we hardly cared to resist his sordid exciting commands, even when he made us kiss the whip.

—I have a treat for you, he said at last.

—He has a treat for us, Edith.

—Shoot, she replied wearily.

From the pocket of his overcoat he withdraw a bar of soap.

—Three in a tub, he said merrily in his heavy accent.

So we splashed around with him. He lathered us from head to foot, proclaiming all the while the special qualities of the soap, which, as you must now understand, was derived from melted human flesh.

That bar is now in your hands. We were baptized by it, your wife and I. I wonder what you will do with it.

You see, I have shown you *how it happens*, from style to style, from kiss to kiss.

There is more, there is the history of Catherine Tekakwitha—you shall have all of it.

Wearily we dried each other with the opulent towels of the hotel. The waiter was very careful with our parts.

—I had millions of these at my disposal, he said without a trace of nostalgia.

He slipped into his raincoat and spent some time before the full-length mirror playing with his mustache and slanting his hair across his forehead in just the way he liked.

—And don't forget to inform the *Police Gazette*. We'll bargain over the soap later.

—Wait!

As he opened the door to go, Edith threw her arms about his neck, pulled him to the dry bed, and cradled his famous head against her breasts.

—What did you do that for? I demanded of her after the waiter had made his stiff exit, and nothing remained of him but the vague stink of his sulphurous flatulence.

—For a second I thought he was an A——.

—Oh, Edith!

I sank to my knees before your wife and I laid my mouth on her toes. The room was a mess, the floor spotted with pools of fluid and suds, but she rose from it all like a lovely statue with epaulets and nipple tips of moonlight.

—Oh, Edith! It doesn't matter what I've done to you, the tits, the cunt, the hydraulic buttock failures, all my Pygmalion tampering, it means nothing, I know now. Acne and all, you were out of my reach, you were beyond my gadgetry. Who are you?

—Ισις ἐγώ εἰμί πάντα γεγονός καί ὄν καί ἐσό-μενον καί τό ἐμόν πέπλον οὐδείς τῶν θνητῶν ἀπε-καλυψεν!

—You're not joking? Then I'm only fit to suck your toes.

—Wiggle.

Later and later.

I remember a story you once told me, old comrade, of how the Indians looked at death. The Indians believed that after physical death the spirit made a long journey heavenward. It was a hard, dangerous journey, and many did not complete it. A treacherous river had to be crossed on a log which bounced through wild rapids. A huge howling dog harassed the traveler. There was a narrow path between dancing boulders which crashed together, pulverizing the pilgrim who could not dance with them. The Hurons believed that there was a bark hut beside this path. Here lived Oscotarach, meaning the Head-Piercer. It was his function to remove the brains from the skulls of all who went by, "as a necessary preparation for immortality."

Ask yourself. Perhaps the treehouse where you suffer is the hut of Oscotarach. You did not know the operation was so long and clumsy. Again and again the blunt tomahawk pokes among the porridge. The moonlight wants to get into your skull. The sparkling alleys of the icy sky want to stream through your eyeholes. The night winter air which seems like "diamonds held in solution," it wants to flood the empty bowl.

Ask yourself. Was I *your* Oscotarach? I pray that I was. The surgery is deep in progress, darling. I am with you.

But who could perform the operation on Oscotarach? When you understand this question, you will understand my ordeal. I had to apply to public wards in pursuit of my own operation. The treehouse was too lonely for me: I had to apply to politics.

The thumb of my left hand was all that politics relieved me of. (Mary Voolnd does not mind.) The thumb of my left hand is probably rotting this very moment on some downtown Montréal roof, or splinters of it in the soot of a tin chimney. That is my relic case. Charity, old friend, charity for the secularists. The treehouse is very small and we are many with an appetite for the sky in our heads.

But with my thumb went the metal body of the statue of the Queen of England on Sherbrooke Street, or as I prefer, Rue Sherbrooke.

BOOM! WHOOSH!

All the parts of that hollow stately body which had sat for so long like a boulder in the pure stream of our blood and destiny—SPLATTER!—plus the thumb of one patriot.

What a rain there was that day! All the umbrellas of the English police could not protect the city from that change of climate.

QUEBEC LIBRE!

Alarmclock Bombs!

QUEBEC OUI OTTAWA NON.

Ten thousand voices that only knew how to cheer a rubber puck past a goalie's pads, now singing: MERDE A LA REINE D'ANGLETERRE.

ELIZABETH GO HOME.

There is a hole on Rue Sherbrooke. Once upon a time it was plugged with the rump of a foreign queen. A seed of pure blood was planted in that hole, and from it there shall spring a mighty harvest.

I knew what I was doing when I wedged the bomb into the green copper folds of her imperial lap. I rather liked the statue, as a matter of fact. Not a few studious cunts I fingered under those shadowy royal auspices. So I ask your charity, friend. We who cannot dwell in the Clear Light, we must deal with symbols.

I have nothing against the Queen of England. Even in my heart I never resented her for not being Jackie Kennedy. She is, to my mind, a very gallant lady, victimized by whoever it is who designs the tops of her uniforms.

It was a lonely ride the Queen and Prince Philip took through the armored streets of Québec that October day in 1964. The real-estate tycoon of Atlantis couldn't have been more lonely the day the wave rolled in. The feet of Ozymandias had more company in the sandstorm of '89. They sat very straight in the bullet-proof auto like children trying to read the subtitles of a foreign movie. The route was lined with yellow riot squads and the backs of a hostile crowd. I do not gloat over their solitude. And I try not to envy yours. After all, it was I who pointed you to a place where I cannot go. I point there now—with my lost thumb.

Charity!

Your teacher shows you *how it happens*.

They walk differently now, the young men and women of Montréal. Music floats out of manholes. Their clothes are different—no smelly pockets bulging with Kleenex bundles of illegal come. Shoulders are thrown back, organs signal merrily through transparent under-wear. Good fucks, like a shipload of joyous swimming rats, have migrated from marble English banks to revo-lutionary cafés. There is love on Rue Ste. Catherine, pa-troness of spinsters. History ties the broken shoelaces of a people's destiny and the march is on. Do not be de-ceived: a nation's pride is a tangible thing: it is meas-ured by how many hard-ons live beyond the solitary dream, by decibels of the female rocket moan.

First secular miracle: La Canadienne, hitherto victim of motel frost, hitherto beloved of nun's democracy, hitherto upholstered by the black belts of Code Na-poléon—revolution has done what only wet Hollywood did before.

Watch the words, watch *how it happens*.

It is not merely because I am French that I long for an independent Québec. It is not merely because I do not want our people to become a quaint drawing on the corner of a tourist map that I long for thick national borders. It is not merely because without independence we will be nothing but a Louisiana of the north, a few good restaurants and a Latin Quarter the only relics of our blood. It is not merely because I know that lofty things like destiny and a rare spirit must be guaranteed by dusty things like flags, armies, and passports.

I want to hammer a beautiful colored bruise on the whole American monolith. I want a breathing chimney on the corner of the continent. I want a country to break in half so men can learn to break their lives in half. I want History to jump on Canada's spine with sharp skates. I want the edge of a tin can to drink America's throat. I want two hundred million to know that everything can be different, any old different.

I want the State to doubt itself seriously. I want the Police to become a limited company and fall with the stock market. I want the Church to have divisions and fight on the both sides of Movies.

I confess! I confess!

Did you see *how it happened?*

Before my arrest and subsequent incarceration in this hospital for the criminally insane, I spent my days writing pamphlets against Anglo-Saxon imperialism, glueing clocks to bombs, the ordinary subversive program. I missed your big kisses but I couldn't detain you from or follow on a trip I charted for you precisely because I couldn't go myself.

But at night! Night spilled like gasoline on my most hopeless dreams.

The English did to us what we did to the Indians, and the Americans did to the English what the English did to us. I demanded revenge for everyone. I saw cities burning, I saw movies falling into blackness. I saw the maize on fire. I saw the Jesuits punished. I saw the trees taking back the long-house roofs. I saw the shy deer murdering to get their dresses back. I saw the

Indians punished. I saw chaos eat the gold roof of Parliament. I saw water dissolve the hoofs of drinking animals. I saw the bonfires covered with urine, and the gas stations swallowed up entire, highway after highway falling into the wild swamps.

Then we were very close. I was not so far behind you then.

O Friend, take my spirit hand and remember me. You were loved by a man who read your heart very tenderly, who sought your unformed dreams as his resting place. Think of my body from time to time.

I promised you a joyous letter, didn't I?

It is my intention to relieve you of your final burden: the useless History under which you suffer in such confusion. Men of your nature never get far beyond the Baptism.

Life chose me to be a man of facts: I accept the responsibility. You mustn't meddle any longer in this shit. Avoid even the circumstances of Catherine Tekakwitha's death and the ensuing documented miracles. Read it with that part of your mind which you delegate to watching out for blackflies and mosquitoes.

Say good-by to constipation and loneliness.

F.'S INVOCATION TO HISTORY IN THE OLD STYLE
The miracle we all are waiting for
is waiting until Parliament falls down
and House of Archives is a house no more
and fathers are unpoisoned by renown.
The medals and the records of abuse
can't help us on our pilgrimage to lust,
but like whips certain perverts never use,
compel our flesh in paralyzing trust.
I see an Orphan, lawless and serene,

standing in a corner of the sky,
body something like bodies that have been,
but not the flaw of naming in his eye.
Bred close to the ovens, he's burnt inside.
Light, wind, cold, dark—they use him like a Bride!

F.'S INVOCATION TO HISTORY IN THE MIDDLE STYLE

History is a Scabbie[1] Point[2]
For putting Cash[3] to sleep
Shooting up[4] the Peanut[5] Shit[6]
Of all we need to keep.[7]

1. Dirty, germ-laden, infected, leading to the Scabbies or inflammation of puncture holes, blood poisoning and Hepatitis. Also blunt or rusty.
2. Drug addict's argot for the hypodermic needle (No. 12).
3. Underworld argot for the conscience, the brain, or any kind of painful consciousness. I have not heard the word used outside of Montréal and environs, and there mainly on Blvd. St. Laurent and the now defunct Northeastern Lunch. It is popular among the criminal element of both French and English extraction. A long period without narcotics, an accidental encounter with a relative or former parish priest, an interview with a social worker or jazz anthropologist is known as "Cash-Work" or "Un job de cash."
4. The introduction of the narcotic into a vein. The hypodermic needle is secured to a common eyedropper by means of a narrow cardboard "collar."
5. Coprophagist's[ab] argot for anything fake or artificial. Originally a term of scorn, it is sometimes employed as an expression of surprised endearment, as in "Why, you little peanut!" or the more explicit French "Quelle cacahuète!" The term originated among the orthodox when a splinter group of "Marranos" in Ontario began using peanut butter in cult rituals in a bid for respectability and community acceptance. In the addict's vocabulary it describes a pure drug which has been adulterated with flour, milk sugar, or quinine so as to increase its volume and multiply its market value.
6. Originally heroin and the "hard drugs," but now in general use for any euphorant from the harmless Indian hemp to the innocuous aspirin. It is interesting to note that users of heroin are chronically constipated,[c] the drug rendering the bowels inactive.
7. "To keep" or "to hold" can mean, in addicts' argot, the condition

THE LAST FOUR YEARS OF TEKAKWITHA'S LIFE
AND THE ENSUING MIRACLES

1.

There was a convert to Christianity named Okenratarihen, who was an Onneyout chief. He was very zealous in
his new faith, just as he had been in his old life. His
name means Cendre Chaude, or Hot Cinder, and this
was a description of his nature. It was his dream that
all the Mohawks would embrace the new pale God.
In 1677 he organized an apostolic mission into the territory of the Iroquois. He took with him a Huron from
Lorette, and another convert who, by "coincidence" (if
we wish to diminish Providence by the term), was a
relative of Catherine Tekakwitha. The first village they
came to was Kahnawaké, the same village where lived
our neophyte and her confessor, le P. de Lamberville.
Okenratarihen was a superb orator. He held the village
spellbound, and Catherine Tekakwitha listened as he
told about his new life in the mission of Sault Saint-
Louis.

—The spirit was not with me before. I lived like an

---

of possessing narcotics with a view to selling them rather than con-
suming them oneself.

a. κοπρος (kopros) — Greek for dung, of course. But compare
with the Sanskrit čakrt, meaning manure. Think of yourself as a
sponge diver, darling. Do you comprehend how many fathoms
crush your mossy fumbling?

b. φαγειν (phag-ein) — to eat, in Greek. But look at the Sanskrit:
bhájati — to *share*, partake; bháksati — to *enjoy*, consume; bhágaš
— *happiness*, wealth. The very words you use are shadows on the
sunless ocean floor. None of them carries a lesson or a prayer.

c. Con-stipatum, Latin past participle of stipare — to pack, press,
stuff, cram. Cognate with the Greek στῖφος (stiphos) — "a heap
firmly pressed together." Today in modern Athens το στῖφος
means a thick crowd, a swarm, a horde. I'm feeding the cables
down to you, friend, so that you can begin to breathe, and soon,
because of me, you will grow your own lovely silver gills.

animal. Then I heard about the Great Spirit, the true Master of the sky and the earth, and now I live like a man.

Catherine Tekakwitha wanted to go to this place which he described so vividly. Le P. de Lamberville wished to secure the remarkable child in a more hospitable Christian environment, so he listened sympathetically to her request. Happily, her uncle was at Fort Orange (Albany) trading with the English. The priest knew that her aunts would not resist any plan that removed the girl from their midst. Okenratarihen wished to continue his mission, so it was decided that Catherine should escape with his two companions. The preparations were brief and secret. Early in the morning they launched their canoe. Le P. de Lamberville blessed them as they paddled into the drifts of mist. In her hand Catherine held a letter to the Fathers at Sault. She whispered to herself.

—Good-by, my village. Good-by, my homeland.

They followed the Mohawk River in its eastern course, then north up the Hudson River, which was laced with vegetative obstacles, huge overhanging branches, tangled vines, impenetrable thickets. They entered Lac Saint-Sacrement, which today is called Lake George, grateful for its still waters. They continued due north, into Lake Champlain, up the Richelieu River to Fort Chambly. Here they abandoned the canoe and traveled by foot through the thick forests, which, even today, cover the south bank of the Saint Lawrence River. In the autumn of 1677 the three reached the mission Saint-François-Xavier de Sault Saint-Louis. That is all you have to know. Do not ponder the promise to her uncle which Catherine Tekakwitha broke. It will soon come clear that Catherine Tekakwitha was not bound by secular vows. Do not worry about her old uncle humming a desolate love song, as he tried to pick her trail out of the falling leaves.

2.

I've got to go fast because the organs of Mary Voolnd will not buzz forever in sexual surprise like an eternal pinball machine and maybe even my four-fingered hand will tire. But I will give you everything you have to know. The priests in charge of the mission were le P. Pierre Cholenec and le P. Claude Chauchetière, our old sources. They read the letter which the girl carried: "Catherine Tegakouita will live at Sault. Kindly assume responsibility for her direction. Soon you will know the treasure we have given you. Qu'entre vos mains, il profite à la gloire de Dieu and to the health of a soul which assuredly is dear to Him." The girl was assigned to the cabin of Anastasie, an old woman who was one of the first converted Iroquois, and who, "coincidentally," had known Catherine Tekakwitha's Algonquin mother. The child loved the mission, it seemed. She knelt at the foot of the wooden cross on the shore of the Saint Lawrence, and there beyond the boiling water, the distant green horizon, and the mountain of Ville-Marie. Behind her was the tranquil Christian village, and all the meaningful tortures which I shall describe. The place of the cross by the river was her favorite spot, and I imagine she spoke to the fishes and raccoons and herons.

3.

Here is the most important incident of her new life. In the winter of 1678-1679 another marriage project developed. Everybody, even Anastasie, wanted Catherine

Tekakwitha to have her cunt opened. Here in this
Christian village, or there among the heathens, it was
all the same. Every community was, by its nature, ulti-
mately secular. But she had sailed her cunt away and
it did not matter who came to claim it, a Mohawk
brave or a Christian hunter. There was a nice young
fellow they had in mind. Not only that, but the relative
who had rescued her and who provided for her sustenance hadn't thought for a moment that misty morning that he was assuming a lifetime economic obligation.

—I won't eat anything.

—It's not the food, dear. It's just unnatural.

She ran in tears to le P. Cholenec. He was a wise man
who lived in the world, lived in the world, lived in the
world.

—Well, my child, they have a point.

—Arrrrggghhhh!

—Think about the future. The future starves.

—I don't care what happens to my body.

But you care about her body, don't you, my old
friend and disciple?

4.

There was great fervor in the mission. Nobody liked his
skin too much. Their pre-baptismal sins hung about
their necks like the heavy tooth necklaces they had
thrown away, and they sought to erase those old shadows with rigorous penitence. "Ils en faisaient une
rigoureuse pénitence," says le P. Cholenec. Here are
some of the things they did. Think of the village as a
mandala or a Brueghel game painting or a numbered
diagram. Look down at the mission and see the bodies
distributed here and there, look down from a hovering

helicopter at the distribution of painful bodies in the snow. Surely this is a diagram to be memorized on the cushion of your thumb. I haven't got time to make this description gory. Just read it through the prism of your personal blisters, and of those blisters choose the one you got by mistake. They liked to draw blood from their bodies, they liked to pull some of their blood outside. Some wore iron harnesses with spikes on the inside. Some wore iron harnesses to which they attached a load of wood which they dragged everywhere they went. Here is a naked woman rolling in the 40-below snow. Here is another woman buried up to her neck in a drift beside the frozen river, reciting her Rosary in this strange position, and let us remember that the Indian translation of this angelic salutation takes twice as long to say as the French one. Here is a naked man chopping a hole in the ice, and then he lowers himself in up to his waist, and then he recites "plusieurs dizaines de chapelet." He pulls out his body like an ice mermaid, the erection perpetuated as it formed. Here is a woman who took her three-year-old daughter into the hole, because she wanted to expiate the child's sins in advance. They waited for the winter, these converts, and they stretched their bodies before it, and it passed over them like a huge iron comb. Catherine Tekakwitha got an iron harness and she stumbled through her duties. Like St. Thérèse she could say, "Ou souffrir, ou mourir." Catherine Tekakwitha came to Anastasie and asked:

—What do you think is the most horrible painful thing?

—My daughter, I don't know anything worse than fire.

—Me neither.

This is a documented conversation. It took place on a

Canadian winter across the solid river from Montréal in 1678. Catherine waited until everyone was asleep. She went down to the cross beside the river and built a fire. Then she spent several slow hours caressing her pathetic legs with hot coals, just as the Iroquois did to their slaves. She had seen it done and she always wanted to know what it felt like. Thus she branded herself a slave to Jesus. I refuse to make this interesting, old friend, it wouldn't be good for you, and all my training might be for nothing. This is not an entertainment. This is play. Besides, you know what pain looks like, that kind of pain, you've been inside newsreel Belsen.

5.

Kneeling at the root of the wood cross Catherine Tekakwitha prayed and fasted. She did not pray that her soul should be favored in heaven. She did not fast so that her marriage would never nourish history. She did not cut her stomach with stones so that the mission would prosper. She did not know why she prayed and fasted. These mortifications she performed in a poverty of spirit. Never believe that the stigmata do not hurt. Never make a decision when you have to pee. Never stay in the room when your mother has her fortune told. Never think that the Prime Minister envies you. You see, darling, I have to trap you on an altar before I can tell you anything, otherwise my instruction is just a headline, just a fashion.

6.

She wandered through the leafy woods on the south bank of the Saint Lawrence River. She saw the deer start from the thicket, listening even in the arc of his leap. She saw the rabbit disappear into his burrow. She heard the squirrel rattling in his hoard of acorns. She watched a pigeon building a nest in a pine tree. In two hundred years the pigeons would sell out and loaf on statues in Dominion Square. She saw the flocks of geese shaped like unstable arrow heads. She fell to her knees and she cried, "O Master of Life, must our bodies depend on these things?" Very still, she sat on the shore of the river. She saw the leaping sturgeon scattering drops like beads of wampum. She saw the bony perch, fast as a single flute note in a wild song. She saw the long silver pike and below him she saw the crawfish, each on his separate layer of water. Letting her fingers drift, she cried, "O Master of Life, must our bodies depend on these things?" Slowly she walked back to the mission. She saw the field of corn, yellow and dry, plumes and tassels rustling in the wind like a crowd of aged sacrificial dancers. She saw the little blueberry bushes and strawberry bushes and made a tiny cross out of two pine needles and a drop of spruce gum and erected it beside a fallen gooseberry. A robin listened as she wept, a fucking robin stopped in his tracks and listened. I have to start you off with fiction, such is your heritage. Now it was night and the whippoorwill raised his melancholy song like a ghostly teepee over her weeping, a teepee or a pyramid, from a long way off it has three sides, the tune of the whippoorwill. Some men deal in teepees, some in pyramids, and it does not seem to matter, but in 1966, and in your predicament—it matters! "O Master of Life," she cried, "must our bodies depend on these?" On Saturdays and Sundays Catherine Tekakwitha took no food at all. When they forced her to drink soup she would only do so after stirring ashes into it. "Elle se dédommageait en mêlant de la cendre à sa soupe."

7.

O God, forgive me, but I see it on my thumb, the whole wintry village looks like a Nazi medical experiment.

"On comparing five Iroquois heads, I find that they give an average internal capacity of eighty-eight cubic inches, which is within two inches of the Caucasian mean."—Morton, *Crania Americana*, page 195. It is remarkable that the internal capacity of the skulls of the barbarous American tribes is greater than that of either the Mexicans or Peruvians. "The difference in volume is chiefly confined to the occipital and basal portions"—in other words, to the region of animal propensities. See J. S. Phillips, *Admeasurements of Crania of the Principal Groups of Indians in the United States.*

This is a footnote by Francis Parkman on page 32 of his book about the Jesuits in North America, published in 1867. I memorized it while looking over your shoulder in the library. Do you understand, now, that with my photographic memory it would have been disastrous to hover too long beside your ear?

8.

Catherine Tekakwitha's best friend at the mission was a young widow who had been baptized under the name Marie-Thérèse. She was an Onneyout, her original name being Tegaigenta. She was a very beautiful young woman. At the mission of la Prairie she was famous for her disorderly conduct. In the winter of 1676 she left with her husband on a hunting expedition along the Outaouais River. There were eleven in the party, including an infant. It was a bad winter. Wind blew away the paw prints. Heavy snows made the track impossible. One of the party was killed and eaten. The baby ate some amid jokes. Then there was famine. First of all they ate some little pieces of skin which they had brought to make shoes with. Then they ate bark. Tegaigenta's husband became sick. She stood guard over him. Two hunters, a Mohawk and a Tsonnontouan, went after game. At the end of a week the Mohawk came back alone, empty-handed but burping. The party decided to press on. Tegaigenta refused to abandon her husband. The others left, winking. Two days later she rejoined the party. When she arrived the group was sitting around the widow of the Tsonnontouan and her two children. Before eating the three of them, one of the hunters asked Tegaigenta:

—How do the Christians regard anthropophagist meals? (repas d'anthropophage).

It didn't matter what she answered. She ran into the snow. She would be roasted next, she knew. She looked back over her sweaty sex life. She had come on the hunt without confessing. She asked God to forgive her and promised to change her life if she got back to the mission. Of the eleven persons who comprised the hunting party only five returned to la Prairie. Marie-Thérèse was one of them. The mission of la Prairie moved to Sault Saint-Louis in the autumn of 1676. The girls met shortly after Easter in 1678, in front of the little church which was nearing completion. Catherine began the

—Let's go inside, Marie-Thérèse.
—I don't deserve to, Catherine.
—Neither do I. What did it taste like?
—What part?
—In general.
—Pork.
—Strawberries taste like pork too.

9.

One always saw the girls together. They avoided the company of everyone else. They prayed together at the cross beside the river. They spoke only of God and things pertaining to God. Catherine looked at the young widow's body very carefully. She inspected the nipples which had been chewed by men. They were lying on the soft moss.

—Turn over.

She looked down at the naked haunches, etched delicately with fern prints.

Then Catherine described to her friend exactly what she saw. Then it was her turn to lie face down.

—I can't see anything different.

—I didn't think so.

10.

She gave up eating on Wednesdays. On Saturday they prepared for Confession by whipping each other with birch switches. Catherine always insisted on getting undressed first. "Catherine, toujours la première pour la pénitence, se mettait à genoux et recevait les coups de verges." Why did she insist on being beaten first? Because, when it was her turn to whip, her effort would aggravate the lash opening she had received at the hand of her friend. Catherine always complained that Marie-Thérèse was not doing it hard enough, and permitted her to stop only when her shoulders were covered with blood, enough blood to drip onto leaves: that was the test of how much blood. Here is one of her prayers, as recorded by le P. Claude Chauchetière:

—My Jesus, I have to take chances with you. I love you but I have offended you. I am here to fufill your law. Let me, my God, take the burden of your anger. . . .

Here is the prayer in French, so that even in English translation this document will serve the Tongue:

—Mon Jésus, il faut que je risque avec vous: je vous aime, mais je vous ai offensé; c'est pour satisfaire à votre justice que je suis ici; déchargez, mon Dieu, sur moi votre colère. . . .

Sometimes, le P. Chauchetière tells us, she could not finish the prayer, but the tears in her eyes could. This material has a power of its own, doesn't it? So it wasn't all work in the library, was it? I think this writing is going to ruin the baskets in O.T.

11.

The war between the French and the Iroquois continued. The Indians asked some of their converted brethren at Sault to join them, promising them absolute freedom to practice their religion. When the converts refused the Iroquois kidnaped them and burnt them at the stake. One Christian named Etienne burned so bravely, crying the Gospel as he died, praying for the conversion of his tormentors, that the Indians were greatly impressed. Several of them applied for Baptism, desiring that ceremony which appeared to confer such courage. Since they had no intention of discontinuing their attacks on the French, they were refused.

—They should have got it, Catherine whispered to the blood smears. They should have got it. It doesn't matter what it's used for. Harder! Harder! What's the matter with you, Marie-Thérèse?

—It's my turn now.

—All right. But while I'm in this position I want to check something. Move your feet wider apart.

—Like this?

—Yes. I thought so. You've become a virgin.

12.

Catherine Tekakwitha secretly gave up eating on Mondays and Tuesdays. This is of prime interest to you, especially in regard to your bowel complication. I have other vital intelligence for you. Theresa Neuman, a Bavarian peasant girl, refused to take any solid food after April 25, 1923. A little while later she declared that she no longer felt the need to eat. For 33 years, right through the Third Reich and Partition, she lived without food. Mollie Francher, who died in Brooklyn in 1894, received no food for years. Mother Beatrice Mary of Jesus, a Spanish contemporary of Catherine Tekakwitha, fasted for long periods. One of them lasted 51 days. During Lent, if she smelled meat, she went into convulsions. Try and think back. Do you remember Edith ever eating? Do you remember those plastic bags she wore inside her blouse? Do you remember that birthday when she leaned over to blow out the candles and ruined the cake with vomit?

13.

Catherine Tekakwitha became seriously sick. Marie-Thérèse told the priests the details of their excess. Le P. Cholenec gently forced Catherine to promise not to perform her penitence so rigorously. This was the second secular promise which she broke. She regained her health slowly, if the word health can be used to describe her chronically feeble state.

—Father, may I take the Oath of Virginity?

—Virginitate placuit.

—Yes?

—You will be the first Iroquois Virgin.

It was on the day of the Annunciation, March 25,

1679, that Catherine Tekakwitha formally offered her body to the Savior and His Mother. The marriage question was resolved. She made the Fathers very happy with this secular offering. The little church was filled with bright candles. She loved the candles, too. Charity! Charity for us who love the candles only, or the Love which the candles make manifest. In some great eye I believe the candles are perfect currency, just as are all the Andacwandets, the Fuck Cures.

14.

Le P. Chauchetière and le P. Cholenec were baffled. Catherine's body was covered with bleeding wounds. They watched her, they spied at her kneeling before the wooden cross beside the river, they counted the lashes she and her companion exchanged, but they could detect no excessive indulgence. On the third day they became alarmed. She looked like death. "Son visage n'avait plus que la figure d'un mort." They could no longer attribute her physical decline to her ordinary infirmity. They questioned Marie-Thérèse. The girl confessed. That night the priests came into Catherine Tekakwitha's cabin. Wrapped tightly in blankets, the Indian girl was sleeping. They tore off the blankets. Catherine was not sleeping. She only pretended. Nobody in the midst of that pain could sleep. With all the skill she had used to weave the belts of wampum, the girl had sewn thousands of thorns into her blanket and mat. Every movement of her body opened up a new source of outside blood. How many nights had she tortured herself like this? She was naked in the firelight, her flesh streaming.

—Don't move!

—Stop moving!

—I'll try.

—You moved!
—I'm sorry.
—You moved again!
—It's the thorns.
—We know it's the thorns.
—Of course we know it's the thorns.
—I'll try.
—Try.
—I'm trying.
—Try to keep still.
—You moved!
—He's right.
—I didn't exactly move.
—What did you do?
—I twitched.
—Twitched?
—I didn't exactly move.
—You twitched?
—Yes.
—Stop twitching!
—I'll try.
—She's killing herself.
—I'm trying.
—You're twitching!
—Where?
—Down there.
—That's better.
—Look at your thigh!
—What?
—It's twitching.
—I'm sorry.
—You're mocking us.
—I promise I'm not.
—Stop!
—The buttock!

—It's twitching!

—Elbow!

—Wha?

—Twitching.

—Kneecap. Kneecap. KNEECAP.

—Twitching?

—Yes.

—Her whole body is twitching.

—She can't control it.

—She's tearing her skin off.

—She's trying to listen to us.

—Yes. She is trying.

—She always tries.

—Give her that, Claude.

—Those thorns are ugly.

—They make an ugly thorn.

—Child?

—Yes, Father.

—We know you're in terrible pain.

—It's not so bad.

—Don't fib.

—Did she tell an untruth?

—We think you're up to something, Catherine.

—There!

—That wasn't a twitch.

—That was a deliberate move.

—Bring the fire closer.

—Let's have a look at her.

—I don't think she can hear us any more.

—She seems so far away.

—Look at her body.

—It seems so far away.

—She looks like a painting, sort of.

—Yes, so far away.

—This is some night.

—Hmmm.

—Like one of those paintings that bleed.

—Like one of those icons that weep.

—So far away.

—She is at our feet but I have never seen anyone so far away.

—Touch one of those thorns.

—You.

—Ouch!

—I thought so. They're real.

—I'm glad we're priests, aren't you, Claude?

—Terribly happy.

—She's losing a lot of blood.

—Can she hear us?

—Child?

—Catherine?

—Yes, my Fathers.

—Can you hear us?

—Yes.

—What do we sound like?

—You sound like machinery.

—Is it nice?

—It is beautiful.

—What kind of machinery?

—Ordinary eternal machinery.

—Thank you, my child. Thank her, Claude.

—Thank you.

—Will this night ever end?

—Will we ever go back to bed?

—I doubt it.

—We'll stand here for a long time.

—Yes. Watching.

15.

Shakespeare is 64 years dead. Andrew Marvell is 2 years dead. John Milton is 6 years dead. We are now in the heart of the winter of 1680. We are now in the heart of our pain. We are now in the heart of our evidence. Who could have told it would take so long? Who could have told when I entered the woman with my quick and my wit? Somewhere you are listening to my voice. So many are listening. There is an ear on every star. Somewhere you are dressed in hideous rags and wondering who I was. Does my voice sound like yours at last? Did I assume too much when I sought to unburden you? I covet Catherine Tekakwitha now that I have followed her last years. I the pimp am I the customer. Old friend, was all this preparation for nothing but cemetery triangle? We are now in the heart of our pain. Is this what longing is? Is my pain as valuable as yours? Did I give up the Bowery too easily? Who tied the reins of government into a love knot? Can I ride in the Magic I enfueled? Is this the meaning of Temptation? We are now in the heart of our agony. Galileo. Kepler. Descartes. Alessandro Scarlatti is 20 years old. Who will exhume Brigitte Bardot and see if her fingers bleed? Who will test the sweet smell in the tomb of Marilyn Monroe? Who will slip with James Cagney's head? Is James Dean flexible? O God, the dream leaves fingerprints. Ghost tracks on the powdered varnish! Do I want to be in the laboratory where Brigitte Bardot lies? I wanted to meet her on the leather beach when I was 20. The dream is a sheaf of clues. Hello, famous blonde naked, a ghost is speaking to your suntan as they unshovel you. I saw your open mouth hovering in formaldehyde. I think I could make you happy if we keep the money and guards. Even after the lights came up, the Cinerama screen continued to bleed. I quiet the crowd with a raised scarlet finger. On the white screen your erotic auto accident continues to bleed! I wanted to show Brigitte Bardot around revolutionary Montréal. We will meet when we are old, in an old dictator's cafeteria. Nobody knows who you are except the Vatican. We stumble on the truth: we could have made each other happy. Eva Peron! Edith! Mary Voolnd! Hedy Lamarr! Madame Bovary! Lauren Bacall was Marlene Dietrich! B.B., it is F., ghost from green daisies, from the stone pit of his orgasm, from the obscure mental factory of English Montréal. Lie down on my paper, little movie flesh. Let your towel preserve impressions of your bosom. Develop into a pervert in our private. Shock me with chemical or tongue request. Come out of the shower with your hair wet and rest your crossed shaved legs on my one-handed desk. Let the towel slide as you fall asleep during our first argument, while the fan heaves the same long wisp of golden path every time it faces you. O Mary, I have come back to you. I have returned up my arm to the true swatch of black body windows, the cunt of now, soak of the present. I led myself from Temptation and I *showed it happening!*

—You needn't have, says Mary Voolnd.

—No?

—No. It's all included in the so-called fuck.

—I can imagine whatever I want?

—Yes. But hurry!

16.

We are at the heart of the winter of 1680. Catherine Tekakwitha is cold and dying. This is the year she died. This is the big winter. She was too sick to leave the cabin. Secretly starving, the thorn mat continues to bounce her body like a juggler. Now the church was too far away. But, le P. Chauchetière tells us, she spent a part of each day on her knees or balanced on a crude bench. The trees came to beat her. We are now at the beginning of Holy Week before Easter, 1680. Holy Monday, she weakened considerably. They told her she was dying fast. As Marie-Thérèse caressed her with birch, Catherine prayed:

—O God, show me that the Ceremony belongs to Thee. Reveal to your servant a fissure in the Ritual. Change Thy World with the jawbone of a broken Idea. O my Lord, play with me.

At the mission there was a curious custom. They never carried the Holy Sacrament to the cabin where the sick lay. Instead, they carried the sick people on a bark stretcher to the chapel, hazardous as the trip was. The girl was definitely too sick for the stretcher ride. What were they to do? Customs were not that easily come by in early Canada, and they longed for a Jesus of Canada dignified by convention and antiquity, as He is today, pale and plastic above the guilty traffic tickets. This is why I love the Jesuits. They argued about to which they had the deepest obligation, History or Miracle, or to put it more heroically, History or Possible Miracle. They had seen a strange light in Catherine Tekakwitha's mucous eyes. Dare they deny her the supreme consolation of the Body of the Savior in His Viatique Change, the Wafer Disguise? They gave their answer to the dying girl, half naked among her thorn-torn rags. The crowd cheered. An exception was justified in the case of Perfectly Shy, as some of the converts had begun to call her. To dignify the occasion, we have the humble detail, Catherine asked Marie-

Thérèse to cover her with a new blanket or anything to hide her half-nakedness. The whole village followed the Holy Sacrament as it was borne to the cabin of the invalid. The crowd pressed around her mat, all the converted Indians of the mission. She was their best hope. The French were murdering their brethren in the forests, but this dying girl would somehow certify the difficult choices they had made. If ever there was gloom thickly laced with unmaterialized miracles, it was here, it was now. The voice of the priest began. After the general absolution, with ardent filmed eyes and bruised tongue, she received the "Viatique du Corps de Nôtre-Seigneur Jésus-Christ." Visibly she was dying now. Many of the staring crowd wanted to be remembered in the prayers of the departing girl. Le. P. Cholenec asked her if she would receive them individually. He asked her softly because she was in agony. She smiled and said she would. Throughout the whole day they filed by her mat with their burdens.

—I stepped on a beetle. Pray for me.

—I injured the waterfall with urine. Pray for me.

—I fell on my sister. Pray for me.

—I dreamed I was white. Pray for me.

—I let the deer die too slowly. Pray for me.

—I long for human morsel. Pray for me.

—I made a grass whip. Pray for me.

—I got the yellow out of a worm. Pray for me.

—I tried to grow an ointment beard. Pray for me.

—The west wind hates me. Pray for me.

—I darkened the old crop. Pray for me.

—I gave my rosary to the English. Pray for me.

—I soiled a loincloth. Pray for me.

—I killed a Jew. Pray for me.

—I sold beard ointment. Pray for me.

—I smoke manure. Pray for me.

—I forced my brother to watch. Pray for me.

—I smoke manure. Pray for me.

—I spoiled a singsong. Pray for me.

—I touched myself while paddling. Pray for me.

—I tortured a raccoon. Pray for me.

—I believe in herbs. Pray for me.

—I got the orange out of a scab. Pray for me.

—I prayed for a famine lesson. Pray for me.

—I dirtied on my beads. Pray for me.

—I'm 84. Pray for me.

One by one they kneeled and passed her bristling Lenin couch, leaving with her their pitiful spirit luggage, until the whole cabin resembled one vast Customs House of desire, and the mud beside her bearskin was polished by so many kneecaps that it shone like the silver sides of the last and only rocket scheduled to escape from the doomed world, and as the ordinary night fell over the Easter village the Indians and the Frenchmen huddled beside their barking fires, fingers pressed to their lips in gestures of hush and blowing kisses. Oh, why does it make me so lonely to tell this? After the evening prayers, Catherine Tekakwitha asked permission to go into the woods once more. Le P. Cholenec granted her the permission. She dragged herself past the cornfield under its blanket of melting snow, into the fragrant pine trees, into the powdery shadows of the forest, on the levers of broken fingernails she pulled herself through the dim March starlight, to the edge of the icy Saint Lawrence River, to the frozen root of the Crucifixion. Le P. Lecompte tells us, "Elle y passa un quart d'heure à se mettre les épaules en sang par une rude discipline." There she spent 15 minutes whipping her shoulders until they were covered with blood, and this she did without her friend. It is now the next day, Holy Wednesday. It was her last day, this day of consecration to the mysteries of the Eucharist and the Cross. "Certes je me souviens encore qu'à l'entrée de sa dernière maladie." Le P. Cholenec knew it was her last day. At three o'clock in the afternoon the final agony began. On her knees, praying with Marie-Thérèse and several other whipped girls, Catherine Tekakwitha stumbled over the names of Jesus and Mary mispronouncing them. ". . . elle perdit la parole en prononçant les noms de Jésus et de Marie." But why didn't you record the exact sounds she made? She was playing with the Name, she was mastering the good Name, she was grafting all the fallen branches to the living Tree. Aga? Muja? Jumu? You idiots, she knew the Tetragrammaton! You let her get away! We let another one get away! And now we have to see if her fingers bleed! We had her there, nailed and talkative, ready to undo the world, and we let the sharp mouths of the relic boxes gnaw at her bones. Parliament!

17.

She was dead at 3:30 in the afternoon. It was Holy Wednesday, April 17, 1680. She was 24 years old. We are in the heart of the afternoon. Le P. Cholenec was praying beside the new corpse. His eyes were closed. Suddenly he opened his eyes and cried out in amazement, "Je fis un grand cri, tant je fus saisi d'étonnement."

—Eeeeeoooowwww!

The face of Catherine Tekakwitha had turned white!

—Viens ici!

—Look at her face!

Let us examine the eyewitness account of le P. Cho-

lenec, and let us try to suppress our political judg-
ments, and remember that I promised you good news.
"From the age of four years, Catherine's face had been
branded by the Plague; her sickness and her mortifications had further contributed to the disfigurement. But
this face, so battered and so very swarthy, underwent
a sudden change, about a quarter of an hour after her
death. And in a moment she became so beautiful and
so white . . ."

—Claude!

Le P. Chauchetière came running, and a village of
Indians followed him. As if in peaceful sleep, as if under a parasol of glass, she floated into the dark Canadian
afternoon, her face serene and bright as alabaster. Thus
she launched her death, upturned face of white, under
the concentrated gaze of the village. Le P. Chauchetière
said:

—C'était un argument nouveau de crédibilité, dont
Dieu favorisait les sauvages pour leur faire goûter la foi.

—Shhhhhhh!

—Hush!

Two Frenchmen happened to be passing by later on.
One of them said:

—Look at that pretty girl sleeping there.

When they found out who it was, they knelt in
prayer.

—Let us make the coffin.

At that precise moment the girl entered the eternal
machinery of the sky. Looking back over her atomic
shoulder, she played a beam of alabaster over her old
face as she streamed forward on the insane grateful
laughter of her girl friend.

18.

Red and white, skin and pimples, open daisies and burning weeds—*pace*, old friend and all you racists. Let it be our skill to create legends out of the disposition of the stars, but let it be our glory to forget the legends and watch the night emptily. Let the mundane Church serve the White Race with a change of color. Let the mundane Revolution serve the Gray Race with a burning church. Let the Manifestoes attach all our property. We are in love with a tower view of rainbow bodies. Suffer the change from red to white, you who weave insignia, which is all of us in our night. But we are merely once upon a time. Another second from our raw fingers, now we are in love with pure flags, our privacy is valueless, we do not own our history, it is borne away in a shower of tiny seed dust and we filter it as in the network of a high drift of wild daisies, and our fashions change beautifully. A kite climbs over the hospital, some O.T. prisoners follow or ignore it, Mary and I, we slip into the orgy of vase Greeks and restaurant Greeks. A new butterfly rollercoasts on the jerky wax shadows of the greenery, small circus falls like air-pocketed kite, the village parachutist essays the tipping fern, plunging in blur Icarus postage stamps. Montréal laundry flaps from the high rent—but I fail perfectly naturally, since I've elected to swell the Fact Charity. Here is good news for most of us: all parties and churches may use this information. St. Catherine of Bologna dies in 1463, a nun of fifty. Her sisters buried her body without a casket. Soon the sisters felt guilty, wondering about all the weight of mud on her face. They were given permission to exhume the body. They scrape her face clean. It is found to have been only slightly distorted by pressure of the mud, perhaps a collapsed nostril the only trophy of 18 days' interment. The body smelled sweet. As they examined it, "the body that was white as snow turned slowly red and exuded an oily liquid of an ineffable fragrance."

19.

The funeral of Catherine Tekakwitha. Anastasie and Marie-Thérèse worked softly over the body. They washed her limbs, stroked away the dried blood. They combed her hair and rubbed oil into it. They dressed her in white beaded robes of skin. With new moccasins they covered her two feet. Usually a corpse was carried to the church on a bark stretcher. The Frenchmen had made her a real coffin, "un vrai cercueil."

—Don't close it!

—Let me see!

The crowd had to be satisfied. They longed to contemplate her new beauty for another hour. We are now in Holy Thursday, day of sadness, day of joy, as her biographers observe. From the church they carried her to the great cross of the cemetery situated beside the river, where the girl loved to forge her prayers. Le P. Chauchetière and le P. Cholenec had argued about the location of the grave. Le P. Chauchetière wanted to bury her inside the church. Le P. Cholenec wished to avoid this singularity. During another grave-digging in which Catherine had participated, the priest had heard her state her own personal preference—beside the river.

—Then I give in.

The next day was Holy Friday. The missionaries preached the passion of Christ Jesus to an audience seized with the deepest emotion. They wanted to weep for longer time. They wouldn't let the celebrant get past the first two words of the *Vexilla*.

—Vexilla re—

—No! No! Sob! Arrgghh!

—Vexilla regis—

—Stop! Time! Sob! Please!

That whole day and the next day, the priests witnessed the most excessive mortifications that they had ever seen.

—They're tearing themselves apart!

—It's happening!

On Friday night a woman rolled on thorns until the morning. Four or five nights later another woman did the same.

—Bring the fire closer.

They beat themselves until they bled. They crawled on their bare knees through the snow. Widows vowed never to remarry. Young married women took the vow and renounced remarriage should their husbands die. Married couples separated and promised to live as brother and sister. Le P. Chauchetière cites the good François Tsonnatoüan, who turned his wife into a sister. He made a little rosary which he called "Catherine's Rosary." It consisted of a cross on which he said the *Credo*, two "grains" for the *Pater* and the *Ave*, and three other "grains" for the three *Gloria Patri*. The news was passed from fire to fire, from convert to convert, from convert to heathen, from heathen to heathen, across the land of the Iroquois.

—La sainte est morte.

—The saint is dead.

In the early Church this type of popular recognition was called *la béatification équipollente*. Look down, look down, see the snowy mandala, see the whole village, see the figures writhing on the white field, try and see through the opaque prism of personal blister of accidental burn.

20.

Here is the testimony of Captain du Luth, commandant of Fort Frontenac, a man after whom a Montréal street is named. He was, says le P. Charlevoix, "un des plus braves officiers que le Roy ait eus dans cette colonie." He also gave his name to an American city on Lake Superior.

I, the undersigned, certify to whomever it may concern, that, having been tormented with the gout for twenty-three years, with such pain that for a space of three months I had no rest, I addressed myself to Catherine Tegahkouita, Iroquois virgin, deceased at Sault Saint-Louis a saint in the general opinion, and I promised to visit her grave, if God would give me back my health because of her intervention. I have been so perfectly cured, at the end of a novena which I arranged to be done in her honor, that for fifteen months now I have not suffered a single attack of gout.

Fait au fort Frontenac, ce 15 août 1696.

Signé J. du Luth

21.

Like a numbered immigrant in the harbor of North America, I hope to begin again. I hope to begin my friendship again. I hope to begin my rise to President. I hope to begin Mary again. I hope to begin my worship again to Thee who has never refused my service, in whose flashing memory I have no past or future, whose memory never froze into the coffin of history, into which your children, like amateur undertakers, squeeze the carelessly measured bodies of each other. Not the pioneer is the American dream, for he has already limited himself by courage and method. The dream is to be immigrant sailing into the misty aerials of New York, the dream is to be Jesuit in the cities of the Iroquois, for we do not wish to destroy the past and its baggy failures, we only wish the miracles to demonstrate that the past was joyously prophetic, and that possibility occurs to us most plainly on this cargo deck of wide lapels, our kerchief sacks filled with obsolete machine guns from the last war but which will astound and conquer the Indians.

22.

The first vision of Catherine Tekakwitha appeared to le P. Chauchetière. Five days after the girl's death, at four o'clock in the morning of Easter Monday, while he was hard at prayer, she came to him in a blur of glory. At her right was a church upside down. At her left was an Indian burning at the stake. The vision lasted two hours, and the priest had time to study it in ecstasy. This is why he had come to Canada. Three years later, in 1683, a hurricane hit the village, tipping over the 60-foot-long church. And in one of the attacks on the mission, an Iroquois convert was captured by the Onnontagués and burnt slowly while he proclaimed his Faith. These applications of the vision may satisfy the Church, dear friend, but let us beware of allowing an apparition to leak away into mere events. A useless church, a tortured man—are these not the usual factors in a saint's flourishing? Eight days after her death she appeared to the old Anastasie in a blaze of light, her lower body beneath the belt dissolved in the brilliance, "le bas du corps depuis la ceinture disparaissant dans cette clarté." Had she lent her other parts to you? She appeared also to Marie-Thérèse when she was alone in her cabin and gently reproached her for some of the things she was doing.

—Try not to sit on your heel when you're beating your shoulders.

Le P. Chauchetière was favored with two more

visions, one on July 1, 1681, the other on April 21, 1682. On both occasions Catherine appeared to him in her beauty, and he heard her say distinctly:

—Inspice et fac secundum exemplar. Regarde, et copie ce modèle. Look, and copy this model.

Then he painted many portraits of his visionary Catherine, and they worked perfectly when placed on the head of the sick. At Caughnawaga today there is a very ancient canvas. Is this the one that le P. Chauchetière painted? We will never know. I pray that it will work for you. But what about le P. Cholenec? All the others had their candy. Where were his movies? It is he whom I most resemble, as he endures without so much as a cartoon spark, hunted only by the Papacy.

23.

". . . An infinity of miraculous cures," writes le P. Cholenec in 1715, "une infinité de guérisons miraculeuses." Not only among the savages but even among the French at Québec and Montréal. It would take volumes. He calls her *la Thaumaturge du Nouveau-Monde*. With a sense of pain you must now be able to imagine, I record some of the cures.

The wife of François Roaner was 60 during January 1681 and close to death. She was an inhabitant of la Prairie de la Magdeleine, where le P. Chauchetière was also serving. The priest hung a crucifix around her neck. It was the same crucifix that Catherine Tekakwitha had grasped to her rags while dying. When Mme. Roaner was cured she refused to surrender the relic. The priest insisted but gave the woman a little bag of mud from the tomb of Catherine to hang in place of the crucifix. Some time later, she happened to take it off for one reason or another. As soon as it was clear of her head she collapsed, stricken to the ground. It was only when the bag returned to her chest that she recovered once again. A year later, her husband was seized by a violent pain in the kidneys. In a reckless instant of charity she removed the mud from her person and hung it over his neck. His pain stopped immediately, but she staggered, stricken again, crying out that her husband was murdering her. He was persuaded by several bystanders to return the little sack to his wife. She was instantly cured but his kidneys began again. Let us leave them here, in their new cruel service to Catherine Tekakwitha, as she invites their souls. Is this familiar, dear comrade? Did Edith move between us like a package of mud? Oh God, I see the miserable old Roaners, who had not touched each other for years, clawing each other like animals on the stone floor of their kitchen.

In 1693 the Superior at Sault was le P. Bruyas. Suddenly his arms became paralyzed. He was removed to Montréal to receive treatment. Before he left he asked the *Sisters of Catherine*, a group of devotees which had formed around her memory, to do a novena on behalf of his cure. In Montréal he refused all treatment. On the eighth day of the novena there was still no change in his stiff arms. Faithful, he kept the doctors away. Four o'clock on the next morning he awakened waving his arms, not surprised, but ravished with joy. He hurried to thank.

1695. The cures began to creep into the upper classes like a dance step. They began with the Intendant, M. de Champigny. For two years he had had the same cold, which worsened day by day, until now he could barely make himself heard. His wife wrote the Fathers at Sault, begging them to have a novena done to their holy girl in order to obtain her husband's cure. The prayers they chose for the novena were one *Pater*, one *Ave*, and three *Gloria Patri*. M. de Champigny's throat cleared up day by day, and on the ninth day it was normal—indeed, his voice possessed a special new resonance. Mme. de Champigny extended the cult of the Iroquois Virgin. She had thousands of Catherine Tekakwitha pictures distributed everywhere, including France, and even Louis XIV looked carefully at one.

1695. M. de Granville and his wife mixed the mud with a little water and fed it to their little daughter, who was dying. She sat up laughing.

"The power of Catherine extended itself even to animals," writes le P. Cholenec. In Lachine lived a woman with only one cow. One day, for no apparent reason, the cow became so bloated, "enflée," that the woman thought the beast would die. She fell to her knees.

—O good holy Catherine, have pity on me, save my poor cow!

She had barely spoken the words when the cow began to unswell, returning to its ordinary size right before her eyes, "et la vache s'est bien portée du depuis."

Last winter, writes le P. Cholenec, a steer fell through the ice in Montréal. They hauled him out but his body was so frozen that he couldn't walk. He was obliged to spend the winter in his stable.

—Kill that animal! commanded the master of the house.

—Oh, let him live one more night, a servant girl pleaded.

—Very well. But he dies tomorrow!

She put some of the tomb mud which she cherished into the steer's drinking water, saying:

—Pourquoi Catherine ne guérirait-elle pas les bêtes aussi bien que les hommes?

This is the actual quotation. The next morning the steer was found on his feet, to the great astonishment of all except the girl and the animal. The most important question the histories naturally ignore. Were the cow and the steer eventually eaten? Or did nothing really change?

Thousands of cures, all recorded, among children and among the senile. A thousand novenas and a thousand bodies glow again. Twenty years after her death the miracles were not so frequent, but we have evidence as recent as 1906. Let us examine the April 1906 edition of *Le Messager Canadien du Sacre-Coeur*. The miracle took place at Shishigwaning, an Indian outpost on Ile Manitouline. Living there was a good Indian woman (une bonne sauvagesse) who had been afflicted, for the past 11 months, with syphilis ulcers in the mouth and throat. She had contracted the disease by smoking the pipe which belonged to her syphilitic daughter, "en fumant la pipe dont s'était servie sa fille." The disease advanced hideously, the ulcers spreading and widening their circumferences and their crater depth. She couldn't even take a little soup, so swollen with sores was her mouth. The priest arrived September 29, 1905. Before becoming a Jesuit he had been a doctor. She knew this.

—Help me, Doctor.

—I am a priest.

—Help me as a doctor.

—No doctor can help you now.

He told her that her cure was beyond human dominion. He pressed the victim to ask for the intercession of Catherine Tekakwitha, "your sister by blood!" That night she began a novena in honor of the long-dead Iroquois Virgin. One day passed, two days passed, nothing happened. On the third day, she sent her tongue searching over the roof of her mouth, but the syphilis Braille had disappeared like the volumes of Alexandria!

24.

In 1689 the mission of Sault Saint-Louis moved farther up the Saint Lawrence River. The reason for the exodus was soil exhaustion. The old location (at the place where the Portage River enters the Saint Lawrence) had been called Kahnawaké, or, at the rapids. Now it took the name *Kateri tsi tkaiatat*, or, the place where Catherine was buried. They took her body with them to the new village which was called Kahnawakon, or, in the rapids. They called the abandoned site *Kanatakwenké*, or, place of the removed village. In 1696 they moved once again up the south bank of the great river. The last migration took place on 1719. The mission installed itself in its present location, across the rapids opposite Lachine, now connected by a bridge to Montréal. It took the Iroquois name of 1676, Kahnawaké, or in its English form, Caughnawaga. There are still some relics of Catherine Tekakwitha at Caughnawaga, but not all. Some of her skeleton had been given away at different periods. Her head was carried to Saint-Régis in 1754, to celebrate the establishment of another Iroquois mission. The church in which the head was placed burned to the ground, and the skull did not survive.

KATERI TEKAKWITHA
Apr. 17, 1680
Onkweonweke Katsitsiio
Teotsitsianekaron

KATERI TEKAKWITHA
17 avril, 1680
La plus belle fleur épanouie
chez les sauvages

THE END OF F.'S HISTORY OF THE LAST FOUR YEARS OF CATHERINE TEKAKWITHA'S LIFE

There! Done! Dear old friend, I did what was necessary! I did what I dreamed about when you, Edith, and I sat on the austere seats of the System Theatre. Do you know the question with which I tormented myself during those silvery hours? At last I can tell you. We are now in the heart of the System Theatre. We are in the dark jockeying for elbow dominion on the wooden armrests. Outside on Ste. Catherine Street, the theater marquee displays the only neon failure in miles of light: dropping two letters which will never be repaired, it signals itself as stem Theatre, stem Theatre, stem Theatre. Secret kabals of vegetarians habitually gather under the sign to exchange contraband from beyond the Vegetable Barrier. In their pinpoint eyes dances their old dream: the Total Fast. One of them reports a new atrocity published without compassionate comment by the editors of *Scientific American*: "It has been established that, when pulled from the ground, a radish produces an electronic scream." Not even the triple bill for 65¢ will comfort them tonight. With a mad laugh born of despair, one of them throws himself on a hotdog stand, disintegrating on the first chew into pathetic withdrawal symptoms. The rest watch him mournfully and then separate into the Montréal entertainment section. The news is more serious than any of them thought. One is ravished by a steak house with sidewalk ventilation. In a restaurant, one argues with the waiter that he ordered "tomato" but then in a suicide of gallantry he agrees to accept the spaghetti, meat sauce mistake. But this is far away from the glass pillar of stubs which the three of us passed and satisfied hours ago. Let us not forget that these doorway ticket depositories are not altogether docile. On more than several occasions I have stood behind a customer whose stub the chute rejects absolutely, and he is forced to get his money back from the contemptuous female sentry booth. They are not pleasant to deal with, these women posted in the entrances of every cinema: they are bound by choice to guard Ste. Catherine Street against self-destruction: the little streetside offices which they dominate protect the army of traffic by an administration which combines the best functions of Red Cross and G.H.Q. And what of the unacceptable patron with his money back? Where can he go? Was the cruel rejection arbitrary, in the sense that Society invents Crime so as to make itself indispensable? There is no dark for him to eat the Oh Henry!—all candy is threatened! Mere suicide vaudeville for the living? Or is there some ointment on the refusal of the toothed throat of the stub depository? Is this the kingly oil of election? Does some new hero discover his ordeal? Is this the birth of the hermit, or his equally passionate complement, the anti-hermit, seed of the Jesuits? And this chess side choice between saint and missionary, is this his first tragic testing? No matter to Edith, you and I, who have safely passed two aisles and half an alphabet, well into the bright amusement. We are now in the heart of the last feature in the System Theatre. Within severe limits, like smoke in a chimney, the dusty projection beam above our hair twisted and changed. Like crystals rioting in a test-tube suspension, the unstable ray changed and changed in its black confinement. Like battalions of sabotaged parachutists falling from the training tower straight down in various contortions, the frames streamed at the screen, splashing into contrast color as they hit, just as the bursting cocoons of arctic camouflage spread colorful organic contents over the snow as the divers disintegrate, one after the other. No, it was more like a ghostly white snake sealed in an immense telescope. It was a serpent swimming home, lazily occupying the entire sewer which irrigated the auditorium. It was the first snake in the shadows of the original garden, the albino orchard snake offering our female memory the taste of—everything! As it floated and danced and writhed in the gloom over us, I often raised my eyes to consult the projection beam rather than the story it carried. Neither of you noticed me. Sometimes I conceded surprising territories of the armrest so as to distract your pleasure. I studied the snake and he made me greedy for everything. In the midst of this heady contemplation, I am invited to formulate the question which will torment me most. I formulate the question and it begins to torment me immediately: *What will happen when the newsreel escapes into the Feature?* What will happen when the newsreel occurs at its own pleasure or accident in any whatever frame of the Vistavision, willy nilly? The newsreel lies between the street and the Feature like Boulder Dam, vital as a border in the Middle East—breach it (so I thought), and a miasmal mixture will imperialize existence by means of its sole quality of total corrosion. So I thought! The newsreel lies between the street and the Feature: like a tunnel on the Sunday drive it ends quickly and in creepy darkness joins the rural mountains to the slums. It took courage! I let the newsreel escape, I invited it to walk right into plot, and they merged in aweful originality, just as trees and plastic synthesize new powerful landscapes in those districts of the highway devoted to motels. Long live motels, the name, the motive, the success! Here is my message, old lover of my heart. Here is what I saw: here is what I learned:

Sophia Loren Strips For A Flood Victim
THE FLOOD IS REAL AT LAST

Joy? Didn't I promise it? Didn't you believe I would deliver? And now I must leave you, but I find it so hard. Mary is restless now, she is jiggling restlessly, neither of us has any pleasure now, and some of her fluids are so ancient and unreplenished that there are pinchy paths of evaporation down my arm. Patients in O.T. are signing unfinished baskets so they can be identified in the nurse's collection. The short spring afternoon has darkened and the tight lilac buds beyond the barred window are barely redolent. The afternoon linen has been sterilized and crisp folded beds require us.

—Bow wow wow! Bow wow! Grrrrrrr!

—What's that commotion outside, Mary?

—Just the dogs.

—The dogs? I didn't know there were going to be dogs.

—Well, there are. Now hurry! Pull it out!

—My hand?

—The package! The oilskin package!

—Must I?

—It's from our friends!

With some fishlike movement she maneuvered her haunches, altering all the internal architecture of her cunt reception. Like a trout dragging the hook into the roof of its mouth, some blunt delicious shelf of miniature fountains applied the oilskin package to my hooked four fingers, and I withdrew it. Her wide white uniform shielded me from curiosity as I read the message. I am reading it now, as Mary Voolnd insists.

ANCIENT PATRIOT

FIRST FATHER PRESIDENT

THE REPUBLIC SALUTES YOUR SERVICE

WITH ITS HIGHEST HONOR

the escape is planned for tonight

is scribbled in invisible ink which her lubrications have activated! Tonight.

—Grrrrrr! Arrooooof!

—I'm frightened, Mary.

—Don't worry.

—Can't we stay here a little longer?

_____

_____

_____

—See the pretty lines, Mary?

—Too late for sex, F.

—But I think I could be happy here. I think I could acquire the desolation I coveted so fiercely in my disciple.

—That's just it, F. Too easy.

—I want to stay, Mary.

—I'm afraid that's impossible, F.

—But I'm right on the edge, Mary. I'm almost broken, I've almost lost everything, I almost have humility!

—Lose it! Lose everything!

—Help! Haaaaaaallllllpppp! Somebody!

—Your screaming can't be heard, F. Come along.

—HAAAAAAAAAAAAALLLLLLLPPPPP!

—Click, clickclick. Bzzzzzzzzz. Sputter!

—What's that funny noise, Mary?

—Static. It's the radio, F.

—The radio! You didn't say anything about the radio.

—Quiet. It wants to tell us something.

(DOLLY IN TO CLOSE-UP OF THE RADIO ASSUMING THE FORM OF PRINT)

—This is the radio speaking. Good evening. The radio easily interrupts this book to bring you a recorded historical news flash: TERRORIST LEADER AT LARGE. Only minutes ago, an unidentified Terrorist Leader escaped from the Hospital for the Criminally Insane. It is feared that his presence in the city will touch off new revolutionary extremes. He was aided in his get-away by a female accomplice who had infiltrated the Hospital Staff. Mutilated by routine police dogs in a diversionary tactic, she is now undergoing surgery, but is not expected to survive. It is believed that the escaped criminal will attempt to contact terrorist strongholds in the forests beyond Montréal.

—Is it happening, Mary?

—Yes, F.

—Grrrrr! Chomp! Arararara! Erf!

—Mary!

—Run, F.! Run. Run!

—Bow wow! Hoooowwwwllll! Grrrrrrr! R-i-i-i-i-p!

(SALIVATING POLICE DOG JAWS TEAR INTO THE FLESH OF MARY VOOLND)

—Your body!

—Run! Run, F. Run for all of us A———s!

(CLOSE-UP OF RADIO EXHIBITING A MOTION PICTURE OF ITSELF)

—This is the radio speaking. Eeeek! Tee hee! This is the ah ha ha, this is the hee hee, this is the radio speaking. Ha ha ha ha ha ha, oh ho ho ho, ha ha ha ha ha ha, it tickles, it tickles! (SOUND EFFECT: ECHO CHAMBER) This is the radio speaking. Drop your weapons! This is the Revenge of the Radio.

And this is your lover, F., finishing the joyous letter which I promised. God bless you! Oh darling, be what I want to be!

Yours truly,
Signé F.

Book Three

Beautiful

Losers

An Epilogue in the Third Person

SPRING COMES into Québec from the west. It is the warm Japan Current that brings the change of season to the west coast of Canada, and then the West Wind picks it up. It comes across the prairies in the breath of the Chinook, waking up the grain and caves of bears. It flows over Ontario like a dream of legislation, and it sneaks into Québec, into our villages, between our birch trees. In Montréal the cafés, like a bed of tulip bulbs, sprout from their cellars in a display of awnings and chairs. In Montréal spring is like an autopsy. Everyone wants to see the inside of the frozen mammoth. Girls rip off their sleeves and the flesh is sweet and white, like wood under green bark. From the streets a sexual manifesto rises like an inflating tire, "The winter has not killed us again!" Spring comes into Québec from Japan, and like a prewar Crackerjack prize it breaks the first day because we play too hard with it. Spring comes into Montréal like an American movie of Riviera Romance, and everyone has to sleep with a foreigner, and suddenly the house lights flare and it's summer, but we don't mind because spring is really a little flashy for our taste, a little effeminate, like the furs of Hollywood lavatories. Spring is an exotic import, like rubber love equipment from Hong Kong, we only want it for a special afternoon, and vote tariffs tomorrow if necessary. Spring passes through our midst like a Swedish tourist co-ed visiting an Italian restaurant for mustache experience, and they assail her with ancient Valentino, of which she chooses one random cartoon. Spring comes to Montréal so briefly you can name the day and plan nothing for it.

It was such a day in a national forest just south of the city. An old man stood in the threshold of his curious abode, a treehouse battered and precarious as a secret boys' club. He did not know how long he had lived there, and he wondered why he no longer fouled the shack with excrement, but he didn't wonder very hard. He sniffed the fragrant western breeze, and he inspected a few pine needles, blackened at their points as if winter had been a brush fire. The young perfume in the air produced no nostalgic hefts in the heart beneath his filthy matted beard. The vaguest mist of pain like lemon squeezed from a distant table caused him to squint his eyes: he scraped his memory for an incident out of his past with which to mythologize the change of season, some honeymoon, or walk, or triumph, that he could let the spring renew, and his pain was finding none. His memory represented no incident, it was all one incident, and it flowed too fast, like the contents of a spittoon in recess jokes. And it seemed only a moment ago that the twenty-below wind had swept through the snow-laden branches of the second-growth fir trees, wind of a thousand whisk brooms raising tiny white hurricanes between the dark of the branches. Beneath him there were still islands of melting snow, like the bellies of beached and corrupted bloated fish. It was a beautiful day as usual.

—Soon it will get warm, he said out loud. Soon I'll begin to stink again, and my thick trousers which are now merely stiff will become sticky, probably. I don't mind.

The obvious problems of the winter he hadn't minded either. It hadn't always been that way, of course. Years (?) back, when some fruitless search or escape had chased him up the trunk, he had hated the cold. The cold seized his shack like a bus stop, and froze him with a fury that was positively personal and petty. The cold chose him like a bullet inscribed with a paraplegic's name. Night after night he cried out in pain during the freezing appliance. But this last winter the cold had only passed through him in its general travels, and he was merely freezing to death. Dream after dream had torn shrieks from his saliva, imploring the name of someone who might have saved him. Morning after morning he rose from soiled leaves and papers which comprised his mattress, frozen snot and tears in his eyebrows. Long ago, the animals fled each time he broke the air with his suffering, but that was when he screamed *for* something. Now that he merely screamed, the rabbits and weasels did not frighten. He presumed that they now accepted his scream as his ordinary bark. And whenever this fine mist of pain made him squint, as it did on this spring day, he stretched open his mouth, torturing the knots of hair on his face, and established his scream throughout the national forest.

—Aaaaaaarrrrrrrggggggghhhhhhhh! Oh, hello!

The scream switched into a salutation as the old man recognized a boy of seven running toward his tree, taking great care to wade through every drift. The child was out of breath as he waved. He was the youngest son of the keeper of a nearby tourist hotel.

—Hi! Hi! Uncle!

The child was not a relative of the old man. He used the word in a charming combination of respect for the ancientry and a rubbing of the forefingers in Naughty, Naughty, for he knew the fellow was shameless, and half out of his head.

—Hello, darling boy!

—Hello, Uncle. How is the concussion?

—Climb up! I've missed you. We can get undressed today.

—I can't today, Uncle.

—Please.

—I haven't got time today. Tell me a story, Uncle.

—If you haven't got time to climb up you haven't got time to listen to a story. It's warm enough to get undressed.

—Aw, tell me one of those Indian stories that you often swear you're going to turn into a book one day, as if I cared whether or not you were successful.

—Don't pity me, boy.

—Shut up, you filthy creep!

—Climb up, oh, c'mon. It's a short tree. I'll tell you a story.

—Tell it from up there, if you don't mind, if it's all the same to your itchy fingers, if it's half a dozen and six, I'll squat right where I am.

—Squat here! I'll clear a space.

—Don't make me sick, Uncle. Now let's hear it.

—Be careful! Look at the way you're squatting! You're ruining your little body like that. Keep the thigh muscles engaged. Get the small buttocks away from the heels, keep a healthy space or your buttock muscles will overdevelop.

—They asked me if you ever talk dirty when the children come across you in the woods.

—Who asked you?

—Nobody. Mind if I pee?

—I knew you were a good boy. Watch your leggings. Write your name.

—Story, Uncle! And maybe later I'll say maybe.

—All right. Listen carefully. This is an exciting story:

IROQUOIS	ENGLISH	FRENCH
Ganeagaono	Mohawk	Agnier
Onayotekaono	Oneida	Onneyut
Onundagaono	Onondaga	Onnontagué
Gweugwehono	Cayuga	Goyogouin
Nundawaono	Seneca	Tsonnontouan

The Iroquois ending *ono* (*onon* in French) merely means people.

—Thank you, Uncle. Good-by.

—Do I have to get down on my knees?

—I told you not to say bad words. This morning, I don't know why, but I informed the Provincial Police about us.

—Did you tell them details?

—I had to.

—Such as?

—Such as your cold freakish hand on my little wrinkled scrotum.

—What did they say?

—They said they've suspected you for years.

The old man stood by the highway, jerking his arm in the hitchhiker's signal. Car after car passed him. Drivers that didn't think he was a scarecrow thought he was an outrageously hideous old man, and wouldn't have touched him with *your* door. In the woods behind, a Catholic posse was beating the bushes. The best he could expect at their hands was a death whipping, and to be fondled unspeakably, as the Turks Lawrence. Above him on the electric wires perched the first crows of the year, arranged between the poles like abacus beads. His shoes sucked the water out of the mud like a pair of roots. There would be a mist of pain when he forgot *this* spring, as he must. The traffic was not heavy but it scorned him regularly with little explosions of air as the fenders snapped by. Suddenly, as the action freezing into a still on the movie screen, an Oldsmobile materialized out of the blur streaming past him. There was a beautiful girl behind the wheel, maybe a blond housewife. Her small hands, which hung lightly from the top of the wheel, were covered with elegant white gloves, and they drifted into her wrists like a pair of perfect bored acrobats. She drove the car effortlessly, like the pointer on a Ouija Board. She wore her hair loose, and she was used to fast cars.

—Climb in, she spoke only to the windshield. Try not to dirty things.

He shoveled himself into the leather seat beside her, having to shut the door several times in order to free his rags. Except for footwear, she was naked below the armrest, and she kept the map light on to be sure you noticed it. As the car pulled away it was pelted with stones and buckshot because the posse had reached the edge of the forest. At top speed he noticed that she had slanted the air ventilator to play on her pubic hair.

—Are you married? he asked.

—What if I am?

—I don't know why I asked. I'm sorry. May I rest my head in your lap?

—They always ask me if I'm married. Marriage is only a symbol for a ceremony which can be exhausted as easily as it can be renewed.

—Spare me your philosophy, Miss.

—You filthy heap! Eat me!

—Gladly.

—Keep your ass off the accelerator.

—Is this right?

—Yah, yah, yah, yah.

—Come forward a little. The leather hurts my chin.

—Have you any idea who I am?

—Ubleubleubleuble—none—ubleubleubleuble.

—Guess! Guess! You thatch of shit!

—I'm not in the least interested.

—Ισις ἐγῶ—

—Foreigners bore me, Miss.

—Are you quite finished, you foul stump of rot? Yi! Yi! You do it wonderful!

—You ought to use one of those anti-sweat wood ladder seats. Then you wouldn't be sitting in your juices in a draft all day.

—I'm very proud of you, darling. Now get out! Clean up!

—Are we downtown, already?

—We are. Good-by, darling.

—Good-by. Have a magnificent crash.

The old man climbed out of the slow-moving car just in front of the System Theatre. She rammed her moccasin down on the gas pedal and roared into the broadside of a traffic jam in Phillips Square. The old man paused for a moment under the marquee, eyeing the huddled vegetarians with two slight traces, one of nostalgia, one of pity. He forgot them as soon as he bought his ticket. He sat down in the darkness.

—When does the show start, pardon me, sir?

—Are you crazy? And get away from me, you smell terrible.

He changed his seat three or four times waiting for the newsreel to begin. Finally he had the whole front row to himself.

—Usher! Usher!

—Shhh. Quiet!

—Usher! I'm not going to sit here all night. When does the show start?

—You're disturbing the people, sir.

The old man wheeled around and he saw row after row of silent raised eyes, and the occasional mouth chewing mechanically, and the eyes shifted continuously, as if they were watching a small pingpong game. Sometimes, when all the eyes contained exactly the same image, like all the windows of a huge slot machine repeating bells, they made a noise in unison. It only happened when they all saw exactly the same thing, and the noise was called laughter, he remembered.

—The last feature is on, sir.

Now he understood as much as he needed. The movie was invisible to him. His eyes were blinking at the same rate as the shutter in the projector, times per second, and therefore the screen was merely black. It was automatic. Among the audience, one or two viewers, noting their unaccustomed renewal of pleasure during Richard Widmark's maniac laugh in *Kiss of Death,* realized that they were probably in the presence of a Master of the Yoga of the Movie Position. No doubt these students applied themselves to their disciplines with replenished enthusiasm, striving to guarantee the intensity of the flashing story, never imagining that their exercises led, not to perpetual suspense, but to a black screen. For the first time in his life the old man relaxed totally.

—No, sir. You can't change your seat again. Oops, where's he gone? That's funny. Hmmm.

The old man smiled as the flashlight beam went through him.

The hot dogs looked naked in the steam bath of the Main Shooting and Game Alley, an amusement arcade on St. Lawrence Boulevard. The Main Shooting and Game Alley wasn't brand new, and it would never be modernized because only offices could satisfy the rising real estate. The Photomat was broken; it accepted quarters but returned neither flashes nor pictures. The Claw Machine had never obeyed an engineer, and a greasy dust covered the encased old chocolate bars and Japanese Ronsons. There were a few yellow pinball machines of ancient variety, models from before the introduction of flippers. Flippers, of course, have destroyed the sport by legalizing the notion of the second chance. They have weakened the now-or-never nerve of the player and modified the sickening plunge of an unobstructed steel ball. Flippers represent the first totalitarian assault against Crime; by incorporating it into the game mechanically they subvert its old thrill and challenge. Since flippers, no new generation has really mastered the illegal body exertions, and TILT, once as honorable as a saber scar, is no more important than a foul ball. The second chance is the essential criminal idea; it is the lever of heroism, and the only sanctuary of the desperate. But unless it is wrenched from fate, the second chance loses its vi-

tality, and it creates not criminals but nuisances, amateur pickpockets rather than Prometheans. Homage to
the Main Shooting and Game Alley, where a man can
still be trained. But it was never crowded any more. A
few teen-age male prostitutes hung around the warm
Peanuts and Assorted machine, boys at the very bottom
of Montréal's desire apparatus, and their pimps wore
false fur collars and gold teeth and pencil mustaches,
and they all stared at the Main (as St. Lawrence Boulevard is called) rather pathetically, as if the tough passing crowds would never disclose the Mississippi Pleasure
Boat they might rightfully corrupt. The lighting was
early fluorescent, and it did something bad to peroxide
hair, it seemed to x-ray the dark roots through the
yellow pompadours, and it located every adolescent
pimple like a road map. The hot-dog counter, composed mainly of bells and pits of aluminum, exhibited
the gray hygiene of slum clinics, which depends on a
continual distribution, rather than elimination, of grease.
The counter men were tattooed Poles, who hated each
other for ancient reasons, and never got in each other's
way. They wore the possible uniforms of an infantry of
barbers, spoke only Polish and a limited Esperanto of
hot-dog conditions. It was no use to complain to one
of them over an unanswered dime. An apathetic anarchy
mounted OUT OF ORDER signs over the slots of broken
telephones and jammed electric shooting galleries. The
Bowl-a-Matic habitually divided every strike between
First and Second Player regardless of who or how many
threw. Still, here and there among the machines of the
Main Shooting and Game Alley a true sportsman would
be losing coin in gestures that attempted to incorporate
decay into game risk, and, when an accurately blasted
target did not fold away or light up, he understood it

merely as the extension of the game's complexity. Only the hot dogs had not declined, and only because they have no working parts.

—Where do you think you're going, Mister?

—Aw, let him in. It's the first night of spring.

—Listen, we got *some* standards.

—C'mon in, Mister. Have a hot dog on the house.

—No thank you. I don't eat.

As the Poles argued, the old man slipped into the Main Shooting and Game Alley. The pimps let him go by without an obscenity.

—Don't get near him. The guy stinks!

—Get him out of here.

The pile of rags and hair stood before William's De Luxe Polar Hunt. Above the little arctic stage set an unilluminated glass picture represented realistic polar bears, seals, icebergs, and two bearded, quilted American explorers. The flag of their nationality is planted in a drift. In two places the picture gave way to interior-looking windows which registered SCORE and TIME. The mounted pistol pointed at several ranks of movable tin figures. Carefully the old man read the instructions which had been Scotchtaped along with fingerprints to a corner of the glass.

Penguins score 1 point—10 points second time up
Seals score 2 points
Igloo Bull's Eye when entrance is lit, scores 100 points
North Pole when visible, scores 100 points
Walrus appears after North Pole has been hit 5 times & scores 1000 points

Slowly, he committed the instructions to memory, where they merely became part of his game.

—That one's broken, Mister.

The old man pressed his palm against the pineapple

grip and hooked his finger on the worn silver trigger.

—Look at his hand!

—It's all burnt!

—He's got no thumb!

—Isn't he the Terrorist Leader that escaped tonight?

—Looks more like the pervert they showed on TV they're combing the country for.

—Get him out!

—He stays! He's a Patriot!

—He's a stinking cocksucker!

—He's very nearly the President of our country!

Just as the staff and clientele of the Main Shooting and Game Alley were to succumb to a sordid political riot, something very remarkable happened to the old man. Twenty men were swarming toward him, half to expel the disgusting intruder, half to restrain the expulsionists and consequently to boost the noble heap on their shoulders. In a split second the traffic had stopped on the Main, and a crowd was threatening the steamy plate windows. For the first time in their lives, twenty men experienced the delicious certainty that they were at the very center of action, no matter which side. A cry of happiness escaped from each man as he closed in on his object. Already an accumulation of tangled sirens had provoked the strolling mob like an orchestra at a bull fight. It was the first night of spring, the streets belong to the People! Blocks away, a policeman pocketed his badge and opened his collar. Hard women in ticket booths sized up the situation, whispering to the ushers as they secured their plow-shaped wood window plugs. The theaters began to empty because they face the wrong way. Action was suddenly in the streets! They could all sense it as they closed in on the Main: something was happening in Montréal history! A bitter smile could be detected on the lips of trained revolutionaries and Witnesses of Jehovah, who immediately dispatched all their pamphlets in one confetti salutation. Every man who was a terrorist in his heart whispered, At Last. The police assembled toward the commotion, ripping insignia away like it was scabs which could be traded, but preserving their platoon formations, in order to offer an unidentified discipline to serve whatever ruled next. Poets arrived hoping to turn the expected riot into a rehearsal. Mothers came forth to observe whether they had toilet-trained their sons for the right crisis. Doctors appeared in great numbers, natural enemies of order. The business community attained the area in a disguise of consumers. Androgynous hashish smokers rushed in for a second chance at fuck. All the second chancers rushed in, the divorced, the converted, the overeducated, they all rushed in for their second chance, karate masters, adult stamp collectors, Humanists, give us, give us our second chance! It was the Revolution! It was the first night of spring, the night of small religions. In another month there would be fireflies and lilacs. An entire cult of Tantric love perfectionists turned exocentric in their second chance at compassion, destroying public structures of selfish love with beautiful displays of an acceptable embrace for street intercourse of genitalia. A small Nazi Party of adolescents felt like statesmen as they defected to the living mob. The Army hovered over the radio, determining if the situation was intensely historical, in which case it would overtake Revolution with the Tortoise of a Civil War. Professional actors, all performing artists including magicians, rushed in for their last and second chance.

—Look at him!

—What's happening?

Between the De Luxe Polar Hunt and the plate-glass windows of the Main Shooting and Game Alley the gasps were beginning that would spread over the heads of the astounded crowd like a leak in the atmosphere. The old man had commenced his remarkable performance (which I do not intend to describe). Suffice it to say that he disintegrated slowly; just as a crater extends its circumference with endless tiny landslides along the rim, he dissolved from the inside out. His presence had not completely disappeared when he began to reassemble himself. "Had not completely disappeared" is actually the wrong way of looking at it. His presence was like the shape of an hourglass, strongest where it was smallest. And that point where he was most absent, that's when the gasps started, because the future streams through that point, going both ways. That is the beautiful waist of the hourglass! That is the point of Clear Light! Let it change forever what we do not know! For a lovely briefness all the sand is compressed in the stem between the two flasks! Ah, this is not a second chance. For all the time it takes to launch a sigh he allowed the spectators a vision of All Chances At Once! For some purists (who merely destroy shared information by mentioning it) this point of most absence was the feature of the evening. Quickly now, as if even he participated in the excitement over the unknown, he greedily reassembled himself into—into a movie of Ray Charles. Then he enlarged the screen, degree by degree, like a documentary on the Industry. The moon occupied one lens of his sunglasses, and he laid out his piano keys across a shelf of the sky, and he leaned over him as though they were truly the row of giant fishes to feed a hungry multitude. A fleet of jet planes dragged his voice over us who were holding hands.

—Just sit back and enjoy it, I guess.

—Thank God it's only a movie.

—Hey! cried a New Jew, laboring on the lever of the broken Strength Test. Hey. Somebody's making it!

The end of this book has been rented to the Jesuits. The Jesuits demand the official beatification of Catherine Tekakwitha!

"Pour le succes de l'enterprise, for the success of this enterprise, il est essential que les miracles éclatent de nouveau, it is essential that the miracles sparkle again, et donc que le culte de la sainte grandisse, and thus extend the cult of the saint, qu'on l'invoque partout avec confiance, that one may invoke her with confidence everywhere, qu'elle redevienne par son invocation, that she becomes again by her mere invocation, par les reliques, by her relics, par la poudre de son tombeau, by the dust of her grave, la semeuse de miracles qu'elle fut au temps jadis, the sower of miracles that she was in former times." We petition the country for miracle evidence, *and we submit this document, whatever its intentions, as the first item in a revived testimonial to the Indian girl.* "Le Canada et les États-Unis puiseront de nouvelles forces au contact de ce lis trés pur des bords de la Mohawk et des rives du Saint-Laurent. Canada and the United States will achieve a new strength from contact with this purest lily from the shores of the Mohawk and the banks of the St. Lawrence River."

Poor men, poor men, such as we, they've gone and fled. I will plead from electrical tower. I will plead from turret of plane. He will uncover His face. He will not leave me alone. I will spread His name in Parliament. I will welcome His silence in pain. I have come through the fire of family and love. I smoke with my darling, I sleep with my friend. We talk of the poor men, broken and fled. Alone with my radio I lift up my hands. Welcome to you who read me today. Welcome to you who put my heart down. Welcome to you, darling and friend, who miss me forever in your trip to the end.

Afterword

BY STAN DRAGLAND

Beautiful Losers was extremely popular between the time of its release in 1966 and the mid-seventies. It's still considered a breakthrough in fiction, perhaps the first postmodernist Canadian novel, by those who monitor the Canadian literary scene. But general interest in this astonishing work seems to have waned. Why?

Some of the novel's first admirers may have been fairweather friends, uncritically applauding the content that seemed in tune with the spirit of the sixties: drugs, free inventive sex, revolution, and all that – all the exploratory experience that makes F. a sort of superhippy. Another factor may have been Leonard Cohen's withdrawal from the Canadian literary scene. He hasn't, except briefly, promoted either his books or the Leonard Cohen mystique in this country for many years. And then the books that followed *Beautiful Losers*, especially *The Energy of Slaves* and *Death of a Lady's Man*, put off many readers with their sour self-referential takes on Cohen's earlier career and his relationship with his audience. These "dismal" books have been seriously misunderstood, I think – they are not repudiations but rather extensions and variations of Cohen's more accepted work – and one side-effect may have been a lowering of the profile of *Beautiful Losers*.

Though the era that produced it is long gone, this bizarre, moving, hugely funny Canadian masterpiece still has a freshness that tells us it never did depend on content.

261

It flies as it always did, on the wings of its art. The art – the way the content is deployed – is anything but simple. The novel is never boring, but it can be bewildering, and a reader who has enjoyed the book may yet welcome an account of its workings that especially reflects on the way it dramatizes and orchestrates the tensions between order and chaos in life and literature that inhabit everyone. One of several ways to do this is to focus on F. in his relationship with his friend, the narrator of Book One, and with the reader.

The most immediately comprehensible strand of the novel's plot – the seventeenth-century story of Catherine Tekakwitha – begins inside a present-day fiction, the story of the unnamed narrator, a scholar desperately courting the Indian virgin with his words as an alternative to continuous grief. The failure of his life has been underlined by the deaths of his wife Edith and his friend and self-appointed guru, F. Retrospectively and unchronologically, he fills in what, in the medley of these relationships, got him stuck in his sub-basement apartment, shut away from the Montreal that he loves. His section, or Book, is called "The History of Them All," though he hardly offers history as logical plot. In fact the narrative is all over the place, as you might expect from a narrator whose "Brain Feels Like It Has Been Whipped."

Gradually, the exploded mind in its mortified body does appear to be on its way to the physical and spiritual metamorphosis that climaxes in Book Three, "*An Epilogue in the Third Person.*" But for most of Book One, it feels unlikely that this man might be symbolically journeying to a star. Much of this section is a howl, not only of pain but of bewilderment, because the narrator was/is the reluctant disciple of a teacher whose "classroom is hysteria," whose teachings are at once persuasive and incomprehensible.

It's one thing to see as through a glass darkly, and another to have to try to see through a prism of funhouse mirrors, through F., best friend since orphanage days, charismatic charlatan – he likes to sing "The Great

Pretender." "Take one step to the side and it's all absurd," the narrator realizes, and the reader (to *Beautiful Losers* as this man is to F.) wants to consider how very easy it is to take that side-step. But F.'s "system" (sketched in Book One and fleshed out in Book Two, "A Long Letter From F."), his outrageous salad of world myths and religions tossed with contemporary advertising, movies, porn, comics, cartoons, the Top Forty, you name it – all accepted as sacred material – is couched in such passionate rhetoric and poetry that it is almost possible to give in to it.

How one interprets *Beautiful Losers* depends on how much authority over the text one grants to F. (is he meant to teach the reader as well as his reluctant student?), and, further, whether one stresses the endorsement of order or chaos – or "balance" – in what he says. How does the world mean/how does the book mean? These complementary questions are probably best explored by trying, like his disciple (but more critically), to keep up with F. as he dodges through the novel.

The fascination of F., the temptation to believe what he says, is astonishing, provoked as it is by a novel so little bound by the conventions of realism. The reason is that the stakes are high. If F. were real and if he knew what he was talking about, then everything in the modern world would make sense, the whole painful puzzle would be whole, as it once was, in "an eternal eye." Any amount of suffering could be endured. "Oh, F.," says the disciple to his master, "do you think I can learn to perceive the diamonds of good amongst all the shit?" "It is all diamond," F. replies. Yes, F. is seductive. His system has its attractions but not, I expect, to the squeamish. Some readers, finally, are unable to overlook the distinction between diamonds and shit.

The whole of *Beautiful Losers* seems to stream through certain set-piece passages composed of the contradictory stresses of existence that both characters and readers must wrestle with. These passages are part of a self-reflexive inquiry into order and chaos in life and art, and they interest a reader in something other than how the plot turns out. They magnetize a reader's attention with the prospect of meaning, even a "necklace of incomparable beauty and unmeaning"; with an offer of "the exercise of a sort of balance in the chaos of existence"; with "a dance of masks" in which "there was but one mask but one true face which was the same and which was a thing without a name which changed into itself over and over"; with the lure of "the sound of the sounds [heard] together."

The well-known passages so abbreviated, those well-springs of aesthetic unity, connect with and supplement each other, and they might all be felt to meet in the statement of faith that F. calls "the sweet burden of my argument." This is the poem, "God is alive. Magic is afoot," that has been wonderfully served in a musical setting by Buffy St. Marie. F.'s message actually involves a further leap, beyond faith in human creative capacity to the divine source of it all.

But in this constellation of remarkable passages lies the meaning of *Beautiful Losers* for those who feel that the novel has something important to say, something the mind can hold and carry away. Both the narrator and F. (the latter in a weak moment) feel the pull of this sort of kernelized meaning. The appetite survives in the "part of [the narrator's] mind that buys solutions," in the "American" part of F.'s mind that wants "to tie my life up with a visit." Small wonder a reader should feel his or her desire for order exercised by this book.

The saint-artist's exercise of balance, the visionary necklace of "beauty and unmeaning" and the rest – these are not images of easy harmony, or they wouldn't be as seductive as they are. All the same, they are reassuring figures that link or contain the constituents of chaos, lending them at least the illusion of coherence. If God is alive, the whole shebang makes sense.

So it's plausible to read *Beautiful Losers* as a modernist novel with an underlying drive towards organic unity because the novel powerfully sponsors that sort of response.

The "celestial manifestation" of the "Epilogue" would then be the plot's fulfilment of the principle of harmony under whose influence one threads the parts of the novel as beads on a necklace. But if the novel were meant to inhere in those transcendent passages, the experience of reading it would not involve, line by line, page by page, such continual readjustment and surprise and joyous evasion of a critic. *Beautiful Losers* will slake the thirst for meaning, for resolution, but only in a reader partially amnesiac.

The few passages that connect, however compelling, are not the book. Cohen has delegated no one to speak for him; neither do the collected voices of the novel add up to Writ. Sometimes the narrative mask all but dissolves to let us see through the words to the man who wrote them, as when a voice one almost seems to recognize cries, "O reader, do you know that a man is writing this? A man like you who longed for a hero's heart. In arctic isolation a man is writing this, a man who hates his memory and remembers everything, who was once as proud as you. . . . " The suddenness of this, rather than any inconsistency with what else the volatile narrator has been saying, persuades me that the author is flirting with self-revelation. It makes more poignant the invocation of mutual exile from bravery and purity of intention. A man like me, only too conscious of his limitations, made *Beautiful Losers* out of his longing. Writer and reader, narrators and characters – we're all in this wilderness together, and only the characters emerge.

Writer and reader are also together, abandoned, in the last passage of the novel, where the melancholy tone is heard again. Those reassuring passages with the family face are not the whole picture: F. speaks only for himself; there is no resting in, say, "God is alive. Magic is afoot." Meaning is not only fluid but collaborative, not only collaborative but reconstituted with each reading.

The desire for order is so palpable in the minds of both narrator/characters, those chips off the old block, that any conclusions they reach ought to be suspect. Their cries of metaphysical loneliness and prayers to silent gods ring through *Beautiful Losers*. "God is alive. Magic is afoot" feels genuinely affirmative, but it pales beside the pain of a mind bereft of certainties in Book One, and it's undercut in Book Two when F. all but admits that spiritual loneliness scares human beings into affirmation.

Beautiful Losers has a great deal to do with the response of artists like F. to the lonely wrack of contemporary life. The novel is largely about the principles and workings of F.'s weird "system." He is using it to mould out of the lumpen clay of his friends superbeings with perfect bodies and wide open minds. He wants things different, "any old different," and not just for the hell of it. "What is original in a man's nature," runs one of his aphorisms, "is often that which is most desperate. Thus new systems are forced on the world by men who simply cannot bear the pain of living with what is."

A poet's allegiance, the passage goes on, "is to the notion that he is not bound to the world as given, that he can escape the painful arrangement of things as they are." F.'s examples are two "creators" not often associated: Hitler and Jesus. Hitler? Is there a revisionism capable of erasing the difference between Jesus and Hitler? The plot shows that F. is not talking through his hat, at least. He and Edith would likely be as happy to go three in a tub with Jesus as with Hitler, though Jesus might not bring the soap. Hitler's soap is human soap; it's six million Jews. In what sort of system is this a comic turn? In the system called *Beautiful Losers*. F. is not laughing. His "lust for secular gray magic" makes him covet that soap. He feeds on *any* power.

To write his letter, F. says, he has "had to stretch my mind back into areas bordered with barbed wire, from which I spent a lifetime removing myself." He never suffered any scruples to interfere with the gratification of his lust for life, and the Argentinian hotel scene shows that he has erased the border between good and evil. One would think that he should be far from Jesuit territory, then, away from the Christian system with its tales of Hero and Adversary in settings of heaven and hell, but he isn't.

The Jesuits use ghastly paintings of hell (in the seventeenth-century narrative of Book One) to frighten the Indians out of their own less dualistic system into "a new loneliness," the death of their heaven. The novel makes this tragedy moving, but it does not stay on the side of the losers. Renting the end of the book to the Jesuits is not the first sign that what they stand for, unfair players and winners though they are, has its admirable side. The narrator of Book One includes in his paean of homage to the Jesuits ("because they saw miracles") a section easy to skip or forget, unless one comes to it thinking of F. and Hitler: "Homage to those old torturers who did not doubt the souls of their victims, and, like the Indians, allowed the power of the Enemy to nourish the strength of the community." Like F., though hardly in the same way, the Jesuits have congress with the devil. In a novel of collapsing identities (the major characters have merged in the Epilogue) it shouldn't be surprising that Hitler's exit leaves behind "the vague stink of [the Adversary's] sulphurous flatulence." There is no passage celebrating the fact that the Devil is afoot, but the narrators of Books One and Two both fold his energy of darkness into their thinking.

If God is alive, is F. even on his side? In the orgy that climaxes with the Danish Vibrator, F.'s "Pygmalion tampering" with Edith is revealed. "You've gone against God," she says to him, placing him in the Archetypal Rebel camp, and that association is extended in a passage that darkly parodies his friend's vision of unity, early in the novel, created by the "needle" of his mind that, when relaxed, sews everything together: "everything which has existed and does exist, we are part of a necklace of incomparable beauty and unmeaning."

This "comforting message, a beautiful knowledge of unity" has to be seen from the perspective of F.'s contrasting needle-work in Book Two. "Call me Dr. Frankenstein with a deadline," he says at the beginning of the grotesque symbolic passage about his failure to stitch together any semblance of a person from the strewn remains of the car accident of contemporary life, "limbs strewn everywhere, detached voices screaming for comfort." Is he thinking of his failure when he shouts "connect nothing!" in response to his friend's necklace vision of unity? "Place things side by side on your arborite table, if you must, but connect nothing!" Given his confession, given his overreaching, who is going to put much faith in F. as a creator, as a saint? His system is a botch.

Or is it? Now we're only listening to the dark side. Reflecting on *Beautiful Losers*, it's very easy to lose balance. Eventually there comes a time to abandon the search for consistency in F.'s system and resolution in this novel, to put aside all that irritable reaching after fact and reason. "Shhh" is "the sound made around the index finger raised to the lips. Shhh, and the roofs are raised against the storm. Shhh, the forests are cleared so the wind will not rattle the trees. Shhh, the hydrogen rockets go off to silence dissent and variety." Shhh, the trickster text will now behave itself. Resisting that step into irony doesn't necessarily mean deciding whose side F. is on. It means keeping the options open.

"We rejoiced to learn that mystery was our home," F. recalls to his friend (and the pronoun welcomes the reader). Their home is this novel. With a true mystery there is nothing to do but play. Mystery is life in the best novels, those tests of whether or not the centre will hold, and play is the creative process at its most cooperative and least judgemental. Accommodating Hitler, of course, Cohen pushes his system right up to the edge of the tolerable. The sheer risk is breathtaking and is echoed in the flamboyant inclusiveness of the novel's technique.

In 1970 Michael Ondaatje wrote that "*Beautiful Losers* is a gorgeous novel, and is the most vivid, fascinating and brave modern novel I have read." Perhaps he would now wish to add some other novels to this select category, but I think the judgement stands up. The Age of Aquarius has passed, and *Beautiful Losers* is no longer considered a holy book by guru-seeking readers, but it isn't dated. Because it broke so successfully with traditional form, showing outrageous new possibilities for fiction to a rather staid Canadian scene, it is one of the most important novels written in this country.

BY LEONARD COHEN

FICTION
The Favourite Game (1963)
Beautiful Losers (1966)

POETRY
Let Us Compare Mythologies (1956)
The Spice-Box of Earth (1961)
Flowers for Hitler (1964)
Parasites of Heaven (1966)
Selected Poems, 1956–1968 (1968)
The Energy of Slaves (1972)
Death of a Lady's Man (1978)
Book of Mercy (1984)
Stranger Music: Selected Poems and Songs (1993)